What the critics are saying...

✂

Desperate Hearts

4 STARS "...wonderful insight into human nature and love." ~ *Romantic Times BookClub*

"Not an everyday romantic storyline...memorable..." ~ *Ivy Quill Reviews*

"A beautifully written tale...Not to be missed!" ~ *In The Library Reviews*

4 Unicorns! ~ *Enchanted In Romance*

Playing His Game

"...well written, with excellent secondary characters. I will certainly be on the lookout for more stories by Kit Tunstall." ~ *Sensual Romance*

"The story line grabs you from the first line and keeps you interested until the very end. Kit Tunstall is likely to have a prosperous future with books like PLAYING HIS GAME." ~ *Love Romances*

"This book is going on my keeper shelf to read again and again." ~ *Timeless Tales*

Timeless

LANI AAMES
KIT TUNSTALL

ELLORA'S CAVE
ROMANTICA PUBLISHING

An Ellora's Cave Romantica Publication

www.ellorascave.com

Timeless

ISBN 1419953214
ALL RIGHTS RESERVED.
Desperate Hearts Copyright © 2004 Lani Aames
Playing His Game Copyright © 2002 Kit Tunstall
Cover art by Syneca

Trade paperback Publication September 2006

Warning:

The following material contains graphic sexual content meant for mature readers. This story has been rated S-ensuous by a minimum of three independent reviewers.

Ellora's Cave Publishing offers three levels of Romantica™ reading entertainment: S (S-ensuous), E (E-rotic), and X (X-treme).

S-*ensuous* love scenes are explicit and leave nothing to the imagination.

E-*rotic* love scenes are explicit, leave nothing to the imagination, and are high in volume per the overall word count. In addition, some E-rated titles might contain fantasy material that some readers find objectionable, such as bondage, submission, same sex encounters, forced seductions, and so forth. E-rated titles are the most graphic titles we carry; it is common, for instance, for an author to use words such as "fucking", "cock", "pussy", and such within their work of literature.

X-*treme* titles differ from E-rated titles only in plot premise and storyline execution. Unlike E-rated titles, stories designated with the letter X tend to contain controversial subject matter not for the faint of heart.

Contents

DESPERATE HEARTS

By Lani Aames

න

Chapter One

ℰᴑ

Talley Robinson snatched up a towel and scrubbed at the spotless bar. Serving drinks at The Rusty Rose was a lonely way to spend Saturday night, but the pay was decent, the tips good, and at least she wasn't home alone wishing she could be with—

The front door opened with a loud creak that cut through the jukebox music. She waited, almost breathlessly, until the customer entered. As far as she could tell, no one else noticed the door and who would come through. Her fingers clenched the towel tightly until the moment he stepped in...but it was only Henry Davis.

Throwing the towel aside, Talley let her breath escape in a rush. This wasn't good, waiting for the creak of the door, holding her breath until someone came through, only to find it wasn't who she wanted it to be, needed it to be.

Kim rushed up to the bar with a couple of empty mugs. "Two more," she called out. "God, they're getting an early start tonight."

Talley took the empties and started filling fresh mugs with draft, tilting the glasses to keep the head as small as possible.

"When's Jeannie coming in?"

"A couple of hours," Talley said after glancing at the big clock on the wall behind the bar. "I can give her a call. She won't mind coming in early."

"Good. They're getting on my last nerve."

Kim took the mugs away, and Henry ordered a beer. After serving him, Talley phoned Jeannie who pretended to be inconvenienced by having to come in early but agreed nevertheless. Talley knew she could use the extra money. Jeannie had it tough with two kids and no husband.

The creak of the door sounded again, but Talley refused to look in hopeless expectation. She jerked up the towel and wiped away the little drops of condensation from the can she'd served Henry. She wouldn't look as she tried to let go of the hope that settled in her breast, very close to a heart that sometimes felt it might split right in two.

"Talley."

Although he spoke quietly, she heard her name and turned her eyes up to see. He was part of what she wanted and needed. She smiled at him even though it was impossible to have it all.

"Hi, Mitch," she said loudly. Her voice didn't carry like his, wouldn't undercut the music so he could hear. He had a deep, rich speaking voice that was mesmerizing when he sang. She stepped over to him, the bar between them, and leaned across.

He kissed her, his fingers splayed along her neck, his thumb at her ear, a familiar gesture that went along with most of his kisses ever since they were kids in high school. They were now twenty-three, their history long and varied, sometimes sweet and sometimes bitter. Now, at this particular time in their lives, it was turning sour—only Mitch didn't know it and Talley couldn't find the words to tell him.

"When do you get off?" Mitch asked when he'd ended the kiss that was sweet and warm and held so much promise. He left his hand where it was, his fingers massaging her neck, his thumb tickling her ear.

"At midnight, when the doors close. You know that."

"Think you can get off early?"

She shook her head. "The crowd's kind of wild tonight. I had to call Jeannie in early. Too bad you couldn't play this weekend, then you wouldn't be here pestering me."

Mitch grinned. "You love for me to pester you."

"Do I?" Talley smiled teasingly and kissed his full sensual lips. Mitch Holloway was a handsome man with a dark complexion, high cheekbones and black brows arching over startling gray eyes. His thick black hair curled at the ends. A nuisance, he claimed, but it looked nice. He'd been a good-looking boy, but the past six years had given him a maturity that could take a woman's breath away.

"It really is too bad we couldn't play. We need the money and the exposure. Mike had to go out of town and Bonnie's mother is sick."

"You never did tell me, is it serious?"

He shrugged. "I don't think so. She has these spells from time to time. Bonnie feels better staying with her."

Although Talley hadn't seen Mrs. Cleary since her return to Randolph a year ago, she remembered her as a pale, nervous woman and always wondered how she could have produced the vivacious and vibrant Bonnie.

"I thought we might have supper at Joe's Bar and Grill."

"Sounds nice, but I don't know. Jeannie should be here in about ten minutes. If the crowd thins out maybe—"

Someone called for a refill and Talley reluctantly left Mitch's caress. One led to another, and Jeannie had arrived before Talley had time to fill a mug and set it before Mitch.

"On the house, but don't tell Dylan."

"One day, sweetheart, you won't have to work behind a bar ever again."

"Actually, I enjoy working at the Rose," Talley said and took up the towel again.

"When The Cold Creek Band hits it big, you won't have to work at all."

"Mitch—"

"I know it's a dream." He scowled. "A pipe dream, Dad calls it, but I know we can make it. It's just gonna take some time."

"I don't doubt you'll make it. You know I'm behind you one hundred percent. Your father is wrong, you know. You're good enough for the big time."

"Yeah, but he doesn't see it. He won't even come and watch us perform."

"He loves Shady Hollow."

"That he does. More than me, I think."

"Not true, Mitch. He wishes you had more interest in it, that's all."

"Well, I don't. If I have to play in dives half the size of the Rose the rest of my life then I'll do it." Mitch frowned and fingered the drops of water sliding down his glass. "I think something's wrong."

"With your father?"

"The farm, I guess. He's been awful moody lately. Well, worse than usual. He's been back and forth to Memphis for three days now. Whatever's wrong he's not talking to me about it."

"Why don't you talk to him?"

"And get my head snapped off? No thanks. I'll help him any way I can, he knows that, but I can't make that farm and raising cows my life. So he cuts me off from it all."

Talley frowned and wiped the bar again.

"You know how he is. He's a tough, stubborn son of a—"

"Don't, Mitch."

"Who thinks if it's not done his way then it's not worth doing at all. I can't turn my back on my music any more than he can turn his on Shady Hollow."

"I know it hasn't always been easy for you, but he must be a good father. Look how you turned out. You're a good man."

Mitch smiled bitterly and shook his head. "No thanks to him."

"You know you don't mean that."

"You know I do."

She frowned at him.

"Whatever I am is because my father isn't."

Talley continued to wipe the bar although the drops were long gone. "Anything happening in Memphis?"

Mitch talked, but Talley only half-listened. She had lived in Memphis a while before deciding to return to Randolph. Talley's parents had divorced when she was ten. Her father was a drifter, and she rarely heard from him. Her mother had dated but never seriously until she met and married Frank Wilson. Because of Frank's job, they moved every few years. The last time Talley had talked to her mother, she had said that Frank had been transferred to Knoxville and they would be moving in the fall.

Over the years, Talley had followed along to stay close to her mother and half-sister, but she couldn't imagine ever moving again. She wanted a more stable life. Early last year, Frank's job brought them to Memphis, near the town where she grew up, and she had decided to move back home to Randolph. Over the years, she couldn't forget Mitch and how much she had loved him. If Mitch was still free, then she had hoped they could recapture what they'd once shared. They had begun dating again six months ago, but in the last three months her life had become more complicated than she'd ever dreamed possible.

If she had any sense at all, she'd be in Memphis now. Unfortunately, she was human, her choices made from her heart, not common sense.

The evening was long. The crowd swelled, and by the time Talley took a break she found Mitch playing pool in the back room. They settled into a corner table, and he put his arm around her, nuzzling her ear with his tongue. Talley laughed and pushed him away. It was a gesture that sent a chill down her spine and a throb through her belly, but she ignored it. He settled at her side again, kept his tongue to himself, but his fingers played along her arm.

"What's the name of the club in Memphis you're going to play?"

Mitch told her and became lost in the talk of his music. She didn't have to respond or even really listen. Mitch did all the talking. She hated using the ploy, but sometimes she didn't feel like talking and any question in connection to his music took care of the conversation.

A slow, romantic song came on the jukebox and Mitch jerked his head toward the dance floor. "Wanna dance?"

"Sure."

Before Mitch could stand, Jack Sandler caught her hand and pulled her to her feet. Talley tried to pull free of his grasp, but his hand crushed hers. She could have made a scene, but Jack and his buddies were drunk and she wanted no trouble. She just shrugged at Mitch's glowering face.

Talley was almost disappointed when Mitch didn't come to her rescue. Not that Jack was a real threat even if he held her too close, his body too rough against hers. Talley tried to draw away, but Jack held her that much tighter. Mitch's face had turned red with fury, but she shook her head at him. There really was no need for trouble.

Talley had made the mistake of going out with Jack when she first returned to Randolph. Mitch had been involved with Bonnie, and Talley had no intention of breaking them up. She took the job at The Rusty Rose to be near Mitch, but she never flirted or teased. Eventually she had decided to get on with her life, so when Jack had asked her out, she'd accepted.

She'd only vaguely remembered him at the time since he was a few years older. He was tall, good-looking in a dark, dangerous way. He had seemed nice when he was sober. Drunk, he was snake-mean and, Talley soon learned, boring as hell. He had no personal hygiene habits to speak of and always stank of stale sweat and old beer.

On their one and only date, she had barely escaped him and his insistent hands. The only thing that had saved her was the fact that he was drunk and could therefore accomplish nothing more than tearing her blouse.

Since then she occasionally had to fend off Jack's vulgar advances. But Jack's usual hangout was Snake's, a bar with a bad reputation. It seemed to Talley that he stopped by the Rose just to give her grief. Tonight had been the first time he'd laid a hand on her since that ill-fated date.

When the song ended, Jack didn't want to let go. He kept one arm clamped around her. "Ain't you through with Mitch the Snitch yet?"

"Come on, Jack, the song's over." She tried to ease out of his arms, but he wouldn't let her go.

"Gimme another chance, baby," he whispered, his sour liquor-laden breath filling her nostrils. She stopped breathing. "How about tonight?"

"Let me go, Jack."

The lull in the music brought the situation to everyone's attention since they were the only ones remaining on the dance floor. Mitch leaped to his feet and came toward them.

"Ol' Mitch the Snitch!" Jack shouted loud enough for everyone to hear. Then he bent close to Talley's ear and whispered, "When you get tired of Mitch the Snitch, remember me."

Jack released her suddenly, and she almost fell into Mitch's arms. He laughed as he headed for the door, his buddies following.

"Oh, grow up, Jack!" Talley called after him and rubbed her aching wrist.

"You all right?" Mitch held her at arm's length as if to check her over.

"I'm fine. I'll go talk to Dylan."

Mitch the Snitch. Why hadn't she remembered that? Jack and his buddies had called Mitch that nickname years ago over some incident from grade school. Jack Sandler had been a bully then and was a meaner bully now. How could she have forgotten?

Dylan let her go. Jack had put an uncomfortable finish to the evening for many and others were leaving anyway. Talley grabbed her purse and left with Mitch's protective arm around her shoulders.

Chapter Two

ຂ

After a late supper at the Grill, Mitch drove Talley home. The blue and white mobile home stood on a small lot near the top of Morning Glory Hill. The small trailer was clean, in good condition, and the rent was cheap. Morning Glory Lane saw little traffic, and Talley enjoyed the seclusion. Her small backyard was a haven. Surrounded by woods, she could almost imagine she was alone in the world.

The night air was heavy with the heat and humidity of the day as Mitch walked her to her door. She turned to him beneath the star-sprinkled sky. Mitch wrapped her in his arms and closed his mouth over hers. She shut her eyes and let her arms slide up around his neck. Her breath deepened, her pulse quickened, and the throb in her belly became a drumbeat that echoed along her nerves.

"Is tonight the night, sweetheart?" he murmured against her lips and pushed his hips toward hers. Desperately, he scattered soft, moist kisses over her face. One hand cupped her breast, his thumb grazing her nipple. She moaned in spite of herself, hated him for stirring her desires, hating herself for the answer she had to give.

She shook her head quickly. "Mitch, I…"

"When, Tal? It's not like we've never done it before."

"I know—" She stopped, but he hadn't interrupted her this time. She felt foolish—foolish for saying no, foolish for being in this particular mess. She was a coward and she knew it.

She began the process of untangling their bodies. When she pulled away, Mitch's eyes were haunted and bright. He didn't understand. and at that moment neither did she. She couldn't make sense of what had happened to her in the past few months.

They had been lovers when they were teenagers, but since she started seeing him this time, she had refused to let them make love again. She didn't think a relationship could be built on sex and little more. She wanted to make sure it worked with Mitch. She didn't want to rush into physical intimacy with him. It would break her heart again to sleep with him then have to let him go. Those had been her intentions in the beginning. Mitch had agreed, but his patience was wearing thin.

"When, Tal? When we're too old and feeble to enjoy it?" He stepped in close and kissed her again. "I want you, Talley. I want you more than that night when we were seventeen and I wanted you pretty damn bad then."

"Oh, Mitch, don't make it so hard." Instead of pushing him away, she closed her eyes and let his lips trail down to settle on a spot where her neck and shoulder met. He suckled hard.

"No!" She jerked away from him, but it was too late. The love bite stung. That was all she needed! Her hand covered the spot, felt the wetness of his saliva. "Grow up, Mitch!"

Unconsciously, she used the same words she'd said to Jack Sandler.

"Do you think I'm like Jack? Is that what you think, Tal, that that's all I want from you?"

"Of course, I don't think you're like Jack!"

"Then what's wrong with you? You used to love it when I put one there, low enough so you could hide it from your mother. And when I left one here." He lowered his mouth to her breast and tongued her nipple through her shirt.

She pushed him away angrily and sat on the concrete steps. She rubbed the spot where he'd left his mark. "I'm not seventeen anymore. It's been six years, and I've changed. That's what I mean, Mitch. We have to discover all the changes in both of us before we take such an important step. It was so hard saying goodbye the last time. I still remember what you said—"

"Tal, I didn't mean it! I was so mad that your mother and stepfather were taking you away from me, all the way to Chattanooga. I always regretted saying it."

"You told me to go to hell."

"Because you wouldn't stay here and marry me. I was mad."

"We were only seventeen. We wouldn't have made it."

Mitch sat beside her without touching her.

"I know that now. You were right and, hell, I knew it even then." He moved close to her and put his arms around her. "I'm not going anywhere and neither are you this time. There won't be a goodbye."

"Maybe not, but I have to be sure. Please, Mitch, say good night and go home."

"I love you, Talley. I never stopped loving you, but I didn't realize it until I saw you again. That's all I need to know. I want to touch you and hold you and fill you up. I want you to want me."

"Sometimes love isn't enough, and I want to find out before we get in over our heads again."

Mitch stared up at the sky. "You're not giving in on this, are you, Tal? Look, I didn't wait on you these last six years. Maybe I should have, but I didn't. I dated other women, and I slept with them. I even thought I loved some of them. I didn't expect you to jump in bed with me on our first date, but I expected to make love to you again. I don't know how much longer I can wait."

"Is that a threat?" she asked quietly.

"No, I'm not saying that! I'm saying I want it here with you. I feel like I'm gonna bust wide open."

It hurt to hear him beg. She loved Mitch and she wanted it to work for them...but she couldn't give in. It didn't feel right yet.

"I'm sorry, Mitch."

"Dammit, Talley, let me stay the night. I'm a hell of a lot better than I was at seventeen. Not nearly as quick. I've learned how to please a woman. We'll take it slow and easy and find all the answers we were too young to find back then."

"Mitch, please. I love you, but I'm not ready for us yet."

He swore under his breath. If he was angry enough, he might go out and seek satisfaction elsewhere. She certainly had no right to blame him if he did.

Strangely, the idea didn't distress her as much as it should have.

"You haven't told me how your song 'Desperate Hearts' is coming along?"

Mitch grinned proudly. "I didn't? I can't believe I forgot. Bonnie finished the lyrics last night. I was having so much trouble with the words, I just handed the whole thing over to her and told her to fix it."

"You two work so well together."

"Yeah, we do. She cleaned it up. We went straight through it once before we quit rehearsal. Took us all afternoon, but we did it. If Dylan wasn't such a jerk, you could have heard it."

A couple of months before, Dylan had gotten it into his head that the band should be paying him for the use of his place to rehearse. He had forgotten that they provided his customers with live entertainment at no cost to him.

The only other place they could find to rehearse was Snake's in "the bottoms". Every spring, the Mississippi River overflowed its banks and flooded the bottomland. Houses, churches and joints like Snake's were built high on stilts to keep from being flooded out. Some families left their homes until the Mississippi decided to return to its rightful place while those who didn't leave used boats.

Mitch and the rest of the band members didn't like Snake's reputation for trouble, but Snake Drummond agreed to let them use his joint in the afternoons. He was satisfied with the arrangement since his afternoon crowd had increased. Dylan grumbled about the falloff at the Rose, but wouldn't admit it was because the band didn't play there anymore.

Talley had thought about quitting the Rose, but she had come to enjoy working there. Dylan was gruff, but he seemed to like her. He let her choose which afternoons or nights to work as long as she always came in Saturday nights. For the past three months his strict rule had worked in her favor...as well as being her excuse for not traveling out of town with Mitch and the band.

"You'll get to hear it next Saturday night, Tal. We're playing the Fourth festival at the park. You will be there, won't you?"

Held the Saturday before the Fourth of July every year, the celebration was a county tradition. Lots of food, games, and contests filled the afternoon as well as local bands taking turns to provide live entertainment throughout the day and night. After the street dance, a spectacular fireworks display would mark the end of the day's festivities.

"I wouldn't miss hearing you, Mitch. I'm glad Dylan agreed to let me off. Otherwise, he'd have a fight on his hands."

"We're on early in the afternoon, but we've also been asked to play for the street dance."

"That's great! Some people leave early and come back for the street dance and fireworks."

"And some don't show up at all until just before. We're gonna save 'Desperate Hearts' for last. We'll blow 'em away!"

"I know you will." Talley leaned into him and kissed him sweetly on the cheek. "Will your father be there?"

"I doubt it," he said gruffly and scowled. "Before they died, my grandparents used to take me. Ever since we've been playing the festival, he always finds some excuse not to make it."

"Did you tell him you got the prime spot of the evening?"

"Yeah. He just grunted."

"Did you ask him to come and see you?" Talley persisted. "Did you tell him about your song and that you want him to hear it?"

"Wouldn't do any good." Mitch jumped to his feet and paced. "I stopped counting the times I asked him to see us a long time ago, Tal, and then I just quit asking altogether. He always has some excuse or just flat out says no if he's drunk enough."

Talley's heart ached for him. "You can't give up."

"Yeah, I can. I'm tired of trying to get through his stubborn head. And I sure don't try when he's been drinking."

"I'm sorry, Mitch."

"Don't be sorry, Tal. Dad's not worth the bother." Mitch took her hands and pulled her to her feet. "I don't want to talk about him anymore. I want to talk about us."

He kissed her, his tongue flicking against hers. She allowed herself to enjoy the taste of him a few moments, then ended the kiss.

Mitch breathed heavily. "I don't mean to rush you, sweetheart, but I love you!"

"I love you, too, Mitch, but the answer is still no."

He hugged her tight. "I'm not giving up, Tal."

"Good night, Mitch."

He kissed her quickly one last time then walked to his truck and drove away. Talley breathed a sigh of relief. She was still overwhelmed by all the emotions that wracked her body. She wasn't immune to his kisses and caresses. She ached deep within herself.

Inside, the trailer was stifling from the heat and humidity, and she turned on the air conditioner. She ran a bath and washed away the smoke and smell of The Rusty Rose and the fine film of perspiration that still clung to her skin. The hot water felt good as she relaxed in the tub, a folded towel behind her head. Her skin tingled from what had been as well as what was to come. She drifted off and when she woke, the water was almost cold. She dried off and dressed in a knee-length white cotton nightshirt with the words "Come and Get It" in hot pink across the front. She pulled hot pink socks over feet that always grew cold with the air conditioner running.

In the kitchenette, she measured grounds and poured water into the coffee maker. She fixed a glass of iced tea and sipped at it while she smoked a cigarette and finger-combed her hair in the dark. When her hair was dry enough and the last of the ice had melted in the glass, she curled up on the couch. The day had been long and tiring, and she fell asleep quickly.

Sometime later, Talley woke to the sound of the door opening. She had left it unlocked on purpose. Her eyelids fluttered open and she watched her doorway fill with the silhouette of a large man.

Chapter Three

୫ର

He was a tall man, lean but not slender. He wore a denim shirt, sleeves rolled up, unbuttoned almost to the waist. His jeans, worn and faded from hours of work in the sun and many washings, fit snug on his hips and were held up by an old leather belt. His scuffed square-toed cowboy boots were rundown at the heels from years of use.

She watched him fill the doorway then pull the door shut behind him. He came in on a wave of hot humid air, but she shivered from the anticipation of him. Every Saturday night for three months he had come to her like this in the middle of the night—every night except the first night.

"Mace," she whispered. She was, as always, in awe of this man. She couldn't see his face clearly in the shadows, but she knew it by heart—every crease around his eyes and mouth, the sun-browned, soft leathery texture of his skin. Her fingers ached to touch his face.

"Come here, darlin'…"

She was up and in his arms before he finished. Her eagerness and desperation for him disgusted her, but she could control neither. She laid her head against his chest. She was tall but he was taller, and that worked out so well.

He tousled her hair and kissed her forehead. She reached up and laid her lips over his, slipping her arms around his neck. His mouth accepted her eagerly, and his hands slid down her sides to cup her buttocks and press her up against the bulge in his jeans. She felt a quickening between her thighs, and warmth spread throughout her limbs. Her breath came in shallow gasps as he released her.

"I wasn't sure you'd come by tonight," she said as she pulled away from him and he patted her butt. She filled a mug from the coffee maker and handed it to him.

He took it and sat in a kitchen chair, downing a large swallow. He leaned back and smiled with a wink. "You knew."

"No, I didn't know, but I'm glad you're here."

"So am I or I wouldn't be."

"How are things going?"

He shrugged, unwilling to talk about what worried him right then.

"The Rose was a madhouse tonight, but Dylan let me off early." She proceeded to tell him about Jack Sandler.

"You never should have gone out with that bottom rat in the first place."

"I never really knew Jack, and it's been six years. I guess I thought he'd changed. He seemed nice enough sober."

Mace took another large swallow of coffee.

"I don't know what you do to it, but you make the best coffee I've had in years."

She reached for his mug. "More?"

His eyes were smoky and he shook his head.

She smiled. "Me?"

"That's what I came for, darlin'."

Crude, but the truth. Talley stepped into the deep vee of his legs and they kissed long and hard. Mace's hands cupped her breasts, his thumbs tracing lazy circles over her nipples. Shivers ran through her body, and she threaded her fingers through the long waves of brown hair salted with gray. When the kiss ended, she trailed her fingertips over his weatherworn face.

"Mace…"

"Mmmm?"

She shook her head, her honey-colored hair falling over him. "Nothing. I like saying your name. Mace."

His hands slipped off her breasts, meandered down, and caught behind her thighs. He heaved her up and closed his legs so that she straddled him. The pressure of his warm bulge and the roughness of his jeans made her ache with the want of him. His hands moved under her nightshirt and spread over her bare bottom.

He grinned a little, leaned forward, and placed a kiss on the pulse in her throat. "You know, don't you," he murmured directly into her ear, "that only whores don't wear underpants."

She laughed at him and pushed him back. "And how would you know?" she teased, reaching for his belt buckle. His grin widened, but he admitted nothing.

When his jeans were undone, she pulled his erection free. He was already straight up and reaching for heaven. Talley wrapped her hand around his arousal, moving up and down in the slow motion she knew Mace liked. He groaned and his head fell back against the kitchen wall with a soft thump.

Need flowed through her, and she squirmed in his lap. He pulled her forward until she was pressed against the bunch of his jeans at the base of his zipper where the rest of his bulge was hidden. He rocked her against him, and the tingle reached all the way to her toes.

Talley stopped with a shudder and a moan when she was close to the edge. Mace moved his hands to her waist and straightened out his legs. She lifted briefly, then sank onto him with a groan, his long length filling her up. With one hand flat on the wall near Mace's head, her other hand pushed aside his denim shirt. She bent her head and swirled her tongue around one flat nipple, bringing it to a hard point, then did the same to the other. Mace's breath escaped in a rush each time.

Her toes pushed against the floor as Mace's hips surged beneath her. She closed her eyes, and her hips quickened with his. Talley tossed back her head and let the warm burst of pleasure wash over her and through her. When it was over, she rested her head on his shoulder. Mace's hands spasmed on her waist, and he grunted as he spilled himself within her.

When he was still, she removed her hand from the wall and wrapped both arms around him. God, he felt good in her arms, under her body. Every inch of her touched him and she never wanted to let him go.

"Darlin', that was the best," he murmured and kissed her hair, "but you're gonna break my back."

"Oh, Mace, don't make me move." But she unwound her limbs from him anyway, then shivered from the extra ripple of pleasure when he slithered out of her. She straightened her nightshirt and made it to the other chair at the end of the dinette table, her limbs weak and shaky.

Mace groaned as he sat up, adjusting himself. "Damn, but I'm too old for gymnastics."

"Ha!" She laughed. "You did nothing but sit there."

"Nothing, huh?" He grinned crookedly as he zipped up. "I seem to recall having a little something to do with your pleasure."

She exaggerated a shrug. "Maybe...a *little*."

"Maybe? *Little*! You're getting awful cocky for a girl."

"No," she assured him and shook her head. "Cockiness is still your territory."

He lifted the coffee cup to his lips and winked at her. He took a sip, grimacing. "Cold."

"I'll get you some more."

He caught her hand as she reached for the cup. His callused fingers played over hers. "You can get me some more coffee, too...in a little while."

"You'll be asleep in a little while because I'm going to wear you out."

"Is that a promise?"

"Yes, Mace."

She turned out the lights as they headed back to her small bedroom. Talley sat in the center of the bed, pulled off her socks and watched Mace undress. He pulled free what was still tucked in of his shirt, undid the buttons, and let it fall off his lean arms. Talley quickly pulled off her nightshirt and stretched out. Mace toed off his boots, then unzipped and peeled off his jeans, underwear and socks.

"Looks like you've done this before, cowboy," Talley teased.

"A few times."

"A few more times and you might get good at it."

"Might?" He pounced on her on all fours, ravishing her belly with kisses.

"Stop, Mace!" Talley squealed, almost laughing too hard to talk. "You're good, you're very good!"

He stopped immediately and raised his head. "And when I'm bad I'm better."

"No, Mace. When you're bad, you're the best."

He kissed her belly one more time then raised to his knees, one on each side of her. Looking down at her, his eyes glittered silvery from the moonlight pouring through the window. "Flattery will get you everywhere."

She writhed against him. "Mmmm, what will it get me tonight?"

"Laid. Just give me time to recover from sitting in your kitchen chair."

"And how long will that take?"

"Forever, if you just keep staring at it."

Talley laughed softly and stretched, drawing her arms above her head. "But what am I supposed to do in the meantime?"

"I think," he said and fell forward, catching his weight on his elbows on each side of her, "I can keep you busy."

He dipped his head, his lips surrounding a nipple, his tongue raking the point mercilessly. Talley gasped as a tingle of pleasure settled between her thighs. Her legs shifted restlessly, trapped by Mace's body.

"Not yet," he said as his head moved to the other side.

He gave the same delicious attention to her other breast, bringing it to a raw point, intensifying the tingle into a burn. Her hips raised toward him on their own, but he ignored the nudge as his hands slid down her sides and he left a wet meandering trail over ribs, detouring around her navel again and again.

Talley moaned when he moved lower, quivering where he touched. She wiggled free of his weight, but only because he was ready for her to spread for him.

She reached for him, expecting him to crawl into her arms, anxious for him to settle his body against hers and carry her away. Instead, his arms slipped behind her thighs and cocked her legs around his shoulders. His hands slid around her hips, fingers splayed across her skin between her and the bed beneath.

"Mace?" she whispered, hardly able to breathe as he dragged his tongue up along the inside of one thigh and down the other.

"Mmmm," he murmured, his lips and tongue now busy with something else besides talking.

"Oh, Mace…"

Talley lay back, closed her eyes, and let Mace have his way with her. His tongue teased her, flicking all around the spot where she wanted it most. She moved her hips a little, hoping to catch him off guard, but his hands tightened their hold, keeping her in place.

She sighed and relaxed, and that was when Mace marked the spot. She thrust forward, gently at first, then faster as Mace kept time with her rhythm. A whimper started in her throat, then turned into something more primal as her back arched and her legs tightened around Mace. Her fingers clenched the headboard as she came.

Mace's tongue stroked her a few more times as the last of her climax dissolved, then kissed the inside of each thigh. He waited until she had regained her senses and eased her legs from his shoulders before raising up and sitting back on his heels.

Talley hadn't wanted to move, enjoying the thought of Mace trapped between her thighs, but knew she had to let him go eventually. Let him go...

Her eyes fluttered open, and she watched him as he wiped his mouth with her nightshirt.

Touching her intimately in that way, Mace forged a bond between them Talley had never shared with another man. She didn't know if Mace felt the same way, probably not, and she didn't have the courage to ask. Instead, she held out her arms to him. He dropped the nightshirt and crawled up over her.

He surrounded her with his long, strong arms. "Did that keep you busy enough?"

Talley smiled against the rough day's growth of his beard. "Hmmm, a little."

He groaned and shook his head, the shaggy ends of his hair tickling her nose.

"I reckon you want *this*, huh," he said and slid into her.

She was still wet and soft and his hips pressed into hers firmly. He lifted enough to enfold his fingers with hers and raise them above her head. As he reared over her, she wrapped her legs around his waist and enjoyed the way he moved in and out with clean, hard strokes. Thoroughly satisfied, she wasn't caught up in the mindless act, but was aware of every place he touched her body, inside and out, where his hardness touched her softness, from his callused hands to his lean ribcage to his rigid length within her.

"Sorry, darlin'..." he said in a breathless rush, his hands gripping hers tightly.

"It's all right," she assured him as she watched his face by moonlight, watched how the sunburned creases deepened and his eyes squinted shut as he finished up inside her. His hands loosened suddenly, and he slumped over her, planting a kiss on her shoulder. When his breaths were close to normal, he rolled to his side and gathered her in his arms, their bodies damp with sweat and seed.

Talley wished she could purr like a contented kitten just to let Mace know what he did to her. Maybe he already knew. Maybe she did the same for him.

She listened to his breathing even and then, eventually, the soft snores. She couldn't sleep. The guilt hadn't set in yet, would come soon enough, but her mind wouldn't shut down. She eased herself from the tangle of his limbs and got up.

He stirred. "Where you going, Lee?"

"I'll be back in a few minutes."

"Miss you when I'm not here."

She went into the bathroom and washed away the dampness of their lovemaking. She pondered his slurred words. Had he meant them as he'd said them or had he misspoke in his sleepiness? Too many questions in her mind tonight. None she would ask him. She wouldn't risk spoiling what they shared.

At the doorway to her bedroom, she watched him for a few minutes, then walked back into the kitchen. She lit a cigarette from the pack Mace had left on the table.

She loved two men and her heart was torn in half. One she loved openly, but gave only a part of herself. The other she loved secretly and gave her all. It couldn't go on. A choice had to be made. Whether the choice would be hers or forced upon her, it needed to be done.

If they were two different men, she might have been able to carry if off for a while longer, but because of their relationship, it would have to be soon.

Whom should she choose?

Mace or Mitch.

The father or the son.

Chapter Four

ഇ

In the seclusion of her small backyard surrounded by dense woods draped with kudzu, Talley usually found peace. Not this morning. Her guilt had grown too large and crowded out any peace she might have left in her soul.

She glanced at Mace's truck, hidden amid the trees and well out of sight of the road. Tears filled her eyes, but she refused to give in to them. That would come later, after Mace had left. She wiped them away, hoping her eyes wouldn't redden. Mace would be out soon.

Talley thought about their first time together, as she often did while waiting for Mace to join her out here the morning after. She hadn't really met Mace again since returning to Randolph. He and Mitch weren't getting along, and Mitch stayed away from Shady Hollow as much as possible. He hadn't taken her to the farm since they'd started dating. Mace never came to the Rose, but she had seen him in passing a few times. She had never given much thought to Mace Holloway except as a careless father who hurt his son deeply by refusing to accept his choices in life.

That first Saturday night, Talley had no idea things would turn out as they had. Mace had come into the Rose just before closing, and Dylan refused him service. Talley had realized Mace was too drunk to drive. She had caught a ride to work with Kim, so she told Dylan she would take him home and Mitch could bring her back. Unable to face the twenty-mile drive, she had instead driven him to her place. She helped him in and poured him on the couch. Then she went to bed. Hours later, she awoke to the sound of the shower running. A few minutes later, he filled her bedroom door asking, "Talley?"

It was four in the morning. When she couldn't think of anything else to say to him, she asked if he was hungry. He said yes, so she fixed them coffee, bacon, scrambled eggs, and toast. That finished sobering him up. One thing led to another and Talley found herself in his arms, kissing him.

No, it was much more complicated than that.

She had refilled his cup. She had set it in front of him, and Mace had reached up, caressing her arm with tender strokes. Just as suddenly, his fingers were gone, and his face had turned dark red under his tan.

If he had grabbed at her or made some vulgar comment, she would have tossed him out with no second thought. Unfortunately, his fingers had danced up under the short sleeve of her robe and lit a fire to every nerve ending in her body. The blush that crept into his cheeks was endearing and made her really look at him for the first time. Her heart had skipped a beat. But she had told him she was seeing Mitch.

"I know," he said, his voice unnaturally husky.

She had never thought of Mace in that way, yet she couldn't help but touch him too. Lightly, her fingertips ran along the deep creases around his eyes and mouth, over his lips. He responded to her apparent invitation by laying his hands on her hips and pulling her to him. She had closed her eyes and kissed him.

Wherever he touched her she felt his heat—the warmth radiating from the taut bulge in his crotch, the small patches where his hands rested on her hips, his warm whiskey and breakfast scented breath as his lips left hers and traveled downward to cover the point of one breast, then the other.

It had been so long since she'd been with a man that she reacted to him as if she was starving and he was a picnic laid out for her alone. She gave in to her need and enjoyed the sensations he aroused. Fleetingly, she thought of Mitch and that this was Mitch's father, but then her mind clouded over and her decision was made.

Tomorrow she would face her guilt and tomorrow Mace would be gone and that would be the end of it. Tonight would be for passions aroused, and the feel of another body pressed close to hers. She wouldn't have to jeopardize her relationship with Mitch over sex.

Then he had stopped and held her at arm's length. She felt the need to explain but in the smallest amount of words as possible. "Mitch and I aren't sleeping together." She didn't elaborate except to add, "I love Mitch." And although the thought had never crossed her mind before, in that one point in time, she wanted Mace with all her heart and soul and every inch of her body. "I want you."

He had stood and released her hand—leaving it up to her, she supposed, but she had already decided. She took his hand again, and they kissed. She led him to her small bedroom, into her small bed, and afterwards she felt as if one weight had been lifted from her shoulders only to be replaced by a greater one.

At the time, it had seemed sensible to give in to her physical longings with someone other than Mitch. She didn't stop to think there wasn't anything at all sensible about sleeping with Mitch's father.

Reason hadn't returned to her until later that morning, and guilt almost drowned her. The saddest part of all was that she couldn't say she had any regrets.

She had awakened to sunlight streaming across their close bodies and felt as if a cloud of smoke had been swept from her brain. She scrambled from the bed, getting as far away from him as possible. Grabbing her gown and robe, she'd disappeared into the bathroom without looking back even when he called out her name.

In the shower she ran water as hot as she could stand it. She'd cried, great choking sobs that wracked her body as she scrubbed her skin over and over. Nothing could wash away what she had done. Nothing could change what had happened. If only she could go back in time a few hours…

But would she have done it differently?

She had emerged from the bathroom hoping Mace had gone. She didn't even glance toward the bedroom. She'd strip the bed later and burn the sheets. She went out the back door and sat on the step, numbly running her fingers through wet hair to get out the tangles. She couldn't think beyond wanting a cigarette, but she was too afraid to go back inside in case Mace was still there. She supposed she could see if his truck was gone, but what would she do if it was still in the driveway where she'd left it last night?

If he was any kind of gentleman, he would have left while she was in the shower and pretended the night had never happened, she'd reasoned. When next she saw him, there would be no remembrance in his clear gray eyes, and he would act as if he were meeting her again for the first time since her return to Randolph.

The door had opened behind her, and she was up and away before he could step outside. She couldn't look at him. She sat in one of the chairs around the table, her back to him, and closed her eyes. Why didn't he just go away?

The silence between them grew until Mace walked to the other side of the table and sat down. She couldn't open her eyes, but she wouldn't run away again. This was her home, and he was the one who didn't belong. She heard him fumble with a pack of cigarettes and light two.

"Talley," he murmured, and then she did look at him.

He held out a cigarette for her, and she took it. His gray eyes were wide and startled, like he couldn't believe it had happened either. She had half expected to see a satisfied smirk on his face, the look of a man who knew no woman could resist him, not even his own son's girl. She was surprised to find he was as confused and embarrassed as she. The discovery eased her discomfort a little.

"I—" he started but couldn't finish. He ran his hands through his longish hair and shook his head.

"I think you should leave now," she said quietly in a neutral tone. She didn't want him to think she blamed him. They were equally guilty of what had happened.

"All right. But I just wanted to say—"

"No. Don't say anything. We-We just need to forget this ever happened."

"I know. That's what I wanted to say. I want to make sure you understand I'm not looking for anything more. I…" He dragged deeply on his cigarette and blew the smoke out slowly. "I don't know what happened, but it won't happen ever again. I don't need anything, or anyone, permanent in my life. I ain't looking for—"

"You've made that clear, Mace. Just leave."

He nodded again and stood. She sensed that he wanted to say more, but then he finally walked away. She heard his truck start, back out of the driveway, and leave. When she could hear it no more, she had breathed a sigh of relief. It was over.

Until the next Saturday night when he knocked on her door.

She just stood there and looked at him. "What are you doing here, Mace?"

She tried to discourage him by speaking coldly, but her heart had hammered in her chest. Images of lying beneath this man flashed through her mind. She had tried not to think of him all week, but it was impossible. Now, here he was again.

"I-I just wanted to see how you're doing, that's all. I ain't welcome at the Rose or I'd have come by there."

A smile tugged at her mouth, but she didn't give in to it. He seemed a little lost and afraid, and she wouldn't have expected to find either in Mace Holloway.

"You have a phone, don't you?"

"Yeah, I do," he said and grinned a little. "It never crossed my mind. I wanted to see you."

"Well, now you've seen me, and I'm all right."

"Yeah," he agreed, but didn't make a move to leave. He stood on the front doorstep and waited.

She waited too. While she waited she thought of all the reasons she should shut the door in his face and break this off right here and now.

She tried. She even took a step back and tightened her hold on the doorknob. She thought of Mitch and how devastated he would be if he found out. She glanced at her driveway, but only her car sat there.

"Where's your truck?"

"Back there, under the trees."

"What do you want, Mace?"

He shrugged helplessly. "I don't know."

Against her better judgment, she said, "Come on in and I'll make you a cup of coffee. Then you have to go."

"All right."

He didn't go, of course, until the next morning. They weren't quite as embarrassed as they had been the first time, and they agreed it shouldn't happen again. Yet, he couldn't stay away, and she couldn't say no. They never spoke of Mitch in the beginning.

Now, one more Sunday morning she waited for him in the quiet of her backyard. Something had to be done. She was being torn in half, right down the middle, but she couldn't make the final decision she knew had to be made. Not yet.

Mace stepped through the back door, fully dressed, with a steaming cup of coffee in his hand. He stood on the step, squinting into the sunlight. He ran his hand through his hair then unconsciously adjusted himself as men do without any thought to where they are or whom they're with.

He looked at her and winked. "Twice in one night. I'm damned impressed with myself."

She laughed as he came toward her and she raised her head for her morning kiss. When he pulled away, an indefinable look crossed his face. He placed a callused finger at the base of her neck.

"I didn't do that," he said gruffly and walked away from her.

Talley's hand flew to cover Mitch's mark. She'd completely forgotten about it in her excitement over Mace's visit. Tears burned her eyes, and a guilty blush crept over her face.

Why did she suddenly feel guilty over Mitch?

"I'm sorry, Mace—" she began.

"You don't owe me any explanations." Mace smiled a little, but his eyes were filled with sadness.

"It was Mitch—"

"Don't explain, Lee. You have a life to live the other six days of the week."

Now her throat burned as well, and she blurted out, "I haven't started sleeping with Mitch."

"Why not? Ain't my boy good enough for you?"

"That's not funny," she snapped.

He sipped his coffee. "Wasn't meant to be. Are you holding out for marriage? I'd like to know if I'm going to be bedding my son's wife."

She sucked in a breath. "Mace, you've gone too far."

He nodded and set his coffee cup on the table. "I'd best leave then."

"No!" Talley jumped to her feet and went into his arms. He held her as tightly as she held him. "This is our time together. The only time I have you. I won't give it up."

"Even after you marry Mitch?"

She shook her head against him. "We haven't talked about marriage."

"But, darlin', Mitch wants to marry you." Mace eased himself from her arms and sat down in his chair. He pulled cigarettes out of his shirt pocket and lit two, handing one out to her. She took it.

"Mitch and I don't talk much anymore without it ending in an argument, but he's talked about you a lot since you've been seeing each other again. I think he's getting me ready to be your father-in-law." He frowned, puzzled. "He's had girlfriends before, and he never mentioned their names to me. I don't know if he thinks I won't approve or what—"

"Maybe he thinks you'll sleep with them." The words were out before Talley could stop them, but she didn't regret what she said. It was only fair that she hurt him as badly as he hurt her. She returned to her chair, and when she looked at Mace again, his eyes were hard.

"I think we're even now," he said.

"And you know how you made me feel."

"All right, Lee."

"Why do you call me that? No one has ever called me Lee before."

"You know why."

She shook her head. She liked that he had a special nickname for her, but she didn't know why he had come to use it. "No, I don't."

"Mitch calls you Tal and, since we each have a part of you, I take what's left. Lee."

What a bitterly sweet thing for him to say, and Talley wanted to cry. She teetered on the edge of tears a lot lately, but she had mastered how to save them for when she was alone.

"I am sorry that I hurt you. I don't know about you, but I don't like myself much these days. I think I need to go now." He drained his cup and stood.

Talley's heart sank into the pit of her stomach. "Is this goodbye?"

He hesitated, then shook his head. "As long as you can live with yourself, I reckon I can, too."

She went into his arms again, and they kissed, long and slow and sweet.

Then he was gone.

Watching him walk away grew more difficult each time. When she could no longer hear his truck in the distance, she cried.

Chapter Five

ร

Saturday always came around although Talley believed the day took longer than the other days of the week and had more hours. This Saturday was the annual celebration of the Fourth at McKenna Park. Mitch offered to pick her up, but she invented some excuse about errands to run, so she would have her own car. She didn't want to have to go through the awkwardness of turning him down again at her front door. In addition to the set just before the fireworks, The Cold Creek Band would also play early in the afternoon, so Mitch had to go on without her.

Talley arrived as they were setting up on the second stage.

"We won't play 'Desperate Hearts' this time, Tal. We're saving it for tonight," Mitch told her when he took a few minutes away from the preparations to talk to her. "I'm glad you're here."

"Me, too."

"But I have to help out. Don't wander too far. I want to be able to see you while we're on."

The festivities filled the park all the way to the wooded area at the west end. Talley kept her eye on the stage at the east end while she went from booth to booth. The traditional barbecue and fireworks had grown over the years to include vendors selling food, soft drinks, and crafts. She played games of chance and admired the handiwork of local artisans. She ate a hot dog and sipped sweet-and-sour lemonade. She was looking over a table of jewelry made of all natural materials when the hair at the back of her neck prickled.

"Hello, darlin'," a voice whispered close to her ear.

She whirled, spilling the lemonade. "Mace!"

"C'mon, let's walk."

Talley glanced toward the stage, but they were as far as they could get from it, almost to the woods. She couldn't tell which was Mitch from this distance. She tossed her glass of lemonade into a trashcan. "What are you doing here?"

"Every lost soul in town is here, why shouldn't I be?"

"Because Mitch said you haven't attended in years." She halted suddenly and touched his arm to stop him. "Did you come to hear Mitch?"

A muscle twitched in his jaw and he shook his head.

"You have to, Mace. It would make him so happy."

He started walking again. "C'mon," he said again.

Talley followed him. Without glancing around, Mace strode into the dense growth of trees. Talley hurried to catch up with him.

"Are you insane, Mace? What if someone sees us disappear into these trees?"

He whirled on her suddenly, his gray eyes almost black in the shaded woods. "What's wrong with a father talking to his son's girl? It happens every day, Lee. Every father talks to his son's girl at some time or other."

She briefly hesitated. "All right."

He shrugged. "I didn't come to hear Mitch and I didn't come to see you. I don't know why I'm here. I thought Mitch wasn't on till tonight."

"They're playing two sets. One now and the other just before the fireworks. It's an honor, Mace, for them to close the evening and play for the street dance."

He nodded. "I saw him but I don't think he saw me. Don't tell him I was here."

"Just come listen to him. Then it won't matter if he knows."

"I just happened to see you at that booth," he continued as if she hadn't spoken.

Laughter echoed through the trees. They weren't the only ones seeking shade from the hot sun, or maybe a place to be alone.

"This was damn stupid, wasn't it?" He took her hand and led her deep into the woods. When they reached the creek, he turned and they followed it north a ways.

The trees blocked the direct sunlight, but their thick branches trapped the heat and humidity. Talley wore a sundress and had pulled her hair into a pony-tail to keep as cool as possible, but the humidity and exertion left a fine layer of sweat on her skin and almost took her breath away.

They came to a place where a dead tree had fallen across the creek and Mace stopped.

"I know every inch of these woods, every hidey hole. Me and Dylan and Henry Davis spent more time here than in school. When I was sixteen, I brought a girl to McKenna Lane and got laid for the first time." He shook his head at the memory and smiled a little. "Lilith Vandemeer—blonde, built like a brick shithouse. Laid every man in Randolph before I got to her."

"The librarian?" Talley thought of the stout lady with graying hair who used to help her find information for the papers she had to write in high school. The same one who had tried to talk her out of reading the trashy novels in the paperback section.

"We used to say McKenna Lane had more rubber than a tire company. I wonder if it's still the favorite parking spot for horny teenagers."

"Where do you think Mitch and I first did it?" Talley asked and held her breath.

Mace didn't say anything for a moment, then he laughed. "And in the front seat of my truck. I never thought... Damn. Time to get a new truck."

Talley shrugged. "Where else could we go back then?"

Mace moved in close as the laughter left his eyes. He forced her to lean against a tree and laid his hands flat on each side of her head.

"What are you doing, Mace?"

"I want you."

He kissed her deeply, his lips working hard over hers. Against her better judgment, she closed her eyes and let her tongue play with his. She realized then that she'd been aroused ever since he'd whispered *darlin'* in her ear, and the kiss only made it worse. Or better. She wanted him too.

Her mouth felt bruised when he pulled away. "You'll have me. Later tonight. Isn't that enough?"

He didn't answer, but kissed her again, sucking gently on her tongue. She closed her eyes again and let her desire and need for him take over. She didn't consider the fact that it was broad daylight and anyone could find them. She couldn't think at all while Mace's busy tongue enflamed the fire burning in her belly, between her thighs. She was ready to spread her legs, hike up her skirt and let him take her right there, the rough bark digging into her shoulder blades…

But a rare breeze rustled the tops of the trees and a few stray notes of music reached them across the distance. Mitch and the band had started.

The sounds brought her back, and her eyes flew open, meeting his clear gray eyes. With one last pull on her tongue, he drew away.

"I have to go, Mace. Come with me and listen to your son."

He shook his head. "I'll come with you later tonight…"

"Mace—"

"This evening, meet me here."

"I can't. I'll be with Mitch."

"Not while he's singing."

"I want to hear him. We won't be able to hear him from here."

"I know."

She decided it was useless trying to convince him. "I have to go. Mitch will be watching for me."

He didn't move. She ducked under his arm and ran all the way through the trees.

She didn't look back.

* * * * *

All afternoon, as she walked with Mitch around the park and back again, Talley told herself she wouldn't meet Mace. She didn't want to miss hearing Mitch perform "Desperate Hearts". But Mace had been in a strange mood. She hadn't smelled whiskey on his breath, so she didn't know what had caused it. She hated having Mace on her mind when she was with Mitch, but she couldn't seem to think of anything else.

As evening turned to night, they filled up on barbecue and roasted corn and glasses of lemonade. She occasionally glanced towards the woods and wondered if Mace was already there. He'd have a long wait, she kept telling herself.

But after Mitch and the others went off to get ready for the last set of the evening, Talley found herself heading away from the stage. She told herself she was only going to the restroom. After visiting the park facilities, she located her car in the crowded parking lot and retrieved the flashlight from the glove compartment. She stopped lying to herself and made her way to the woods.

The three-quarter moon wasn't strong enough to light her way through the trees. With the help of the flashlight, she found the creek and headed north as Mace had taken her that afternoon.

She took her time, not wanting to tumble over the bank into the water. In the daylight with Mace, the path hadn't seemed nearly as dangerous. A fall into the muddy water was not the most pleasant way to end the evening. Besides, how would she ever explain to Mitch?

The night was sultry and sweat covered her like a second skin. She wiped at the droplets that formed on her upper lip and felt a trickle down the small of her back. She had to be near the place where Mace had taken her. If she didn't find him soon, she would turn around and go back.

She walked a few more yards, flashing the light around and found him perched on the end of the fallen log. He blinked in the brightness of the beam.

"I didn't think you'd come," he said and put a bottle to his lips, letting the dark golden liquid slide down his throat.

"I always come with you," she said, but he didn't smile at her joke like he usually did. He patted the spot beside him and she sat close by but not touching. She cut off the flashlight.

"Was she any good?" Talley asked, not knowing what else to say.

"Who?"

"Ms. Vandemeer." She couldn't bring herself to call the woman by her first name. It was difficult enough imagining Mace at sixteen. It was impossible to imagine him with *her*. She didn't think she'd ever be able to go into the library again.

He shrugged. "I wasn't too worried about how good it was, just that I was finally doing it. When you're that age, that's all that matters."

What did that say about her and Mitch if that had been all that mattered to Mitch? She knew it had meant more to him. In some ways, Mitch was a kinder, gentler man than his father could ever hope to be.

"I scored a few more times that year—"

"Why are you telling me this?"

"—and the next summer, at the Fourth festival, I met Mitch's mother."

He took another drink from the tall bottle.

"Ellen wouldn't let me in her pants, but I wanted there so bad. I stayed away from other women." He hung his head.

"Damn, but you remind me of her in some ways, Lee. Not that you look like her or act like her. The way you trust me completely with your body and your secrets. Took almost a year before she was ready to let me in and I thought it had shriveled up and quit working by then. That first time was a disaster for both of us. We got better at it, but she was so afraid of making love without being married."

He put the bottle to his mouth.

She glanced at the bottle and then at him. "Don't, Mace."

He held the bottle out and looked at it. "I've only had a couple of swallows. Barely cleared out the neck." But he reared back and threw it into the creek. She heard the tinkle of breaking glass, then silence.

"You always talk drunker than you are."

"It keeps people away."

"Even Mitch?"

"Yeah, even Mitch. He always needed me so much, then he grew up. Hell, all of a sudden I didn't know a damn thing and he had all the answers."

"It was nothing personal, Mace. All kids are like that. Don't you remember being a kid yourself?"

"I thought it'd be different with us because it was just the two of us for so long." He belched. "Damn fine whiskey you made me toss."

"I don't make you do anything, Mace."

"Yeah, you do. You just don't know you do."

They sat in silence for a long time. Talley watched Mace. Her eyes had adjusted to the darkness and she could make out the silvery glint of his eyes and the thoughtful expression on his face. Every once in a while a few strains of music floated their way. They sat so long, Talley thought Mace had decided not to finish whatever he wanted to tell her. She moved around, trying to find a more comfortable seat on the log. Maybe she should just go back and catch the last of Mitch's performance. She started to get up.

"Don't go yet. I'm not through."

She sighed and settled back down. She wasn't sure she wanted to hear about Mitch's mother.

"As soon as she turned eighteen we got married. I wasn't much older myself. Too young, of course, but she wanted it. And because she wanted it, I wanted it. I loved her, Lee, but when I look back on what little time we had together, I can't remember why."

His voice was hoarse and broke on the last few words. She didn't dare look at him then. She didn't think she could stand to see him with tears in his eyes.

"We had a few months together, then she was carrying Mitch. Something went wrong and we almost lost him...and Ellen too. I kept thinking I didn't want him if it meant losing Ellen. I know it sounds bad, but I didn't know him, had never seen him. They didn't do those...those pictures back in those days."

"Ultrasounds."

"Yeah, that's it. So in a way, he wasn't real to me." He shook his head. "It makes me sound like the worst father, but hell, I was only nineteen. What did I know?"

"I don't think anybody ever knows how they'd feel in a situation like that until they're in it."

"It wasn't that I didn't want him at all. A boy or girl, didn't matter. Having a baby was the next step. You get married, have babies, live your life the best you can, then you die. That's the way it's supposed to go, only it didn't for Ellen. She had Mitch and survived it. Doctors said she probably shouldn't try to have any more. Then a few months later she got sick all of a sudden. Didn't have anything to do with the problems she'd had with Mitch. Cancer. And a few months after that she was...gone. Mitch wasn't a year old."

Talley blinked back tears. She had known that Mitch's mother had died when he was young, but she had never given any thought to her as a real person, a woman who'd loved Mace.

"It's been so long, Lee, over twenty-two years. Most of the time I can't remember what she looked like, can't remember what her hair felt like in my hands. Mitch has her hair, black as sin, and her dark skin."

"He has your eyes."

"Yeah. Ellen's were blue as the sky on a clear day, not dark and stormy like yours."

"Why are you telling me this, Mace?"

"Because I need to tell someone. I can't tell Mitch, can't make him understand how much I missed his mother for so long. Then one day I didn't miss her so much and now...now I can't really remember her at all. I can't tell him that we were only together three years and it seems like a dream I had. Ellen's folks wanted to take Mitch, but I wouldn't let 'em. How could I give him away? How could I give up the only part of Ellen I had left? My folks helped raised him till they died. They were both gone by the time he was twelve."

Talley vaguely recalled the elderly Holloways. They must have had Mace late in life. An accident on the farm had taken Mitch's grandfather and illness had claimed his grandmother and both had happened within just a few years time. Talley hadn't thought about the fact that they had been Mace's parents as well. She tried so hard to keep Mace and Mitch separate that she sometimes blinded herself to the threads that wove them together.

"She could sing like an angel," he said and stopped.

"Ellen?"

He hesitated, then nodded. "Back in those days, the Fourth festival was a lot smaller. Sometimes local people would sing for the crowds. Ellen and her family had just moved here from Jackson. I watched her sing some old gospel songs with her family and then she did a solo. I think that's when I fell in love with her. When we got married, we lived with my folks on the farm. After Mitch was born and before she got sick, I'd sit out on the porch late in the evening and listen to her sing Mitch to sleep. I'd close my eyes and all I could hear was her sweet voice filling the night."

He said no more. He didn't have to. She now knew why he couldn't bear to see his son perform. She moved closer to him and he wrapped his arm around her. At that moment the patches of night sky visible amid the leaves lit up with the first starburst of fireworks.

"Sorry I unloaded on you." He winked and squeezed her arm where his hand lay. "Seems like that's all I do, unload on you."

"It's okay, Mace. I understand now."

"I hoped you would."

"Mitch will be looking for me."

He nodded. "Go on, then."

She'd have to make some excuse to Mitch. She hated lying to him. When had she started lying? When had this gotten so complicated?

"Will you be by later tonight?"

He nodded again and took his arm away from her. She kissed him on the cheek, turned on the flashlight and started back.

Chapter Six

ଚ୨

With Mitch in Nashville for most of the week, Talley felt a little lost without him. They were staying with another band member's relatives who lived near Nashville. Mitch had been relieved. The generous offer saved them the cost of motel rooms.

Now it was Friday night and Talley tried to imagine Mitch and The Cold Creek Band in a bar at least three times the size of the Rose. She heard his music in her heart. Mitch and the band were good and had a realistic shot at their dreams if only the right people would hear them. They hoped to make the right connections in Nashville.

Then her thoughts drifted to Mace and everything he'd told her nearly a week ago. Her heart ached for him. If only he would talk to Mitch and make him understand why. Talley wished she could make Mace understand that Mitch needed to know some of the things he had confided in her. It would help their troubled relationship more than he could imagine. Mitch had no idea how or why Mace hurt inside.

She picked up a towel to keep her hands busy. She'd had to lie to Mitch about not catching his performance and not watching the fireworks with him. She'd told him the barbecue hadn't agreed with her and she'd been in the restroom throwing up then sat away from the crowd until she felt a little better. The excuse did double duty as a reason to turn Mitch away again easily.

Later that night, Mace had come to her although she really didn't expect him to. There was none of their usual teasing, only a desperate need to find comfort with one another. Afterwards, Talley held him throughout the night, his restless stirrings keeping her awake. He cut their morning ritual in her haven short and left earlier than usual. Talley missed him beyond reason.

The loud creak of the door caught her attention and her wide eyes looked toward it. She hoped it wouldn't be Jack Sandler. Without Mitch to help her, she was afraid Jack's increasing nastiness would explode.

Who came through the door almost made her heart stop beating. As many times as she had watched the door open and wanted it to be him, suddenly she was afraid. Mace filled the doorway then let the old wooden door slam shut behind him. He squinted in the dim lighting until his eyes pinpointed her behind the bar. His long legs ate up the floor between them, and Talley took a step backward at his determined presence.

At the bar, Mace swung one long leg over the stool in front of her, his eyes having never left her.

"Mace?" She asked a thousand questions in that one whispered word.

"I'll have a beer," he said too loudly. His eyes glittered like polished silver and bore into hers.

With shaking hands, Talley filled a mug with draft, leaving hardly any head at all. She set it in front of Mace.

"Howdy, Mace. Been awhile," Dylan said from behind her, causing her to jump. Dylan gave her a questioning look.

"We-e-ell," Mace drawled and downed half the beer. He slammed the glass on the counter hard enough to crack it, liquid sloshing over the side. "Life's a bitch, ain't it, Dylan."

"Take it easy, Mace." Dylan frowned. "Been a long time since you had a drink in this place. And you remember the reason why as well as me. I won't stand for any of your bullshit and you know it." Dylan looked at Talley. "I don't know what's going on between you and Mitch, but I don't want no trouble."

"Trouble," Mace repeated, and he belched loud enough to wake the dead. "Nobody knows the trouble we're gonna see before long. But not tonight, Dylan. No trouble tonight."

"I'll hold you to that," Dylan said and moved on.

"I have work to do, Mace," Talley said, trying to keep her voice steady.

"Work," he repeated in that stupid, patronizing tone. "So do I, darlin'. So do I."

Obviously, it wasn't Mace's first drink of the evening. He was a little drunk, enough to slur his speech and give his words a razor edge, but not enough to pass out and save them from disaster. Or maybe he was pretending again.

"What do you want, Mace?" Talley tried to keep her voice low, but she had to be heard above the music.

Mace chugged down the last of the brew before answering. "My boy's out of town singing his heart out on some stage somewhere and I want his woman."

Warmth crept into her face and she shook her head. "Not like this, Mace."

He cocked his head to one side as if thinking hard. "Seem to recall I was a lot drunker than this the first time I took you."

"Don't, Mace."

"Then come home with me." All the bitter sarcasm was gone and Talley could hear the need in him.

"I—" she began and stopped. It was a mistake giving in to him when he was like this, but what could she do? She was afraid he might jump on the bar and shout to the world what was going on between them. She couldn't chance hurting Mitch. "I get off work in about half an hour. If you go on now and have a cup of coffee at the Grill, I'll meet you there."

"That's it, darlin'." He winked, slid off the barstool and left the same way he came in, long decisive strides across the wooden floor.

Talley took away the mug, checking it for cracks, and wiped down the bar. Dylan appeared at her side again.

"What's eating him?"

"H-He's worried about Mitch," she improvised, but didn't think it was a lie.

"He didn't pay," Dylan pointed out, always the businessman.

"It was my treat. Take it out of my check."

"And Talley, next time you see Mace, tell him not to start his hell-raising at the Rose. We're both too old for it."

At midnight, after everyone had cleared out, Talley grabbed her purse. With Mitch out of town, she had ridden to work with Jeannie. Talley's car needed a tune-up and new tires, but she hadn't gotten around to taking care of either.

Outside, Talley saw Mace's truck still in the parking lot. She told Jeannie she had a lift home.

"Are you sure, hon?"

"I'm sure. Thanks again."

She waited for Jeannie to drive off before walking across the empty parking lot to the pickup. The white Ford was nearly twenty years old and great patches of rust covered the hood and fenders. Yes, the same truck she and Mitch had parked in on McKenna Lane.

She found Mace on his knees, retching into the bushes. She controlled the urge to put her foot on his backside and flatten him into his vomit.

Instead, she leaned against his truck. "I'm not going to pick you up, Mace. I'm not going to coddle you like some helpless baby. You're a grown man so why the hell don't you act like it?"

He pushed himself to the side and sat with his back against a tire. "It's not the beer, Lee. I only had one other drink before I got here." He ran his hand through his shaggy hair. "I'm sick of myself. And us. I don't know how much longer I can go on like this."

Then tell me what you want! her mind screamed, and she bit her lip to keep from saying the words aloud. She had sworn she wouldn't prompt him. Whatever Mace wanted, he had to let her know without having to drag it out of him. She would not corner him nor threaten him. It had to come from his heart.

"I think you gulped down that beer too fast."

With the help of his pickup, Mace stood. His whole body shook from the effort.

"You coming home with me?"

Going with Mace to what was also Mitch's home made her uneasy. Yet, Mace seemed to feel no extra guilt in the act.

"Yes, but I'll drive."

Talley's heart tightened with each of the twenty miles she drove toward Shady Hollow. Mace huddled in the corner of the cab, snoring. Soon enough, Talley steered the truck up the long driveway to the sprawling farmhouse. She stopped, shifted into park, and turned off the lights and ignition. She sat for a while, smoking.

Finally, Mace stirred.

"We're here," she announced and got out of the truck. She followed Mace to the front door and inside. It had been many years since she'd been in this house, not since she was a teenager. She remembered the last time. Mitch had pulled her through the living room where Mace sat with the Sunday paper, steamy cup of coffee and cigarette. Shyly, she had greeted him, calling him Mr. Holloway. He'd barely glanced at them, nodded, and went back to his paper.

She and Mitch had gone into the kitchen, packed a lunch, and spent the afternoon making up for the times they wouldn't be together once her family left for Chattanooga.

"What did you think?" Talley asked after reminding him of that sunny Sunday afternoon.

His brow wrinkled. "I don't remember that particular afternoon, but you were always around. I remember thinking you were a pretty girl and would be a beautiful woman one day. And I was right. I thought my boy was lucky to have you for his girl. I damn sure didn't think of you the way I do now, Lee."

"I know. I didn't think of you that way either. I was a little afraid of you. You were Mitch's father, the voice of authority, just as my mother was. All adults were the enemy. That afternoon was the day my mother told me she was marrying Frank Wilson and we were moving to Chattanooga. I didn't mind her seeing Frank, and I didn't mind that she was getting married. Frank's a great guy, and I wanted her to be happy. But I didn't want to move away and leave Mitch behind."

The silence was deafening.

"It's why I came back, you know. I missed him so much."

"Then why—" he started to ask, but stopped himself. "C'mon, Lee. I'll take a shower while you make us some coffee. I never made it to the Grill."

Talley watched him leave the room. She could guess what his unasked question would have been. *Then why haven't you slept with Mitch?* Or maybe, *Why are you sleeping with me?* How could she explain to him, or Mitch, when she couldn't really explain it to herself?

She looked for coffee grounds and found a jar of unopened instant in a cabinet. Mace wouldn't drink anything but "real" coffee, and Mitch rarely drank coffee at all. Why did he have a new jar of instant? Because of her? Had he expected to bring her to the house at some point? She didn't know what to think. She only wished Mace would hurry up and decide what he wanted.

"Didn't mean to embarrass you at the Rose," he mumbled as he entered the kitchen, his lean ranginess enhanced by not wearing a shirt. He often worked out in the sun with no shirt so his upper body was sun-browned while below the waist he was as smooth and pale as she.

"Yes, you did. That's exactly what you were trying to do," she accused as she poured him coffee. "I kept picturing you standing on the bar, shouting to the world about us. I was afraid you might do it or something equally stupid. I couldn't let you hurt Mitch like that." She handed him his mug and sipped from hers. "I don't want to hurt Mitch at all."

"We've already done that. It can't be undone." He sighed and lit up two cigarettes, handing one to her. "Have you noticed most of our talk is about Mitch lately? We never used to mention him at all."

Tears burned her eyes. "I have to go."

"I won't stop you."

"Good because you have to drive me. I don't feel up to a twenty-mile walk in the middle of the night."

"Don't go, Lee."

Was it really that simple? Stay and make love with Mace, feel good tonight and guilty tomorrow. She couldn't keep them separate anymore. Mitch overflowed into her strange relationship with his father. And Mace had already overshadowed her relationship with his son.

"All right, I'll stay." Yes, it was that simple, that basic. She would be consumed with guilt tomorrow, but she would also have an extra night with Mace.

His bedroom, two doors down from Mitch's, was uncluttered. The bare necessities, but not much else, as if he were a stranger passing through this life. Mace was a man who needed little but what he did need was absolutely essential. Had that come to include her?

She undressed and slipped into his bed, clean but unmade. He pulled off his clothes, but stood and watched her in the faint moonlight streaming through the window.

"I don't know how many times I've imagined you lying in my bed just like that," he murmured then crawled in beside her. She snuggled into his arm, kissed his chest, ran her hand through the sparse hair.

If sex was the point then it was dulled by the presence of Mitch's shadow in the house. He was safely miles away but neither of them could forget him for a moment.

"It feels right, you here beside me," Mace said and nuzzled her hair. She turned on her side, her back against his front, and his strong arms surrounded her. A little while later, his breathing evened and he slept. Strangely, it was enough. She didn't feel frustration or annoyance at him. She agreed with him.

It felt *right* lying beside him, drifting off to sleep. In his sleep, he nudged her backside. She smiled and closed her eyes, knowing she would see his handsomely worn face the first thing in the morning.

Chapter Seven

ॐ

Talley didn't know how long they'd slept, but she awoke to her leg being lifted out of the way and Mace easing himself inside of her. She didn't open her eyes or say a thing, but shifted a little to make it easier for him. When he was firmly in place, his leg underneath hers, he snuggled against her back and laid his free arm along her arm, his fingers folding between hers.

They moved together slowly, and Talley drifted with the rhythm of Mace sliding in and out, in and out of her flesh. His warm breath passed over her ear and cheek, and she smiled.

If she could freeze time, this would be the perfect moment to make last forever. She and Mace moving as one before the urgency took over and ended it. Then she cleared her mind of all thoughts. She didn't want to waste another precious second *thinking*. She only wanted to *feel*.

"Mace," she murmured as he buried himself inside of her over and over again, "yes, Mace."

He groaned, heightening her arousal.

The perfect moment lasted longer than she'd ever imagined was possible, but it was coming to an end. Her skin tingled around her hips and belly and down her thighs, and her fingers and toes flexed on their own. Mace's thrusts now came harder and faster and he felt stiffer deep inside of her.

The orgasm rippled through her suddenly. Caught by surprise, Talley cried out and Mace tightened his hold on her writhing body.

"Darlin'," he rasped out.

As it faded, her muscles throbbed with the release, and her eyes filled with tears.

A pleasant thrum continued where he drove into her even harder. He thrust one last time and stayed there, pulsing, a low growl of satisfaction sounding deep in his throat.

The tenseness left their bodies.

They stayed as they were, bodies joined, their breaths evened, heartbeats slowed, and they fell back to sleep.

* * * * *

She didn't know how long they'd slept again. When she awoke this time, it was still dark and Mace wasn't beside her. She sat up, eyes wide, and found Mace at the gun cabinet. He had pulled out a handgun and was loading it.

"Mace, what are —"

"Hush, Lee. I heard something in the front of the house. I think somebody's broken in. Stay here."

Mace disappeared through the bedroom door.

Talley scrambled to her feet and rummaged in the dark for clothes. She ran across his shirt smelling of sunshine and musky sweat and everything that made up Mace. She tugged it on, buttoning it as she ran to catch up with him.

He jerked her a look and shook his head for her to stay back and keep quiet. Then she heard a noise and her heart rose in her throat.

They passed through the dark kitchen, and Mace stepped into the living room. Talley stayed in the doorway, frozen by the shadowy figure that moved at the other end of the room.

Just as Mace lifted the gun, the lights snapped on and they all blinked in its sudden brightness.

"Dammit, boy!" Mace shouted in fear and anger and dropped his arm. "I almost shot your fool head off."

Then no one said a word.

Mitch's gaze swept from Mace to Talley and back again, then rested on Talley. The sight of Talley wearing nothing except Mace's denim shirt must have been almost as disturbing as seeing his father with a gun trained on him. His jaws worked, but no sound passed through his open lips. He took a step forward then two back.

Mace, in an eloquent if morbid summary of the situation, touched the barrel to his temple and made a soft exploding sound with his pursed lips. Then his shoulders slumped, and he leaned against the back of the couch.

"No. Mitch…" Talley started, but didn't know what to say. Nothing she said would wipe away the hurt and betrayal in Mitch's eyes.

"Well," Mitch said, at last able to make some sound. "Well, damn. This answers a hell of a lot of questions, doesn't it, Tal?"

No, she wanted to scream at both of them, *it doesn't answer anything*! Instead, she said, "Oh, Mitch, it's not what you think."

Mitch swallowed hard. "Then you're not sleeping with my father?"

"Oh." Talley's hand flew to her mouth. She couldn't lie and deny it. Besides the fact that she didn't possess the quick imagination to invent a story to explain why she was here in the middle of the night wearing only Mace's shirt, she wouldn't outright lie to Mitch, not again. "That's not what I meant," she mumbled behind her hand, not knowing what she had meant. She had been searching for words to ease Mitch's pain.

Mitch's gray eyes glinted like steel. "Pardon the interruption, but I really have to get out of here."

Talley wanted to close her eyes and fade away. She wanted the floor to rip open and swallow her up. For a fraction of an instant she had the urge to grab Mace's gun and put her out of both their miseries, but she was too much of a coward to do it.

"You'll understand if I don't stay tonight. Hell, the noise would probably keep me awake." Mitch stalked toward the door.

"Watch your mouth, boy," Mace said.

Mitch whirled around. "You don't have a *boy* anymore. Just remember, *Daddy*, I had her first."

Mitch went out the door before either of them could say anything else.

Talley couldn't move and was unaware of Mace's movements until he spread the afghan from the couch around her shoulders.

"Go after him, Lee. He might do something stupid and get himself killed."

Mace wiped away the tears she didn't know streamed down her face.

"I'm sorry, Mace," she whispered, "I didn't mean—"

"Don't apologize to me. If anybody knows what you didn't mean, it's me. Apologize to him and try to explain." Mace held up the revolver. "I think I'd best unload this and put it away."

Talley placed a hand on his arm. "You-you wouldn't do anything stupid with that thing, would you?"

"Not me. I'm sorry he had to find out like this, but I have no regrets. Go to him, Lee."

Talley ran out of the house, surprised that Mitch's truck was still in the driveway. He sat inside like a cold statue. She opened the door and slid in, huddling into the afghan. The night wasn't cool, but she was trembling anyway. Mitch didn't say a word, stared straight ahead as if he didn't know she was there.

"I love you, Mitch."

He jumped as if he'd been struck with a hot poker, then hit the steering wheel with his fist.

"Hell of a thing to say to me after I find out you've slept with my—with Mace."

"I've always loved you. That first day of school, the first time I saw you, I went home and told my mother I loved you and would marry you when I grew up." Talley laughed but it was a bitter sound. "You don't know how hard it was for me to leave you six years ago. My mother and I battled over that for the longest time. I stayed angry with her for years. Of course she had to go with Frank, but I didn't want to leave you. You're why I came back."

"Then *why*, for God's sake? You haven't let me touch you in the six months we've been seeing each other."

"I've been seeing Mace for about three months—"

"You mean this isn't the first time?" Mitch's face screwed up in confusion and his voice rose in pitch. He beat both fists against the steering wheel then yanked open the door and stumbled out. His scream of anguish cut the still night, and Talley flinched at the raw sound. Fleetingly, her eyes rested on the house. Mace undoubtedly heard his son's wail of unbridled grief.

Talley almost wished she had let him think this was the first time. It would have eased Mitch's grief and he might have gotten over one night of lost reason more easily than a continuous affair. Yet she was glad she hadn't lied. At this point all she had to offer him was the truth. Or as much of it as any of them could handle for now.

The whole truth was too fragile for any of them to face at the moment, even herself.

Talley slid across the seat and set her bare feet on the ground. "Will you listen to me, Mitch?"

"Will you lie to me, Talley?"

"No. As you pointed out, I could have done that at first. You would have believed any silly story I could have come up with because you wanted to believe. Right now, I want to tell you the truth. Mace and I have been sleeping together, but it has nothing to do with you."

Mitch laughed without humor.

"Please, Mitch, just listen. If Mace weren't your father, just another man, it wouldn't hurt nearly as bad."

"I feel like I've been kicked in the stomach twice by an old mule. Talley...Talley, I love you. I thought you loved me. I wanted us to make it this time."

"I did, too. I do want us to make it."

"Damn you both!" he swore.

"Mitch, I didn't sleep with Mace to hurt you. And Mace didn't sleep with me to hurt you either. It just happened. And I know how stupid and useless that sounds. Either of us could have stopped it, but we didn't because…because…"

She faltered. She didn't know how to finish the sentence. "You can't let this come between you and Mace. You have enough problems without this."

"Sure, Tal. I can walk right back in that house and act like my father never slept with my girl. I can sprout wings and fly from here to McKenna Park easier than I can do that."

"I didn't say it would be an easy thing to do. You have to accept this or you and Mace will never have a chance. I am responsible for this and I accept that. Now, I have to do what I can to make it right."

Mitch paced back and forth beside the truck like a caged animal. Talley drew a deep breath of the humid night air.

"Will you take me home?"

"At this moment, Talley, I don't ever want to see you again. You or my f—you or Mace."

She didn't think that was completely true. Otherwise, Mitch would have been gone when she came out of the house. He wouldn't have listened to her. He wanted to find a way around this as desperately as she did.

"I know. I don't blame you. I really want you to take me home."

Reluctantly, he nodded.

"I have to-to get my things."

He nodded again.

Talley returned to the house. She dropped the afghan on the couch and cautiously walked from room to room and down the hall to Mace's bedroom without seeing him. She dressed with numb fingers, fumbling with buttons and a zipper, and when she turned around, Mace filled the doorway watching her.

"Mitch is taking me home. I'll try to talk him into staying with me. I doubt if he'd come back here anyway."

Mace said nothing, watched her.

"I think he hates me," Talley admitted.

"And me."

"No! You're his father. He can't hate you. I'll make him hate me enough so he won't have any left for you."

"Don't do that, Lee. I'll take my share of the hate and the blame."

Tears filled her eyes and overflowed. She felt them track hotly down her cheeks. "No, I'll take it all. I won't come between you."

"You already are."

Mace walked toward her and Talley met him halfway. She leaned against his chest and let her tears soak into the old denim shirt he now wore. His arms enclosed her and his hands ran through her hair. She listened to Mace's heart beat its strong, steady rhythm. In truth, she didn't want to go, but she didn't know how else to repair the damage between them.

"Goodbye, Lee," he murmured gruffly into her hair.

Talley thought she heard his heart breaking in two.

She turned her face up to his and they kissed, long and sweet, what she thought would be for the last time. She couldn't say goodbye, she couldn't say anything. She forced herself out of Mace's arms and ran through the house, all the way to Mitch's truck.

Breathless, she climbed in and Mitch turned the ignition. They didn't say a word during the long drive.

Mitch left the motor running when he stopped in front of her place.

"Please come in with me, Mitch."

Mitch shook his head. "I don't think so," he said tiredly.

"You can't go home tonight. Please, Mitch, we have a lot to talk about. And the couch is comfortable." She reached over, cut off the motor, and took the keys.

"Talley—" He reached for them, but she held them back.

"Please, Mitch," she begged and a part of her didn't understand why she pleaded with him to stay.

She got out of the truck and unlocked the front door. Uncomfortably, he stood just inside while she turned on the air conditioner. "Are you hungry?"

"Give me my keys. I won't go back to Shady Hollow, but I can still find some other place to stay."

"You sound too tired to do any more driving tonight. Please, Mitch."

He removed his hat and laid it on the table. Talley sighed in relief. Perhaps the night could be salvaged after all.

.

Chapter Eight

ℛ

Talley fixed two glasses of iced tea and handed one to Mitch. She looked at his hat. It looked new and unused, like all of Mitch's clothing. So unlike Mace whose clothes always looked as if he'd just come in from a hard day's work. Of course, Mitch had had a gig that evening and wanted to look his best.

Talley frowned at the strange comparison. She had vowed to keep them separate in her life. No thoughts of one while with the other. Lately, all she and Mace had talked about was Mitch. Now, all she could think of was Mace. A line had been crossed, and she wished she'd been able to avoid it.

She brought out a pillow and a quilt and set them on the couch. "Do you feel like talking tonight?" she asked uncertainly.

"I don't feel much of anything right now." Mitch sat in a chair and set aside his cup. "Bonnie fell while we were setting up this afternoon. She broke her arm."

"Oh, how awful. How is she?"

"Well, she didn't let on at first. Said she couldn't hold a guitar, but she could still sing. We played the gig. Mike played rhythm instead of piano. Mike just can't play rhythm worth a damn, but we made do. Bonnie was hurting real bad by the time we finished. I tried to get her to let me take her to a hospital in Nashville, but she wanted to come home. She was in so much pain by the time we got here, I took her straight to the emergency room. They doped her up and they're keeping her overnight. They'll do X-rays in the morning. When I left, she was asleep."

"I'm sorry, Mitch."

"I thought I'd stay home tonight and go back to Nashville tomorrow. We have one more night at the club."

"We didn't expect you back until Sunday."

"Obviously," he murmured.

"I am sorry, Mitch. I can't say it enough."

"Actually, you haven't said it at all. I can't help but wonder if you're sorry you slept with Mace or if you're sorry you got caught."

"I'm sorry we hurt you. And I'm sorry Mace and I didn't have the sense to stop this before it went too far."

Mitch closed his eyes.

"Everything I said about you and me is true. I didn't want us to ruin our chances this time. We moved too fast when we were teenagers."

"We're not kids anymore, Talley. Did you always have a thing for Mace? Was I just a way to be close to him back then…and now?"

"No, I barely noticed him back then. He was just your father, another parent who made stupid rules. I noticed him less this time until…well, that night he came into the Rose and he was drunk. The Rose was closing, and you were off playing somewhere and wouldn't be back for hours. I was going to drive him back to Shady Hollow and wait for you, but it was late and I was tired. I brought him here and put him to bed on the couch."

Mitch jumped to his feet. "It happened *here*?"

"Tonight was the first night I'd ever been to the farm." Talley took a deep breath. "Anyway, that night Mace woke up about four in the morning and I fixed us something to eat. We made small talk, like polite strangers. I don't think either of us took any special notice of the other until that moment. One thing just led to another and…it just happened."

Mitch made a sound of disgust deep in his throat.

"You wanted the truth and this is the truth. It had been so long since I'd been with anyone. I needed to be held and touched and Mace just happened to be there. I tried to justify it, of course. I kept telling myself that sleeping with you just because I needed sex would not do our relationship any good. I wanted to be sure this time. Mace was someone I could trust even though I didn't know him well. And, I suppose, I thought he was the only person in the world who would want to keep it a secret as desperately as I did."

Mitch tried to speak, cleared his throat and tried again. "And Mace?"

"I don't know, really. I think it had been a long time for him, too. And I suspect he needed closeness without any attachments. Maybe he knew I was the one person in the world who wouldn't expect anything from him. I do know that he wasn't trying to hurt you." Talley sighed. "It just happened."

"You keep saying that, but it kept happening."

"I'm sorry, Mitch. I don't know what else to say."

Mitch sat on the edge of the couch and pulled off his boots. "Don't mind me. I'll be gone in the morning. I'm just so damned tired right now."

"I'll go with you to see Bonnie."

"You don't have to pretend anymore."

"I've never pretended anything."

He rubbed his face with his hands. "I don't understand!"

"It had nothing to do with you and me. I love you, Mitch, and I've been seeing you and spending time with you because I want to."

"And you just happen to be sleeping with my father?"

"Yes, that's it. I don't want to stop seeing you because of Mace. If you can forgive us a little and try to get past it—"

"And you won't see Mace again?"

"No, not after tonight. I don't expect an answer this minute. Take as long as you need. I just don't want it to be over for us."

He stretched out on the couch. "Neither do I, Tal. I need to get some sleep. I want to be with Bonnie when they do the X-rays."

Talley went to him and spread the quilt out for him. Tentatively, she kissed his cheek. Mitch reached up for her, his fingers splayed against her neck, his thumb at her ear. He brought her to him and pressed his lips to hers.

When he let her go, she straightened.

"'Desperate Hearts' got a standing ovation tonight," he told her.

"It's a beautiful song, and you and Bonnie sing it perfectly together. I am so proud of you."

"I just wish…" His voice trailed off as if he thought better of finishing the sentence.

"Mace is proud of you, too. He wishes you had more interest in the farm, but he's proud of anything you do."

"Has he told you that?"

"No, but I know Mace well enough to know that he couldn't wish you anything but success. He just doesn't know how to show it."

"I don't believe it, Tal. All he has to do is come and listen to us just once."

She held her tongue. Mace hadn't asked her not to say anything to Mitch, but it wasn't her place. He needed to hear it from Mace himself. Somehow she would have to convince Mace to tell him…

Then it hit her and her stomach twisted into a hard knot. She would probably never see Mace again. For Mitch's sake, they could never allow themselves to be alone.

"Talk to him, Mitch. Tell him it's what you want." If she couldn't talk to Mace, maybe she could convince Mitch to open up to his father.

"I don't think I'll be talking to Mace about anything for a long time, Tal," Mitch said stiffly. "Now, I need to sleep."

"All right, Mitch. Good night."

"No, it hasn't been a *good* night at all."

72

* * * * *

The next morning Talley went with Mitch to see Bonnie. After her arm had been put in a cast, they drove her home. Talley and Mitch spent the rest of the day together, and she tried not to think of Mace. She tried not to remember it was Saturday. She tried to give her undivided attention to Mitch, but only half succeeded.

When Mitch had left her that evening without attempting to talk her into bed, she'd almost missed it. It had become a part of their relationship and felt strange without it. After he had gone, she shut the door behind him, tears burning her eyes as she turned the lock. Mace wouldn't come to her tonight or ever again. Nothing had ever kept him away except the loss of his son, and she couldn't blame him. She could miss him and ache for him, but she couldn't blame him. She slept on the couch that night.

The more time she spent with Mitch, when he wasn't on the road, the less she thought of Mace. She decided when she could look into Mitch's gray eyes and not see hurt or betrayal, then he would be ready to go to bed with her. But there never was a time when she looked into his eyes that she didn't see some trace of what she and Mace had done to him.

Mitch was spending more and more time on the road. The Cold Creek Band was being booked all over the state. They played nightclubs and fairs and private parties. "Desperate Hearts" was a hit everywhere they went.

When Talley listened to the song for the first time since her breakup with Mace, she realized, with a pang in her heart, it was *their* song—Bonnie and Mitch's, her and Mace's. Bonnie had written most of the words, but she had written them from her heart. Bonnie longed for Mitch as much as Talley missed Mace. The heart-wrenching melody of lonesome guitar riffs only emphasized the melancholy lyrics filled with lost love and empty hearts desperate to find some way to go on.

She never should have come between Mitch and Bonnie. Both of them loved their music and their life on the road. They could spend hours deep in conversation or working on a song. Talley watched them often. She'd felt left out at first until she realized this was the way it was meant to be. She believed things happen for a purpose, and her renewed relationship with Mitch had been the only way for her to find Mace.

If she hadn't come back to Mitch, she never would have returned to Randolph in the first place. If she hadn't been seeing Mitch, she never would have felt compelled to take care of Mace when he came into the Rose that fateful night. She never would have brought him to her house. Nothing else could have brought them together like their common bond to Mitch.

Sometimes she felt as if Mitch was on the verge of telling her it was over. She always managed to make him forget by reminding him of something that happened years ago. Talking about their past relationship helped them both. While she believed they still loved one another in the special way that first lovers do, their love hadn't grown up with them.

So she clung to Mitch because she couldn't have Mace, and she hated herself for it. Mace had never offered her anything. He'd told her that first time he wasn't looking for anyone to be a permanent part of his life, and he had never said anything to make her think he had changed his mind.

One day, Mitch had come to her and told her he had had a long talk with Mace and he understood his father better now. Mace had explained about Mitch's mother and why it was so difficult for him to hear his son perform. She could see the relief in Mitch's eyes now that he knew. All this time he had thought Mace was disappointed in him because he wasn't the son Mace wanted.

Talley was happy for them both, but she now knew she could never be the one to leave Mitch. If she left and tried to return to Mace, accepting him on his own terms, Mitch would never be able to forgive either of them a second time. Since father and son had reached an understanding, Talley could never come between them again.

Chapter Nine

🔊

Talley tried. It had been a few months since she'd seen Mace. He had stayed away from the Rose and hadn't come to her again on Saturday night. She had hurt badly while she and Mace were slipping behind Mitch's back, but the pain had been nothing compared to the ache she experienced now.

Traveling with Mitch was something she didn't want to do. She went with him if the gigs were close and he could drive her home afterward. Since the band was being booked farther and farther away, Talley found herself home alone many nights. Mitch tried to convince her to come with them, but she had her job at the Rose and couldn't give it up. She had to keep her job, and Dylan wouldn't agree to her working whenever she felt like it.

In October, her stepfather's company sent him to Knoxville, and Talley spent Thanksgiving with her family there. Now, a week and a day later, on a cloudy Friday afternoon, Talley suddenly found herself in her car, heading for Shady Hollow. Mitch wouldn't be there. The Cold Creek Band had booked a club in Chattanooga for the weekend. He wouldn't be back until Sunday.

Talley couldn't control this irresistible urge to see Mace. It came out of nowhere, the need to see his weatherworn face, to help ease the ache in her heart.

The car sputtered occasionally. She'd had the car tuned up several months ago, but now something else was wrong. She didn't have the money to get it repaired or to buy new tires. She had been thinking of getting a part-time job, especially with Mitch away so much, but like so many things she let fall by the wayside, she hadn't done anything about it. Sometimes she felt as if she walked around wrapped in a gray fog and, lately, all she could think about was Mace.

Junior, a hired hand that worked part-time at Shady Hollow, said Mace was up at the pasture near the old home place mending fences. He pointed, telling her how to get there.

The dark gray sky spat icy rain at her as she drove along the back roads. She passed by several houses, but didn't see any others the farther she went. Talley wasn't familiar with this road that ran along the ridge overlooking the bluff, and hadn't realized Shady Hollow Farms was this large. She prayed the car would make it and the freezing rain wouldn't turn into the ice the weatherman had predicted until she could get back home. He had announced a winter storm advisory, but assured his listeners it was a precaution. No accumulation of ice was expected.

A few miles before she reached the last turnoff, Talley met a bright red truck she would recognize anywhere. Jack Sandler leered and waved. In the rearview mirror, she saw his brake lights. She expected him to turn around, but then the lights went out and he moved on. Relief flooded her tense body. That one date with Jack was a mistake she'd regret as long as she lived.

She almost missed the turnoff to the old Shady Hollow home place. The narrow road was paved, but not well maintained. She hit bumps and potholes and icy rain still spluttered from dark, brooding clouds.

A few miles down the road, she started searching for signs of Mace. Then she saw the dirt track and his truck parked out in the pasture and farther away a little shack with a crooked stone chimney. Talley stopped on the side of the road, afraid she might get stuck if she drove to Mace's truck. The ground was still soft and muddy in places.

The cold air hit her in the face when she opened the door. The temperature had dropped since her drive had begun. With luck, she'd make it home before the weather turned any worse.

All she wanted was to see Mace.

She should have chosen a better time and place, but the overwhelming force had hit her suddenly, without warning. She barely recalled making the decision. Her arms and legs had seemingly moved of their own accord, and she'd found herself going to him. She had never expected to have to drive to the backside of nowhere to see him.

Just a few minutes, enough time to look at him and see how he was doing, then she would leave.

He was stringing new barbed wire from post to post and Talley stopped and watched him awhile. He must have known she waited. He had to have heard the car and looked back to see who it was. She watched him tighten the wire then fasten it down.

The thought crossed her mind that he might not want to see her at all. Earlier her feet had moved on their own, but now she couldn't make them go any farther. Time passed and finally Mace straightened, seemed almost to brace himself, and turned. He looked at her, motioning for her to come to him.

Only then did her body respond—in more ways than one. She walked toward him, but her knees were weak and her heart beat faster. She missed Mace with a desperation that frightened her.

Mace walked to his truck and leaned against it, pulling off his heavy gloves. He lit two cigarettes, then drew on one as he held the other out to her. When she reached him, she took it and dragged deep.

She missed smoking with him. And having coffee with him. And their Sunday morning ritual. And their Saturday night delight. She still wanted to find out how it would feel to wake up to his weatherworn face after a night of only sleeping in his arms.

Talley stood very close to him, their arms touching.

"Good to see you, Lee."

Thick drops of rain mixed with ice stung her face, but didn't bother her. She felt such a perfect peace standing next to Mace, listening to his dry, quiet voice.

"Hell of a time to be mending fences," she said, then caught the double meaning of the words.

Mace caught it too. "Never too late to mend fences. Or burn bridges. Which is it, Talley?"

She shrugged. The temperature seemed to be dropping by the minute. Or maybe it was Mace who caused her to feel colder. He'd called her Talley—that should tell her something. If she left right now, she might make it home before it was fully dark.

"Junior told me you were here. I wanted to see you. It's been awhile."

"Twenty weeks tonight. Mitch and I talked. We made our peace."

"I know. He told me you explained everything about his mother. I'm so glad you did. He understands now." When Mace didn't say anything, just stared at her, she asked, "Are you angry with me?"

"No more angry with you than myself. No, Talley, I don't hold any of it against you. I was drunk, but I knew what I was doing that first night."

"I don't even have the excuse of being drunk."

"It's not my excuse!" he snapped with a flare of anger. He tossed his cigarette and stomped it out.

"I didn't mean—"

"I got work to do, Talley. You set fire to this bridge and it's all burned down."

He strode over to the fence, pulling on his gloves. He knelt and began stringing wire again, effectively dismissing her.

"The rain is turning to ice, Mace. You might get stuck up here."

He searched the sky and shook his head. "It won't accumulate on the roads."

"Mace?"

"Yeah," he grunted, tightening the wire.

Talley walked closer to him. "Mace."

He didn't answer her that time. One word, any word, and she would…

"You'd best be getting back. That car of yours ain't the most reliable. And you need new tires. Go on, now."

"Yes, Mace."

Darkness had come sooner than she'd expected, so she could barely see her way to the car. The tears that filled her eyes didn't help. She ran, stumbled, fell into the car, and started it. She turned up the heat. God, she was cold, so cold, and only part of it was the weather. Mace had left her frostbitten.

She sat awhile, too shaken and cold to drive. She couldn't believe he hadn't done or said anything more personal than giving her a lit cigarette. He hadn't called her darlin', hadn't called her Lee after that first slip. And what did she expect? He had reconciled with his son over their stupid mistake. He couldn't risk losing Mitch a second time. She knew she shouldn't have come.

The freezing rain had turned to fine bits of ice by the time she pulled on the lights, turned the car around and drove away. Patches of ice covered everything, no matter what the weatherman and Mace had said.

Hypnotically, the wipers worked to scrape the slush off the windshield. Wasn't it time to face the truth yet? Wasn't it time to say to herself—

Her thoughts were interrupted by the sight of a red truck, crossways in the road ahead. The same pickup she'd seen earlier. Jack Sandler. What was he doing out here, blocking the road, unless he had trouble…or was bent on causing trouble?

Without hesitation, Talley swung the car to the right to go around the truck. With no room on the narrow road, she had to drive onto the soft shoulder. She hit the mud with a bump and moved along nicely for ten feet, then the front of her car bogged down, pitching her forward.

Lock the doors! the warning screamed in her head. As she raised up and reached for the button, the door was yanked open beneath her fingers. Rough hands grabbed her and pulled, but Talley screamed and fought him, striking out at him with her fist.

"Stop it, bitch!" Jack Sandler yelled. It was then Talley saw the knife in his hand and she froze. He pressed the blade to her neck. "Get out of the car."

Mace, she thought, *hurry*!

She did as Jack told her. When she was out, Jack moved the knife away and tightened his grip on her arm. Without the blade at her throat, she dug in her feet and resisted, twisting her arm to break free. Jack swung around, the knife coming toward her. Desperately, she threw all her weight backwards. His hand slipped and she tumbled into the ice-covered mud.

Before she could scramble away and get to her feet, Jack was on top of her. He clenched a handful of hair at the top of her head and put the blade to her throat once again.

"Mace," she croaked. "Mace Holloway will be along any minute."

Jack glanced uneasily up the road.

His grip tightened in her hair and her head throbbed. Where was Mace? He couldn't be mending his fences in the dark, in the pelting ice. Why didn't he come?

Jack looked back at Talley and grinned wolfishly.

"Mace?" he asked and something clicked in his mind. "You up here with Mace? Where's Mitch the Snitch?"

"I-I…" Talley faltered. She was no good at lying. "Mace is repairing the fence. Mitch is out of town, and I came up here to-to give him a message from Mitch."

The words sounded thin to her own ears and some false tone must have set off alarms in Jack's head. "You and Mace, huh?"

"No, you idiot. What the hell do you think you're doing, Jack? Let me go and help me get my car out of the ditch."

He put his face real close to hers, and it was then that she smelled the heavy aroma of whiskey clinging to him like a cloud.

"Mace can't stay much longer in the dark and the snow. He will be coming along, he will." She didn't know if she tried to convince Jack or herself.

"But he hasta give you a good head start, don't he?"

"You're talking crazy, Jack."

"Naw, I don't think so. I heard something a while back, about you and Mace. Even told my good buddy Mitch, but you know what? He didn't act real surprised. And that shack up here, the old Holloway house'd make a good place to sneak away to." Suddenly, he pulled her to her feet. "Come on, easy like. Don't make me use this. If you can give it away to an old fart like Mace Holloway, you can give me a piece too."

Jack was a bully, too cowardly to follow through on his threats. Even if he did slit her throat, it was no great loss. Mitch couldn't trust her and Mace couldn't want her. Nothing else mattered. She'd rather be dead than at Jack's mercy. "No, Jack. I'm not going with you. Use the knife if you have to, but I'm not moving."

Jack pressed the knife harder and she thought she felt a trickle of warmth from it, but she couldn't be sure. Too much snow and she was too cold. She didn't feel any pain.

He growled, deep in his throat like a wild animal ready to attack, and suddenly let her go. He swung his fist, and stars exploded in her head as pain burst through. She staggered back against her car, and Jack hit her again and again. She wasn't aware of the cold or the snow anymore, or even when she fell to her knees. All she felt was intense pain with each of Jack's blows. There was a final impact to her side and she was only vaguely aware of the sound of a vehicle driving away.

"Mace…" she moaned as she tried to move.

But then darkness crept in and overcame her as she passed into unconsciousness.

Chapter Ten

80

Mace tucked the blankets in around her more securely then brushed a strand of hair from her face. The bruise under her eye had darkened to deep purple since he'd brought her in. He had pulled a chair close to the bed and sat there, watching for signs of discomfort or regaining consciousness. The coffee had grown cold in his cup, but he didn't want to leave her side even for a few minutes in case she woke up and needed him.

He leaned back in the chair. He didn't know who had done this, but he suspected and the son of a bitch was as good as dead.

When Talley had come to him this afternoon, he should have told her. But he and Mitch had found a way around what he had done and as much as he wanted and needed this woman, he couldn't risk losing his son again. He wasn't a man who shed tears except over the most sorrowful of things, but his eyes filled with them now. How could he go on without her?

He wiped at them angrily. He'd have to. She had made her choice. The night Mitch came home unexpectedly and found them, she had gone with him. On the other hand, he hadn't asked her to stay. He'd never given her any reason to choose to stay. He knew if she had chosen him that night, Mitch would have been lost to him forever. So he'd told her to go with his son. Maybe Talley knew it, too.

Mace needed coffee. What he really wanted was a bottle of whiskey, but he had cleared the place of liquor some time ago. Here and at the house. Drinking had no answers, made his problems worse. He jumped to his feet.

Quickly, he tossed the cold coffee, poured fresh from the pot on the stove, and returned to his chair. He wished she'd awaken. It wasn't a good sign that she'd stayed unconscious this long.

He sipped the strong brew and thought of that first night. He had been so drunk he barely remembered going to the Rose. He and Dylan were on the outs over a brawl he'd started some months before. Tore the place up. Even though he'd paid for the damage, Dylan didn't want him around anymore. Mace still couldn't remember what the fight had been about. He had stayed away until that Saturday night. He couldn't recollect why he'd decided to stop in at the Rose on his way home.

Talley had been tending bar. He'd seen her around a few times. He and Mitch weren't getting along. Mitch wanted to follow his dreams, but Mace had a farm to run. Neither would give an inch. Too much alike, he guessed, too damned stubborn for their own good. They were always so angry with one another. Mitch hadn't bothered bringing Talley out to Shady Hollow although he told Mace she was back and he was seeing her again.

Dylan wouldn't let Talley serve him. She offered to take him home, saying Mitch could drive her back when he got in. Instead, she took him to her place, saying she wasn't up to the long drive. She fit perfectly under his arm as she helped him to the door. She let him fall on her couch, and he only remembered a glimpse of her as she walked back toward her bedroom before he passed out.

He woke about four in the morning, wondering where he was and what he was doing there. He lay there in the dark and thought for a while. Gradually, bits and pieces had floated to the surface—the three-day drunk he'd been on, wandering into the Rose when he knew he wasn't welcome, Talley helping him inside. He got up slowly, still a little drunk, and went to the kitchen sink. He found a glass and drank cold water till he thought he'd bust.

In her tiny bathroom, he didn't think he'd ever quit pissing. Then he shucked his clothes and showered until her hot water ran out. Clean, mostly sober, he'd stepped close to the door of her bedroom and called out, "Talley?"

She'd told him she'd be out in a minute. He sat in one of her kitchen chairs, wishing for coffee, and waited. Sleepily, she came out dressed all in white, a thin cotton robe over a thin cotton gown. White cotton socks covered her feet, and he found that incredibly sexy. It aroused him like nothing had in a very long time. She offered to make him breakfast, and he nodded. He stared at her feet as she moved around the small kitchen. He wasn't hungry, but he wanted to watch her walk around on her sock-covered feet.

His appetites stirred as the trailer filled with the smells of bacon, eggs and toast. She had made him a cup of instant coffee, and he grimaced as he sipped it. He liked real coffee made from coffee grounds, the stronger the better, but hers would have to do. She set their plates down and sat across from him.

He shifted in his chair, trying to find a comfortable position for his hard-on. He couldn't very well stand and rearrange things like he needed to. Hopefully, it would go down on its own, and he wouldn't have to worry about it at all.

He wolfed down the food she had prepared while she nibbled at hers. She kept her eyes on her plate, and they didn't say much. He scraped up the last of the eggs with his toast and popped it in his mouth.

"Do you want something else?" she asked, her pretty blue eyes lighting gently on his old, worn-out face.

He shook his head, wiped his mouth and hands on the napkin she'd placed there for him. He took a long drink of coffee, trying to ignore the constriction in his pants and wondering what to say to her.

Mitch's girl, he reminded himself uncomfortably. No, Mitch's *woman*. Mitch was a grown man, and Talley Robinson had grown into a beautiful woman. Beautiful in a way he couldn't describe. She'd never be in a picture ad in a magazine, but that was good. Those perfect women, while nice to look at, were a little scary in their perfection.

Making a pass at his son's girlfriend wasn't the brightest thing he'd ever do, but the desire to do it was irresistible. It had to do with white socks and watching her make breakfast. It'd been years since he'd watched a woman cook for him, one of the little things a man missed when he didn't have a wife anymore.

He had loved Mitch's mother with his whole heart. But Ellen's death was more than twenty-two years past and the raw ache of missing her had dulled long ago. Now, he missed the little things the most. Well, he'd make the pass. She'd turn him down and that would be that. She might tell Mitch. Mace would take the blame, make some excuse that it was a misunderstanding. He'd never touch her again, but right then he wanted to touch her more than anything in the world.

Talley stacked their plates and utensils and stood. The thin robe and gown revealed more than they could ever hope to hide. He drew in a sharp breath, and she looked at him, those pretty blue eyes questioning.

"More coffee?" was all she asked and took his cup along with the other dishes to the sink.

Now or never, Mace decided. One shot is all you get. He knew he wasn't thinking clearly or smartly. He'd never been the sharpest knife in the drawer, but he had never been outright stupid either.

Would she slap him? Or just burn his ears with what she thought of him? If she did either, he'd quietly go away and that would be the end of it. He didn't think he had a snowball's chance in hell of being accepted. Sometimes a man could be pretty damn stupid.

When she walked back to him and set his filled cup in front of him, Mace held his breath and reached for her. His callused hand slid up her arm, beneath the sleeve of her robe. He wasn't surprised at the texture of her skin. It was soft as warm silk, the color of light honey where the sun reached and fresh cream where it didn't. He grew painfully hard.

Talley froze beneath his touch, her hand on his cup. His fingers played along her skin. The blood pounded in his temples, and he snatched his hand back. What a stupid, stupid thing to do! He wasn't prepared for the guilt that washed over him like spring rain.

A hot flush of embarrassment had colored his face when she looked at him. "Mace?"

He shook his head, afraid he might choke on his own stupidity if he tried to speak.

"I'm seeing Mitch," she whispered.

As if he didn't know. As if it wasn't a thorn in his side, a thousand thorns covering every inch of his body. His skin had felt all prickly and itchy and —

He nodded. "I know," he croaked and cleared his throat. He felt like some awkward kid asking a girl out for the first time. He thought of Mary Louise Johnson, whom he'd had a crush on when he was fifteen. She'd turned him down flat. Mary Louise was still in Randolph, married with kids and grandbabies, and Mace was still embarrassed whenever he saw her.

"Mace." Talley's hand was warm against his cheek, but he nearly jumped out of his prickly skin. He almost wished she had slapped him. He couldn't believe she wasn't going to kick up a fuss. He couldn't believe her thumb was trailing over his lips. He couldn't believe she was making a pass back at him.

Before either of them could come to their senses, Mace put his hands on her hips and pulled her close, between his legs. He might get a kiss before she saw reason. He throbbed hard where her legs touched him, and his jeans were too damn tight for comfort.

His mouth reached just below her breasts, and his face was lost in the white cotton fabric as he slid his arms around and crushed her to him.

Both of her hands tangled in his damp hair as she tugged on him to lift his face. She bent hers close and when her lips touched his, Mace thought he must still be on the couch dreaming the sweetest of dreams. Or he'd died and gone to heaven.

Her arms folded around him, and the kiss became a desperate, hungry outpouring of physical longing for both of them. He kissed her hard and long, then trailed his lips down the side of her neck to her breasts and the hardened nipples protruding through the thin white cotton. She tilted back, and he suckled one gently, then the other, and her small moans of pleasure were the sweetest sounds he'd ever heard.

He never thought it would go this far, never thought she could actually want him. He couldn't stop the question that skittered through his mind. Didn't his boy know how to satisfy a woman?

He knew Mitch was a man, and he never wanted to go there in his thoughts, but Talley reacted to him out of desperation. He could feel her need in the tautness of her muscles, smell it in the rich musky odor of her womanhood, taste it on her lips and skin. In his experience, and he'd be the first to admit his experience was limited, a woman who had her needs met didn't react this way, unless she was the kind who was never satisfied.

Yet Talley didn't seem the type. She hadn't openly flirted with him, hadn't come on to him. In fact, she had seemed mildly irritated that she felt obliged to take care of him when he'd swaggered into the Rose.

Whatever the reason, she wanted him and he was confounded. Reluctantly, he removed his mouth from her breast and leaned back in his chair. It was time to take a breather and see where this was headed. Any further and he'd take her right there in the chair, have her straddle him and ride him like a bronco.

That fantasy had come true, he thought and looked over at her sleeping form. He would have smiled at the memory, but he was too worried about her condition. One of the last times they were together, when he had come to her on a Saturday night, they hadn't waited to go to her bed. Mace reached over and tucked the blankets in again. He lit a cigarette and smoked, watching her and remembering.

Talley had looked down at him. "Mace."

Her desire was as real as his, and her confusion just as bad.

"Darlin'" he said but couldn't say any more.

"Mace...Oh, Mace." Her pretty blue eyes were wide as if she were surprised. Maybe she was.

His hands slid down her arms, and he folded his fingers with hers. They could only look at one another.

"Mitch and I aren't sleeping together," she said.

Her confession threw a new light on the situation. She answered his questions, but brought up new ones.

And made things a little easier.

"I love Mitch."

Or harder. He nodded to say he understood.

"I want you."

Then he didn't understand at all.

"Darlin'," he began again, but still couldn't finish. He wasn't going to push her into anything, but he was afraid they'd be there for hours if he didn't nudge her. One way or the other didn't matter, to her bed or to her front door.

He stood and she stepped back giving him room. Now, he could look down at her, and he felt like some big bully forcing her to do it. He let go of her hands suddenly and then just stood there, wishing he was a million miles away...or a dozen feet away, in her bedroom, the decision already made.

Talley's breath came in short shallow gasps, but he left it up to her. Drawing in a deep breath, she at last reached for his hand. He used it to pull her against him, his long hard body fitting nicely to her softly rounded curves. They kissed again, hungrily, and moved down the hall to her bedroom.

They parted long enough to get rid of their clothing, and Talley lay back on the bed, waiting for him. He climbed over her, his hands framing her face.

He hated to bring it up, didn't want to jar her back to reality, but he didn't need any more responsibilities than he already had. Didn't need any surprises nine months from tonight. He had enough trouble with the son he already had. "What about—"

As if she read his mind, she said, "Don't worry, it's taken care of."

He kissed her more gently this time. He made love to her, and she shuddered with the pleasure that flushed her body. Mace caught her moans with his mouth and echoed them when he poured himself into her. Her arms and legs kept him pinned to her and he rested his head on her shoulder, carrying much of his weight on his elbows. His hands still framed her face.

With the urgent, aching need satisfied, guilt flowed over him. How could he? How could he not, when her need had been as great as his. He shifted to the side and slid his arm under her neck and laid his hand across her stomach. She snuggled into him. Never again, he vowed, but he knew better than to say never.

He stayed away as long as he could, but the next Saturday night he was knocking on her door. She opened it, surprised to see him. She watched him, as wary as a stray cat. Finally, she let him in. They made small talk and drank coffee. By the time he kissed her, he was as hard as a rock and without another word, she led him back to the bedroom. Once again, he swore *never*.

But the next Saturday night he was there. At some point she started leaving her door unlocked for him and he stopped swearing *never*.

And somewhere along the way, he fell in love with her. The visits that began out of a desperate need to have sex with her had turned into a need to be with her, to see her and talk with her. Ever since Ellen's death, he had shied away from any commitment. He hadn't wanted a woman permanently in his life. He'd slept with other women, but they usually wanted something he wasn't ready to give and so he cut them off quickly. His crude method worked, but he rarely saw the same woman more than a few times. Until Talley.

The one woman he thought he could finally give of himself was the love of his son's life. Now, he laughed bitterly at the cruel twist of fate and wished he were a better man.

Chapter Eleven

ॐ

Talley dreamed she was swimming in a pond. Ice floes as big as cows bobbed up and down in the icy cold water, although the sun was bright and the pasture was green and dotted with flowers. Mace and Mitch stood side by side on the grassy bank. They waved to her, then threw their arms around one another, turned, and walked away.

"Help me!" she cried out and opened her eyes.

Now, she was awake, but didn't know where she was. A small, primitive room, plain wood walls, beam ceiling. She was piled with blankets, but she shivered so hard her teeth rattled.

And she hurt. Her face hurt, her head and stomach hurt. Her arm. She tried to move, but the pain was unbearable and she cried out.

"Darlin'," she heard and a warm callused hand gently touched her forehead.

"Mace? I'm so cold."

"I'm here, darlin'. I put every blanket in the place on you and stoked the fire as high as I can get it."

"I'm cold," she said again and shivered.

Mace took off his boots, lifted the covers and slid in beside her, the old springs squealing in protest. The rusted iron twin bed wasn't made for two, but he carefully gathered her into his arms and tucked the blankets in around them.

Every movement hurt, but she bit her lip to keep from crying out again. She was afraid he wouldn't stay if he thought he caused her discomfort. She snuggled deep into his arms, into his warmth.

"Where are we?"

"The old home place, the house my grandparents built when they first married. I fixed it up. I come here sometimes when I need to get away from everything." He brushed her tangled hair back. "What happened, Lee? Who did this to you?"

She told him what Jack had done. "When I refused to go with him and told him to use the knife, he started hitting me and wouldn't stop."

"I'll kill him," Mace swore.

Talley didn't try to dissuade him.

"I hurt, Mace."

"I know. I couldn't find anything broken or busted. Some bruises and a black eye. I'm sorry, Lee."

"Hold me, Mace."

"I am holding you."

"Don't let me go."

"I'll hold you as long as you want me to, darlin'."

Talley slept for a long time and when she woke, Mace was still beside her. The chill in her bones was gone, but she didn't want to tell Mace. She wanted to remain in his arms.

"I love you, Mace," she whispered.

"I love you, too, Talley. Now, can I get up for a minute? I need to piss real bad."

Reluctantly, she let him go. She closed her eyes. He loved her too. She had never had any doubt, not really. He just didn't know how to say the words. Didn't know how to get around her involvement with Mitch. If only he had said he loved her long ago. So much of this could have been avoided.

She drifted off again and when she woke, Mace was seated in a chair as close as he could get to the bed, sipping coffee.

"I heated some soup for you." He got the cup and helped her sit up. She wore nothing but a clean denim work shirt that covered everything to her knees.

She sipped the chicken noodle soup through swollen lips. "I need to go to the bathroom."

He helped her up and held her as she limped to the door. Every step was painful, jarring some muscle Jack had punched or kicked. She winced, but tried not to react to the pain so Mace wouldn't know how bad it was.

"It's not really a bathroom," he apologized and lit a kerosene lamp. "But you'll have some privacy."

The room was no larger than a closet. A mirror hung on the wall with a shelf below that held the lamp, soap and shaving gear. A clean towel draped over a nail in the wall. An old bucket and dipper, washbasin and chamber pot served their original purposes.

It hurt to pee, and her urine was dark and strong but not bloody. Maybe she hadn't suffered any major damage from Jack's beating. She dipped fresh cold water into the basin and washed her face, skipping the black and purple bruise under her eye. She cleaned away the crusted blood from the cut on her neck. She lifted the shirt and stared at the array of bruises across her skin. One huge bruise made a circle the size of her fist at her side.

Slowly, she walked back into the other room, her hand at her side. "I think we can head back now. Have my clothes dried out?"

"Come here, darlin'," Mace said, but he went to her and helped her to the front door. He opened it and turned on a flashlight. Talley gasped. The powerful beam illuminated an entire landscape encased in a thick layer of crystal. Bits of ice slanted across the light as they fell.

"I thought you said it wouldn't accumulate."

"I was wrong." He turned off the flashlight, shut the door, and led her back to the bed. He tucked the blankets around her again and handed her the cup of soup.

"Your car is stuck in a ditch. When I found you—"

"What took you so long! It was dark when Jack attacked me. You couldn't have still been working."

"I came here. I was going to stay the night here anyway, but I kept thinking about that piece of junk you drive and your bad tires. That's the only reason I left." His hands shook around his coffee cup. "It scares the hell out of me to think I might not have found you. I tried to get the truck here to the shack, but it got stuck and I carried you the rest of the way."

"Mace."

"I'm right here."

"I like saying your name. Mace."

He remained quiet a few moments, then, "What do you want, Lee?"

She didn't think he meant what she wanted at this moment. What did she want for the rest of her life?

"That's the wrong question," she said and clamped her lips shut. She'd sworn she would never prompt him. She shouldn't have told him she loved him first, but the words spilled out before she could stop them. He had answered her with no hesitation, no indecision, as if it was the most natural thing in the world to speak of his love for her.

His face screwed up in a frown. "Then what's the right question?"

She shook her head and sipped the soup.

"You're not going to tell me. I have to figure it out myself?"

She didn't look at him.

"Okay, Lee, you asked for it. I've known what the right questions are for a long, long time. Are you ready to hear them?"

She shot him a look. "Are you ready to ask them and mean them?"

"I've been ready for some time." He stood and paced to the fireplace. "The most important question is, will you stop seeing Mitch?"

"It's not the most important question, but I'll answer it. Mitch has to let go of us on his own. If I leave him, he'll never be able to forgive you. I don't matter, but you're his father. I know I'm the wedge that has driven you farther away from one another, but I won't be what breaks you apart."

He stiffened. "Then there ain't any more questions to be asked."

"Oh, yes, there is." Talley threw back the covers and her resolve along with them. She had to know that Mace wasn't giving anything up. Slowly she moved her legs over the edge of the bed.

"Don't get up. I'll come to you." He strode across the room and sat in the chair.

"Mitch is no happier than he was the night he found us. He's tried and I've tried, but it's not working. I hate traveling with him and he needs someone to be with him on the road. All he can talk about is his music, and I want more." Talley wrapped her hands around his. "I miss you. You see, that's how I knew. I miss you when I'm with Mitch. I miss you so much I hurt. But when I'm with you, I don't miss him very much at all. That's how I knew I loved you best."

He grinned a little and squeezed her hands. "Then what are the other questions?"

"Eventually Mitch will get tired of this and want to call it quits. He's already hinted at it, but I keep convincing him things will get better."

"Did you ever think that things would be better between you if I weren't in the picture?"

"Yeah, I've thought about that often. It's too late, though. You're already in my heart."

Mace pulled his hands free and fumbled with cigarettes, lit two, and handed her one. She drew deeply on it and sighed.

"The next time he suggests it's over I can simply agree with him."

"Then what?"

Talley smiled. "That's the question I need answered from you."

He blew out a trail of smoke. "You want to know what my intentions are."

She nodded. "You've never given me any reason to think you had any intentions where I was concerned, other than sex. You told me that first time, remember? You said you didn't want anything or anyone in your life permanently. I think you drink yourself into oblivion to make sure no woman will have you."

"You may be right." He crushed out his cigarette. "But before I answer your question, I have one for you. Why did you let me into your bed that first night?"

She grinned sheepishly. "For the sex. I hadn't been sleeping with Mitch, and I needed a warm body next to mine, just for a little while. You were someone I could trust. And I knew you wouldn't use it against me later because you wouldn't want Mitch to find out any more than I would. It was supposed to be a one-night stand, just a way to get through the long, lonely nights until I felt it was the right time for Mitch and me." She made a face. "That sounds so stupid when I say it out loud, but it made perfect sense that night."

"I know what you mean."

"Now, it's your turn. Why did you come to my bed?"

"To get laid. I kept coming back because it was good." His eyes softened and he smiled crookedly. "And then I was coming back because I didn't think I could get through another week without seeing you." He lit up another cigarette. "I know what you want to hear, Lee."

"Don't you dare say it just because I want to hear it! Say it because you mean it."

"I love you. I will come to you again and I will make love to you again and I will ask you to marry me—but not until you're free. Those are my intentions and what you do with them is up to you. Now, finish your soup and get some rest."

"Yes, Mace," Talley said happily. She took another swallow then handed the cup out to him. "I've had enough. Will you see if my socks are dry? My feet are cold."

Mace took the cup, but Talley was puzzled by his foolish grin.

Chapter Twelve

ဆ

Mace went to the stove and retrieved Talley's socks from among her clothes hanging on the ladder-back chairs to dry. He brought them to her, but didn't hand them over.

"Get back in bed," he said.

Talley scooted back, still sitting up, and held out her hand.

"Lie down, Lee. I'll put them on."

"I don't think they'll fit you."

He snorted. "I'll put them on *you*."

She did as she was told, straightening the shirt to keep everything covered. When she had settled, he sat on the edge of the bed, the rusty springs shrieking their disapproval, and placed one foot in his lap. His hand massaged her toes.

"Damn, they're like ice cubes."

"I always have cold feet. I usually wear socks to bed."

He frowned. "You never wore socks when I came to your bed."

"I didn't need to. You warmed me all the way to my toes."

He lightly traced the curve of her arch. She couldn't snatch the foot away. The quick movement would hurt too much. She moved it from side to side trying to evade his fingers.

"Don't, Mace. Don't make me laugh. It'll hurt."

"Sorry, darlin'." He leaned over and gently placed a kiss just under the backside of her toes.

"What are you doing, Mace?"

"Making out with your toes. Maybe Mitch won't mind if I stay below the ankle."

She had to laugh and it did hurt. She wanted to cry.

"Well, my toes are about the only part of me that does feel like making out."

"I'm sorry, Lee. I forgot for a minute why you're here." He reached for her socks.

"Don't stop, Mace." She wiggled her toes at him. "See how excited they are. You've got them all turned on. You can't leave them hanging now."

"We're asking for trouble. You know that, don't you?"

"I know." She moved her heel closer to him, on top of the warm bulge in his jeans.

"Hmmph," he grunted, pushing her foot back to a safer distance. "Don't, darlin'. It's hard enough as it is."

"Mace!" She giggled and held her side. "I said don't make me laugh. It hurts too much."

He winked at her then turned back to her foot.

With tender strokes, he massaged her foot from heel to toe and finished with a kiss to the most sensitive area in her arch. Then he slipped on her sock and carefully folded down the top. Her other foot received the same treatment. When he was done, Talley sighed and wished she weren't battered. She wished it was already over between her and Mitch.

Mace pushed back and leaned against the wall, her sock-covered feet resting in his lap. He fished out two cigarettes from the pack in his shirt pocket, lit them, and handed her one.

"Was it good for you?" he asked, gray eyes twinkling.

"Oh, yeah. How about you?"

"Right now, I wish I raised sheep instead of cows."

"Ooooo, that's awful, Mace!"

"Trying to lighten the mood."

"I think you just lightened it enough to blow it out of the room."

He gave her feet one last squeeze and got up off the bed. He spread the blankets over her and tucked her in.

"I don't need to be on that bed with you. Too much of a temptation."

She nodded. "I wonder how long we'll be trapped up here."

"We can find out." He walked across the room and brought back a battery-operated radio. It took a few minutes to find a clear station.

Waiting for a weather report, they listened to the music.

"I'd ask you to dance, but I think you'd turn me down."

"I wish I could. We've never danced."

"We've never done a lot of things, Lee. I wish it could have been different. I wish I'd seen you first."

"It would have been illegal," Talley teased.

"Now it's just immoral."

That sobered them both. "Don't, Mace. We did the best we could."

He shrugged. "Yeah, I know."

After a while, they heard the weather report. The ice was expected to stop in a few hours and would be melted off in a few days. Mace turned off the radio.

"It'll be daylight in a little while. When the ice stops, I'm going out to call for help."

"You can't walk that far in this weather! It's more than five miles to the nearest house."

"That's going back toward Randolph. Henry Davis lives up the other way about a mile, two at the most."

"But that's the same weatherman that predicted it wouldn't accumulate. We can't trust what he says."

"I've got to get you to a doctor, Lee."

"No, Mace. I'm fine. A few bruises, that's all. They'll heal."

102

"I want you to get checked out. Something might be messed up inside. And I need to call the sheriff, tell him what Jack did to you."

"Mace. If you go to the sheriff, he'll want to know exactly what happened. If I tell him where I was and who did this, then word will get out I came up here to see you. Jack said something about there being talk about us a while back." She rubbed her eyes, careful of her bruised cheek. "There's no reason in the world why I should have come looking for you in an ice storm except the obvious one. Even though I wanted to talk to you and nothing else, no one's going to believe it. Especially Mitch."

"Don't you want Jack in jail?"

"I want him hog-tied and skinned alive, but not at the risk of you losing Mitch again."

Mace's face was stony. "Then I can take care of Jack."

"Mace, you wouldn't…?"

"No, but I'd make him wish I had."

"Just let it go, Mace."

"All right, Lee." He agreed too quickly, and Talley felt it was the first time Mace had ever lied to her. "You still need to see a doctor."

"Same thing, Mace. If I go to a doctor's office or the emergency room, they'll have to know what happened. People will talk."

Mace thought that over for a moment. "If I can get you to Doc Benson's place, it won't be a problem. Doc owes me one."

"He's retired."

"Doesn't mean he's forgot everything he learned in medical school. He can look you over, but if he says you need to go to the emergency room, then you go. No arguments, Lee. We'll just have to face whatever happens."

She nodded. "Mitch won't be in until tomorrow. He might have tried to call, though. He'll call me and he'll call you. And neither of us will be home."

"I was here mending the fence and got caught in the storm. Your phone was turned down, and you didn't know until late."

"Okay, but Junior knows I'm up here."

"Junior'll keep his mouth shut. If he knows what's good for him."

"Good thing I didn't have to work last night, but Dylan will expect me this afternoon."

They thought a while, but neither could come up with a solution.

"Looks like that's that," Mace finally said. "As soon as it stops, I'll head up to Henry's."

"No! There has to be a way. If either of us had a cell phone, I could just call in sick tonight. You ought to have one if you've been staying here alone. Anything can happen."

"Damn nuisance. I don't like to answer the phone when I'm at home. Why would I haul one around with me?"

"For emergencies. Like this."

"Fine. I'll get one as soon as we get back to Randolph."

She ignored his sarcasm.

"There has to be a way," she said again. "If I don't call in, Dylan will know something's wrong. I've always called him even if I'm going to be late a few minutes. He knows I live on Morning Glory Hill and he knows I don't drive in this weather. He might send somebody out to check on me. When they find me and my car gone, they might start looking for me. That will bring a whole lot of attention to where I'm found, Mace."

"Lee, I don't see…" Mace broke off and slapped his forehead with the heel of his hand. "Cell phone. Shit. Henry has one. All I have to do is walk up to his place, borrow his four-wheel-drive and make sure I get his cell phone too. I'll tell him I need to get back into Randolph right away. Then I'll drive you to Doc's, and if he says you're okay, I'll take you home. Mitch won't be in till tomorrow. You can still call in sick. You won't be in any shape to work tonight anyway."

"I can tell him and anybody else I lost control of the car and ran off in a ditch because of the ice."

"After I take you home, I'll get Junior and we'll tow your car out to the farm. You ran off the road at Murphy's Bend, and I found you on my way back home last night. That explains your car at my place."

"Okay, sounds good."

"If we're gonna play it that way, just let me take you to the emergency room."

"No, it's too late for that. I should have gone last night. Besides, they can tell bruises that come from a beating."

"All right." He lit up a cigarette. "We're too damn good at this. It's scary."

"I know."

"Get some sleep, Lee."

"What about you?"

"I'll catch a nap in this chair."

They didn't say anything for a while. Talley yawned and nodded toward the light coming through the window. "It's Saturday, Mace."

"I know, darlin'. I know."

Chapter Thirteen

೩

Talley couldn't believe it, but it all worked out as they'd planned. Sometime after dawn, the ice stopped and the sun had come out. The weatherman was right for once. Mace got ready to go to Henry's and kissed her chastely on the forehead.

"I'll get dressed while you're gone."

He sighed. "I would have to miss that," he said and headed out.

Talley dressed, and within an hour Mace was back with Henry's four-wheel-drive and parked it on the road. Mace put out the fire in the old woodstove. He put his arm around her, and they left the cabin. She curled up on the backseat, and he drove her to Doc Benson's. The going was slow, and Talley dozed off and on during the ride.

Doc took their surprise visit in stride. After he examined her he told them he couldn't find anything wrong other than contusions that would heal. He disinfected the small cut on her throat and gave her some pills for the pain. Mace did all the explaining, telling him what really happened. Doc looked at the back of Mace's hands then looked her straight in the eye and asked if it was the truth. She looked him straight in the eye and said yes. Doc believed her, and told Mace he'd keep their visit to himself.

Once again, Talley lay in the backseat, and Mace drove her home. The going was faster since most of the roads near Randolph had been salted. The warming sun and stirring traffic helped, too. With a running start, they barely made it up Morning Glory Hill, almost sliding into a ditch. At her place, Mace carried her inside and set her down gently.

She couldn't let go of him just yet. She rested her head on his chest. "Stay and have coffee with me, Mace."

"Much as I want to, I can't. You know that."

"I only know—"

"Don't say anything, Lee. It ain't time yet."

She nodded against his coat. "Call me when you get through with everything. I want to know you're safe."

"I will." He laughed. "I feel like we've committed a murder, and we're trying to cover up the evidence."

"It's guilt. But remember, Mace, we don't have anything to feel guilty about this time."

"Tell that to your toes."

He didn't kiss her before he left.

Talley spent the rest of the day anxiously waiting to hear from Mace, but Mitch called first later that afternoon.

"Tal! I've been worried about you. I tried calling last night a dozen times but there wasn't any answer."

"I guess I turned the ringer on low and didn't notice till sometime today. I'm sorry, Mitch." She held her breath. She was no good at lying. Surely, he had to hear the deception in her voice.

"I'm glad you're okay. I heard Randolph got hit with ice."

"It's not too bad. It stopped early this morning and the sun's been shining all day. Uh, Mitch, I was in a little accident yesterday afternoon. I'm okay, but I have a few bruises and I banged up my car."

"Are you sure you're all right, Tal? Do you need me to come home now?"

"No, I'm fine. Like I said, just a few bruises. I have one on my cheek where I popped the steering wheel when I hit the ditch. I was up around Murphy's Bend and the ice caught me by surprise. I took the curve too fast. Before I could get out of the car, Mace came along."

"Mace?"

"Yeah, he'd been mending a fence, by the old home place, I think he said." Talley held her breath again.

"Good thing it was Mace that found you, Tal. Jack Sandler lives up that way."

"Yeah, I know. Mace brought me home then he and Junior towed the car out to Shady Hollow. When the roads clear, I'll get someone out to pick it up."

"Are you sure you're all right, Tal? You don't sound good."

"I'm sure. Still a little shaky from the accident, I guess."

She asked how last night had gone and smiled at the excitement in his voice as he told her. "The guy from the recording company was there last night instead of tonight. He said he liked to show up early to hear how a band really sounds and how it can work a crowd. He's right. We'd have been too keyed up to play well if he'd waited till tonight. He wants us to make a demo and send it to him."

"That's great, Mitch!" Her enthusiasm was real. This was the break he'd been waiting for.

"He really liked 'Desperate Hearts'. He said to make sure that song is on the demo."

"Oh, Mitch, I'm so happy for you. Your dream is coming true."

"Not just yet. We checked into it, Tal. Coming up with the money to make the demo is going to be a problem. Looks like it may be a while before we can get it together."

"You could ask Mace."

There was silence at the other end. "No. No. Mace'd probably do it, but I won't owe him anything. I have to do this on my own. Besides, he has enough financial worries with the farm."

"Okay, Mitch."

He talked more about the talent scout until Talley told him she was tired. They said goodbye and hung up. She stared at the phone a while and wondered when things had really begun to go bad between them. Neither of them had said, "I love you."

Talley kept the phone close to her. Mace was an excellent driver, but anything could happen.

Mace didn't call until after dark. "Everything's taken care of."

She closed her eyes and imagined him in his house holding the phone. She wanted to reach through the line and touch him. It didn't seem fair that she couldn't be with him since he'd told her he loved her and what he wanted.

"Do you realize this is the first time we've ever talked on the phone?"

He was silent for a few seconds. "I don't think there'll be any need for it to happen again...any time soon. How are you feeling?"

"A little better." She drew in a deep breath. He obviously meant to keep her at arm's length even over the phone.

"Good to hear it."

"Mitch called earlier." She repeated their conversation, then gave him the good news.

"I'm glad for him, Lee."

"You don't sound glad."

"I'm tired. It's been a hell of a day." She heard a pouring sound in the background and hoped it was coffee. "I have to go now. If you need anything, call me."

"I will, Mace." But she knew she wouldn't.

"Good night, Lee."

She waited until she heard the click of his receiver, then whispered, "I love you."

Mitch came home the next day and was concerned over her bruises. She didn't show him the huge circular bruise on her side. She had no way to explain it and all the other places covering her body. A dive into a ditch as shallow as the one at Murphy's Bend wouldn't have produced them all.

Mitch stayed with her all evening, and she learned more about the music business than she ever wanted to know. That wasn't fair, she knew. Mitch was so excited about their shot at making it, he couldn't think of anything else.

But Talley could. Her mind wandered most of the evening. Finally realizing how tired she was, he kissed her good night and went away.

Go to Bonnie, Talley thought. She never should have come between them. She had returned to Randolph to try again with Mitch, and although she never flirted with Mitch while he was seeing Bonnie, her presence had been enough. Bonnie had been angry with them both, but the band and their music were in her blood as much as Mitch's. Bonnie loved the traveling and loved to spend every waking moment talking about their music.

It had been a mistake from the beginning, coming back to Mitch…except for one thing.

Days passed, her bruises healed. The band was booked most nights. Talley refused to go with him.

"You really don't like traveling with me, do you?" Mitch complained. "Don't you realize I'm going to be gone two weeks?"

"I know, Mitch, and I'll miss you. I have a job here. Dylan won't let me off for days or weeks at a time then let me waltz back in when it pleases me. He depends on me."

"So get another job!"

"I like working at the Rose!"

It had become a constant argument. Before, she had always given in or let the subject drop. Now, she argued with him. It wasn't fair to Mitch, but she was tired of having to pretend. Once, the night he found her and Mace together, she had assured him she never pretended anything. That had changed since she knew Mace waited for her.

He swiped at his hair with angry strokes. "Where are you, Tal?"

"Right here."

"No, you're not. You're always a million miles away."

Talley lit a cigarette and Mitch wrinkled his nose. He didn't smoke because he didn't want to ruin his voice.

"Do you have to do that now?"

"This is my house, Mitch. If you don't like it, you can leave." She pressed her lips together. She hadn't meant to go so far.

Mitch shook his head. "It's not working, is it?"

"I'm sorry, Mitch." She crushed out the cigarette.

"It's not just that. It's...It's everything."

"I don't like the traveling. I hardly ever see my father because he can't stay long in one place. Then my mother married a man who's job takes him to a different city every couple of years." Talley sighed. "I'd been following them around to be close to my mother and sister, but when we came back here I realized I wanted to have a home in one place. I came back to Randolph to find that as much as to find you again."

"When we get the record deal—"

"When you get the record deal, it's only going to get worse, Mitch. For me."

They sat in silence for a while.

"Is this it, Talley?"

She drew in a deep breath. "It's up to you, Mitch. If you can accept that I won't be traveling with you much and stop nagging me about it."

"Aw, Tal—"

"No, I mean it. I feel bad enough because I can't help the way I feel. Your nagging makes it worse."

He leaned close to her. "I love you."

"I love you, too, Mitch. I always have."

"But we don't have much fun anymore, do we?"

She shook her head.

"I'm sorry, Talley. I guess you were right all along. We have changed. We want different things."

She nodded and tears flooded her eyes. It hurt to lose him this way. For all the wrong reasons.

He reached for her, his fingers spread along her neck, his thumb at her ear. He kissed her slowly and deeply. "Goodbye, Talley."

"Goodbye, Mitch."

Chapter Fourteen

෩

Talley waited.

She didn't know what else to do except wait for Mace to come to her. Every Saturday night she put on a pot of coffee and, while she didn't leave the door unlocked, she slept on the couch waiting for him. By the third Sunday morning as she dumped out yet another full pot of coffee, she felt quite foolish. He had come to her throughout most of their relationship, and she thought it would be appropriate if he came to her to start over.

Talley spent Christmas in Knoxville with her family. While there, she'd almost decided Mace must have changed his mind. She didn't know if she could bear it if, in the end, he had decided he didn't really want her. Hadn't he promised he would come to her? Was she supposed to wait forever?

Now, more than a month after she and Mitch said goodbye and a couple of weeks into the New Year, Talley found herself on the road to Shady Hollow. She had waited long enough. She had to know one way or the other. It was the perfect opportunity since Mitch was out of town.

She pulled up the long driveway and stopped the car. Tiny snowflakes drifted lazily through the air. The same weatherman had forecasted accumulating snow at any time, but she didn't believe him.

She got out of the car and stood a few moments. Mace had to know it was over between Mitch and her. Once again, she didn't know if she was handling things the right way or the best way. She had messed up so much lately she wasn't sure of any of her actions any more. The only thing she was sure of was she had to see Mace because she was overcome by the same irresistible urge that had plagued her the day they became stranded at the old home place. If he made her go away, then she would. He had told her his intentions, and she could only hope he still felt the same way.

She walked up to the house and knocked several times, waiting. She knocked again, but no one answered the door. She turned and looked over the outbuildings. Maybe he was in the barn.

The barn door opened on a creak and a swirl of snowy wind. She closed it behind her. She pushed back the hood of her coat and waited until her eyes adjusted to the dimness.

A bright shaded bulb hung from a beam, and Mace's truck sat in the pool of light. Under the open hood, Mace bent over the side, his head lost in the inner workings of the vehicle. Talley walked closer.

"Mace?"

He raised his head, nodded at her, then leaned back inside. She walked closer.

"Am I interrupting?"

"No," he said without looking up.

"Mace? Talk to me."

"No. You need to talk to me." He grunted as he fought with a stubborn piece of metal.

"I can't talk to you with your head down there. Should I come back later?"

He raised up suddenly. "No."

She watched him as he snatched up a rag and wiped his hands. When he turned just right in the light, she saw the large bruise on his jaw. The color was more green than purple.

"Oh, Mace, what happened?" Instinctively, she stepped closer to him and raised her hand to it.

He tilted his head away from her touch, but he wouldn't meet her eyes. "Damnedest thing, I ran into the bathroom door during the night."

"Mace…"

His voice lowered. "You won't be bothered again, Lee."

She had noticed Jack Sandler didn't come to the Rose anymore. She tried not to think of him at all, but when she did, she'd hoped he had been scared off by his own cowardice. She remembered Mace had threatened to take care of him, but hadn't known if he had followed through.

"I'm sorry, Mace. Are you all right?"

He nodded. "That door got in one good punch before I laid it out."

He kept his hands wadded up in the rag, but Talley reached for them and slowly pulled the rag away. His knuckles were bruised as well and cuts and scrapes had begun to scab over. Any scars that might be left would mingle with those that already marred his skin. She brought his fingers to her lips and kissed them, then held them to her cheeks.

"Thank you, Mace, for taking care of those who get attacked by doors."

His hands turned over and cupped her chin briefly before dropping to his sides. He didn't say anything else. He waited for her to speak.

"It's over. Mitch and me. Has been for a while."

"I know."

"Then why—"

"I know what we did, Talley. It wasn't right and it wasn't good. I can swear that I'll never do anything like that again. Can you?"

"Oh, yes, Mace! I swear."

"Are you done with Mitch?"

"A part of me will always love Mitch. I can't lie about that. But I won't go back to him, even if I never see you again. We're too different now. We want different things." She blinked back the tears that filled her eyes. "For a long time, I didn't want to lose you both. If I couldn't have you, then I wanted Mitch." She shook her head. "But not anymore. If I can't have you, I'm going to Knoxville to be with my family. There'd be nothing here for me anymore."

"All right then."

He turned his back to her and ducked his head under the hood again. She waited a few minutes, then took a few steps closer.

"Mace?"

"I'd like to get this finished up before dark. I have somewhere to go tonight."

"Oh."

"If I don't get this truck fixed, I know a lady who's gonna be mighty displeased."

She couldn't breathe. The pain that ripped through her chest made her think her heart had stopped beating. If he had given up on them, then why all the questions? Just to satisfy his curiosity? Maybe if he didn't want her, he needed to know that Mitch wouldn't have her either. She stepped back a couple of paces.

"I'm sorry, Mace. I-I didn't mean to interfere." She turned and ran for the door. She pulled it open and didn't look back even when he called out her name.

The weather outside had turned as severely as the atmosphere inside the barn. The lazy, fluffy flakes had turned to fine bits of snow that whipped her face as she stumbled to the car.

"Talley, wait!"

He'd called her Talley, and she thought she'd never be able to breathe again. The tears in her eyes flooded down her cheeks. Her hand slipped off the door handle of her car again and again as she tried to open it. Then Mace was beside her, pulling up her hood against the driving snow.

"Dammit, Talley, don't you know what today is?"

She shook her head and tried to pull away from him. At that moment, completely overcome by the terrible hurt she felt, she didn't know what year it was.

"It's Saturday, darlin'. It's Saturday."

She stopped struggling as the meaning of his words made it past the pain. She blinked up at him. "Oh, Mace…" She buried her face in his cold, snow-covered jacket.

"Let's get inside. You can't drive in this weather."

She grabbed his jacket in her numb fingers. "You said you'd come to me, remember? I waited, Mace, I waited as long as I could."

"I know, but I wanted to give us both a little time. I didn't think a few weeks would hurt us any. Talley, I'm freezing my balls off. Let's go inside."

She shook her head. "Why are you calling me Talley?"

"It's your name."

"You know what I mean!"

He smiled a little and brushed snow crystals from her face with shaking hands. From the cold, she supposed, but she wasn't going inside with him until he told her.

"I can call you Talley now because I have all of you."

Only then did she allow him to hustle her into the house. They pulled off wet jackets and boots and huddled on the rug in front of the crackling fire. Mace took her hands in his, rubbing them briskly. His hands were cold, too, but she wouldn't say or do anything to end his touch.

"You scared the hell out of me, Mace!"

"Didn't mean to. I thought you knew what day of the week it is."

"You sounded like you'd changed your mind," Talley said softly. "I wasn't thinking straight after that."

"Darlin'," he said and drew her into his arms, "I was trying not to rush it."

"Well, you tried too hard," she said and looped her arms around his neck. Over his shoulder, she saw the steady snowfall out of the window. Everything was already covered in a layer of white. "I don't think I'll be able to drive home, Mace, unless you want to take me."

"Yeah, I want to take you. Right here, right now," he murmured in her ear.

Talley smiled. She had missed their playfulness almost as much as she'd missed Mace. "I don't know, cowboy. Have you gotten any better at it?"

He snorted. "I wouldn't know. I haven't used it in so long, I think it's dried up and blowed away."

Talley pulled back enough to look up into his gray eyes. "Then you didn't—"

"No, I didn't."

"Neither did I. I don't think Mitch could get over what happened. He never asked again."

Relief flooded his face. She hadn't realized it would mean so much to him to know.

He kissed her forehead. "Will you marry me?"

She frowned up at him. "You're not doing it the way you said you would. You said you'd come to me and make love to me and ask me to marry you."

He laughed. "I meant I'd do 'em all, but not exactly in that order. Will you marry me, Talley? All I can offer you is a broken-down farm mortgaged to the hilt. And me."

"Oh, yes, I'll marry you."

Their lips met in a deep and binding kiss, and Talley let her aching need for him wash over her completely. She pressed as close to him as she could and felt the hard proof of his need for her. Mace responded by trailing kisses along her neck.

"Will you take me now, Mace?"

"Right here?" he asked huskily between kisses.

"Yes…" Talley breathed and tilted her head back.

"Right now?" he teased and planted a kiss in the hollow of her throat. His hands found her buttocks and squeezed.

"Oh, yes," she murmured and helped him remove all the clothing that was in the way.

Talley lay back on the plush rug, and Mace pulled the afghan from the back of the couch to cover them. He settled between her thighs as her legs slipped around his waist. His hands, flat on the rug on each side of her, held his weight, and the tip of his arousal barely touched her. He looked into her eyes.

"I love you, Talley," he said hoarsely as he buried himself inside of her, thrusting in as deeply as he could go.

She arched against him on a moan, accepting him as she had so many times before. But this time was different, better. She was free to love him with her heart as well as her body. She held out her arms, and Mace dropped into them while he continued to thrust in and out of her, holding her close as they moved as one.

Then they came as one.

Trembling, she hugged him tight as he relaxed against her.

"I love you too, Mace," she whispered.

He rolled to her side and drew the afghan closer as they snuggled together. Desperation didn't drive their need anymore.

Only love.

Epilogue
Two years later

&

Talley Holloway shifted the baby from one arm to the other then set the porch rocker in motion again. She looked down into his angelic face, eyes closed in peaceful sleep, and saw the resemblance to both the father and the son. Strange how she'd never noticed any physical similarities between Mace and Mitch, but in her son she saw some of each. The thought made her smile.

Autumn had colored the leaves and a brisk breeze stirred a whiff of wood smoke past her nose. She snugged the blanket closer to Mason—Macefield Tyrel Holloway, Jr., but they called him Mason—Mace's son. The air had a bite to it, and she thought it might be time to take him inside when a new SUV pulled off the main road into their long driveway.

"Mace," she called, then louder, "Mace! They're here!"

Her son stirred in her arms, whimpered, then settled again.

When the SUV stopped, Mitch got out and hurried to the other side. He opened the door and carefully helped a very pregnant Bonnie ease from the passenger side. They slowly made their way to the house, Bonnie with one hand on the small of her back and the other holding onto Mitch securely.

Mace stepped out on the porch and squinted at his son and daughter-in-law. "Damn, did you get that big?" he said low enough for only Talley to hear. "She looks like she could drop any second."

Talley grinned, but said, "Hush, Grampa."

"Pa," Mace decided. "I want the little one to call me Pa."

"Whew, what a drive! I'm so glad it's over," Bonnie said as Mitch helped her up the steps. "Aw, Mason's asleep. I wanted to hold him."

"He'll be awake in a bit," Talley assured her. "Then he'll be raring to go."

"Uh-oh." Bonnie headed for the front door. "I have to go *again*."

Mitch shook his head as she disappeared into the house. "We had to stop twice on the way from Nashville."

Mace tapped Talley on the shoulder. "Three times. The last time we visited her folks before Mason was born. She watered every bush between here and Knoxville."

"Mace! We stopped at service stations and you know it. Fix me a cup of cocoa."

"Cocoa?"

"Yeah, cocoa. And see if Bonnie wants some."

Mace shook his head. "I ain't going near her. She might pop."

When he had gone inside, Talley looked at Mitch. "He's nervous about your visit, but he's driving me crazy. Making cocoa should keep him busy for a while."

"I'm nervous too." Mitch walked over and lightly rubbed his baby brother's cheek. "It's been so long since we've spent any time together. We talk on the phone a lot, but it's not the same. Of course, we don't argue nearly as much as we used to."

Talley nodded. "Want to hold him?"

"He's asleep."

"It's okay. Nap time is almost over anyway."

Talley laid her son in Mitch's arms and stretched out her legs. Crossing her ankles, she leaned back and rocked herself slowly.

"I can't believe how much he's grown in two months," Mitch said quietly.

"They grow too fast. I feel like if I blink he'll be graduating from high school."

"I know. Bonnie's due in a few weeks. Doesn't seem like it's been that long. She wants the baby born here in Randolph. I think she just wants to be close to her mother when the time comes." Mason wriggled in his arms and gurgled. Mitch secured him in the crook of one arm and put his fingers into Mason's hand. Mason latched onto one. "We're going to have a little girl, you know," he said proudly.

"I know." She smiled. Talley didn't remind him that he told them every time he talked to them.

"When I get a chance, I'm going to talk to Mace."

"About what?"

"Shady Hollow."

"We're doing fine. Mace let things get away from him for a while, but he's got it all under control now. He hasn't had a drink in over two years. And he's accepted the fact that you don't want any part of the farm."

Mitch laughed. "Well, he had to accept that, didn't he? *Desperate Hearts* went gold and is bringing in more money than any of us ever dreamed of. It's been optioned by a major company to use in their ad campaign. A cable movie company wants to develop it into a movie and if the movie does well, they want to make a series out of it. Add to that the merchandising, T-shirts, caps, heart-shaped keyrings…hell, even lunchboxes." Mitch sucked in a deep breath. "It's unreal, Tal. The projected amount of money we'll be raking in over the next few years is indecent."

"I'm happy for you and Bonnie and the band. You deserve it. But what does all this have to do with Shady Hollow?"

"I want to pay off the loan. And whatever else Mace needs to get this place running right. I was never interested in taking it over one day, but it's home. I know Mace and he'll refuse. I want you to talk him into it."

"It might help," Talley said quietly, "if you called him Dad again."

Mitch's jaw clenched. He answered with a quick shake of his head.

"What am I supposed to tell Mason when he's old enough to wonder why you call your father Mace?"

Mitch walked the length of the porch and back again.

"We ended up the way we were supposed to, Tal. Bonnie and me. You and Mace. You were right, and I think I knew it a long time before I admitted it. Still…"

Talley didn't say anything and waited for Mitch to finish.

"I tried to forgive and forget. It was easier than I thought, forgiving Mace. But I can't forget. Even though it was the best thing and the right thing, I can't forget what he did."

"He wasn't the only one, Mitch," Talley reminded him.

"I know. I've forgiven you too, Talley. What went on between us seems like another lifetime ago. Or like it happened to two other people. So it's easy to forget *us*." Mason cried out, and Mitch lifted him to his shoulder, swaying back and forth to quiet him. "But Mace is my father and that makes a big difference."

Talley nodded. If Mace had been any other man, it wouldn't have hurt nearly as bad and he'd have been able to put it behind him more easily. She guessed they were lucky Mitch could forgive. "You know better than I do how stubborn he is. I don't know if anything I say will convince him."

Mason squirmed and cried out lustily. Mitch handed him back to Talley, resting one hand on the arm of the rocker. "Tell him I'm doing it for the kid here," he said and rubbed the back of Mason's head. "I don't want the farm, never did, but maybe Mason will make it his life. Tell him that, Talley, and Mace'll take what I offer."

The screen door opened and Mace came through with a steaming mug of cocoa and his own coffee.

"Only two hands, Mitch. If you want coffee, you know where it is." Mace handed the mug to Talley. "Better check on Bonnie. Hope she didn't drop the kid in the toilet."

"Mace!" Talley frowned and swatted at him.

But Mitch chuckled and headed inside.

Mace stepped to the edge of the porch and gazed into the distance.

"Mitch wants to talk with you."

"I heard," he said thickly.

"How much did you hear?"

"Enough."

Talley set the cocoa aside and went to stand beside him. He turned and looked at her with glistening eyes.

"My boy has forgiven me," he whispered.

Talley nodded. Tears welled up and she blinked them back. "I thought he had. You two have been closer these past two years than any I've ever known."

"I hoped he had, but I didn't *know*. 'Til now."

"Accept his offer, Mace."

He nodded as he laid his hand on his younger son's head. He rested his forehead against his wife's. "All right, but I ain't gonna make it easy for him."

Talley grinned. "He would expect no less," she said and kissed him.

Also by Lani Aames

ᔓ

Aphrodite's Touch (writing as Lanette Curington)
Ellora's Cavemen: Tales from the Temple I (*Anthology*)
Enchanted Rogues (*Anthology*)
Eternal Passion
Lusty Charms: Invictus
Santa's Lap

About the Author

ᔓ

Lani Aames was born and raised in west Tennessee. She resides there with her husband, two daughters, and a clowder of cats. She is multi-published in a variety of erotic romance sub-genres. She also writes romance as Lanette Curington. For the latest news, reviews, and excerpts, visit www.laniaames.com and www.lanettecurington.com

PLAYING HIS GAME

By Kit Tunstall

ഇ

Prologue
Bobby's Big Break

ର

"Whoo, baby, I got it." Bobby swept Mya into a hug, and then circled her around the room.

Her hazel eyes shone with excitement when he finally set her down in the middle of their tiny apartment. "Really?"

Bobby's long, flaxen locks waved about his face when he nodded. "You're looking at the co-star. No more two-bit shit for me." The almost completely unbuttoned silk shirt admirably displayed his puffed out chest.

Bobby still held her in a loose embrace and Mya pressed herself closer. She put her arms around his neck and hugged him tightly. "This is it. Your big break." She started to kiss him, but he moved away.

He nodded. "I'm going all the way. This movie is shit, but someday there will be an Oscar waiting for me." Bobby's dreamy blue eyes went slightly out of focus. He stared into the cracked mirror in the hall.

Mya rolled her eyes because she knew he was either lost in his own reflection or in his dreams of the glory days that awaited him. She cast an eye around the hovel they had shared for eighteen months since their arrival in Los Angeles. Now they could finally afford something better — and more than that. "We can get married."

He blinked and turned his deeply tanned face back in her direction. "Yeah. Soon."

She threw herself against him and hugged him again. "I can't believe it's finally happening." It had seemed like forever while they waited for his big break. He worked in whatever bit parts he could find, and she had worked fast food, childcare, and retail. Of the jobs she'd had, Mya preferred her current one as a sales clerk at Macy's makeup counter. "We're going to be rich."

He frowned down at her. "This isn't about being rich, Mya."

Her eyes widened. "But you always say…"

A grin teased his lips. "This is about being fucking rich— and more famous than God."

She laughed along with him.

His expression turned serious. "I'm going to make it. I swear to you now. I'll do whatever it takes."

Mya framed his flawless face in her cupped hands. "We'll do whatever it takes, baby."

Chapter One
Introductions

ဢ

"Please?" Mya stuck out her bottom lip. "You promised to let me come."

Bobby's mouth curled. "It's going to be a heavy shooting day—"

"I won't get in the way." She batted her reddish eyelashes at him as she worked her fingers up the buttons of his shirt. "It's my day off, and I don't have anything to do."

He waved a hand around their new, larger apartment. "You could finish unpacking."

"Oh, Bobby! I'm sick of being stuck in this apartment."

"We've only been here a week, Mya."

She heaved a deep sigh. "I never get to go anywhere. You're always working or meeting with people." She clasped her hands together and rested them against her chest. "Please? Let me watch your brilliant performance again?" Mya batted her eyes at Bobby rapidly. She hoped to persuade him.

He still looked pained, but his blue eyes gleamed. "I know you like watching me, but you didn't have any fun the last two times you came with me."

"I'm sure they were off days," she said quickly.

Bobby shook his head. "You told me you wouldn't want to go back after the last shoot you attended. Have you forgotten?"

She remembered having said that and squirmed—mostly because she remembered why she hadn't enjoyed herself. When Bobby himself called cut, in the middle of a scene, to announce he looked awful in yellow, she had been embarrassed. When he tossed his bagel at an assistant during a break because it had onion cream cheese instead of plain, she had vowed never to return to the set.

That was before the unrelieved boredom of every day began to wear on her. The first time she was on set, he had been just fine. Surely last time had been an aberration. "Oh, please, Bobby? I can't stand to stay here another day." She trailed her fingers up his chest. "It's so boring when you're gone. I miss you so much."

He rolled his eyes. "Fine, but you'll have to stay out of the way."

She nodded eagerly. "I will. I promise."

*   *   *   *   *

To Mya's relief, Bobby's only colorful display had been minor. Earlier in the morning, he had flubbed a line and yelled at the script lady when she corrected him. Later—after prompting from Mya—he apologized to the woman. Since that incident, Bobby had focused strictly on his work.

Mya's attention was drawn from Bobby's scene by the approach of a man with massive shoulders and the physique of a world champion bodybuilder. He wore a black shirt stretched across his bulging muscles. It said Security in gold letters.

"Ma'am?"

"Yes?"

"Mr. Thomas has asked to see you."

She frowned. "Who?"

"The owner of the studio."

Mya lifted the security pass on a string around her neck. "I checked in. "

"You aren't in trouble."

"Then why—?"

He shrugged, which sent the tops of his shoulders up to his ears. "I didn't ask."

She turned away from the scene to follow the security guy through the sound stage and carefully dodged equipment and people as they made their way to a set of split-level metal stairs that led to the top three floors of the studio.

Mya struggled to keep up as the man's long legs took the stairs at a brisk jog. She was a little breathless when they stopped on the second level before a black door with a gold nameplate that read Roarke Thomas.

"Go on in, ma'am." He knocked for her, and then stepped aside.

"Come in." The voice was distinctly masculine, with a hint of velvet.

Mya shivered as she opened the door and stepped into the office. Her eyes widened as she scanned the recesses. Black carpet blended seamlessly into the silvery-white walls. Silver filing cabinets lined half of one wall, and the only other furniture was the massive glass-topped desk, a smaller leather seat across from it, and a presidential style leather chair. Someone occupied the chair, and she tried to discreetly study the man who had summoned her as she waited for him to speak.

His hair was wavy and brushed straight back. The rich sable shade gleamed in the sunlight that spilled through the glass wall opposite the one that looked down into the studio. A neatly trimmed mustache and goatee accented his rugged features. He wore a dark suit jacket and white turtleneck that hid most of his body from view, but she could see definition when he moved his arms. A blush swept across her face when she realized he studied her just as intently with rich brown eyes framed by thick, dark lashes.

"You're here with Waller?"

She stood awkwardly before him as she nodded. Mya clasped her hands together. "You are—"

"Roarke Thomas." He waved to the only chair in front of his desk. "Have a seat, please."

Mya struggled to hide her anxiety as she dropped into the chair with what she hoped was grace. "Have I done something wrong?"

He shook his head and leaned forward to prop his arms on the desk. "I'm not concerned with what you've done, but what you will do."

"Huh?"

"What's your name?"

"Mya Langelles. I'm with Bobby..." She lifted the security pass.

"Are you his sister?"

She unconsciously twisted the modest diamond on her finger. "Fiancée." Mya shifted uncomfortably. "Are you sure I'm not in trouble?"

"Of course not."

"Why did you send for me, Mr. Thomas?"

Roarke leaned back in his chair. There was a strange expression on his face. "Does Bobby want to be more than a one-hit wonder?"

Her concerns lifted and relief swept through her. He wanted to talk about Bobby. "He plans to make it big, sir. He's been in four movies already, and—"

"Yes, I'm sure he's dedicated." Roarke folded his fingers together. "What are you doing to help his career?"

She frowned. "I supported him when we first got here."

"Where did you come from?"

"Serpent Springs in Washington."

A corner of his mouth quirked. "Sounds charming."

She shrugged and averted her eyes to hide her homesickness.

He waved a hand, mentally and physically dismissing her hometown. "Let's cut to the chase, shall we?"

She nodded.

"I want to see Bobby have a long, successful career, and I can make that happen."

Her hazel eyes widened. A wide smile spread across her face, displaying white teeth. "Really?"

"But I can make sure he doesn't ever work in movies again."

A frown chased away her grin. "What are you saying?"

"I want something from you, and you want to help your fiancé, don't you?"

"What do you want?"

His smile bordered on feral. "You, specifically."

Her eyes widened, and her mouth opened and closed several times before she laughed.

Roarke looked confused. "What's so funny?"

Mya was busy scanning the office, searching for a camera. "Bobby arranged this, didn't he? His practical jokes—"

Roarke scowled at her. "This isn't a joke."

"Right…" She trailed off when she realized it wasn't a joke. "You can't be serious!"

"I'm very serious."

Mya jerked from the chair and strode to the door of his office. "You're a sick man."

"Poor Bobby," he said as she grasped the handle. "He's going to be crushed when I fire him from this movie. And he'll have to reimburse us since he didn't fulfill his contract."

Her hand dropped from the doorknob while she mentally tallied how much of the money they had already spent. New clothes for his image, the expenses of the move to the new place, and a large down payment on the Cadillac SRX Bobby had wanted sprang to mind. It went well into the thousands. She felt sick when she turned back to him. "Why are you doing this?"

"I'm a powerful man, and I get what I want. I want you."

"But, why?" Mya waved a hand down her body. "I'm nothing. I love someone else. Why would you go to all this trouble?"

"It's a game, darling. Some play it, and others get played."

Her mouth fell open. "This is all about some game?"

He nodded.

"You can't be serious."

"I am. All I want is your lovely body in exchange for Bobby's secure future."

All the money they would have to repay—and Bobby's aborted dreams—weighed heavily on her. She held his future—their future—in her hands. Could she do it though? It was tantamount to prostitution. However, so much was at stake. She swallowed back tears and asked in a thick voice, "When?"

He opened a drawer on his desk and extracted a key ring. "Catch."

As he tossed it to her, Mya held out her hand to intercept the key chain. It was one of the simple clear kind, tinted purple, with a handwritten label inside. "What is this?"

"Where we rendezvous—1427 Flower de Boliva Avenue. The penthouse, of course."

Sick, Mya shoved the key chain into the pocket of her jeans. "When?" she asked again.

"Every Tuesday and Thursday from one until...whenever we finish."

She shook her head. "I have to work on Thursday afternoons."

"How about Fridays?"

"I work in the mornings, until one."

Roarke shrugged. "Fridays, we'll meet at two-thirty instead."

"What about Bobby?"

"I'm not going to tell him." His mouth twisted. "I'll make sure you're home in plenty of time."

"How long do I have to…" she lifted her chin as she paused, "…whore myself to you?"

He seemed to flinch, but his voice was still cool and level. "Until this movie's in the can."

Mya shook her head. "That could take weeks."

"Months, probably," he said, and sounded entirely too happy.

"I—"

"Having second thoughts?"

She glared at him. "No." He didn't speak again, so she turned on her heels and touched the handle for the second time. Once again, his voice stopped her.

"Are you clean?"

She turned back to him, puzzled. "Clean?"

"Disease-free?'

Her eyes widened. "Are you?"

"Fair question. Bring your test results with you to our first meeting, and I'll do the same."

"Test results?"

He nodded. "Go see a doctor. Have the usual tests, and we'll compare notes."

With a cry of outrage, Mya turned back to the door, threw it open, and stormed out. It wasn't until she was in the ladies' room on the first floor that she gave in to the tears. What had she agreed to? But what choice did she have? She loved Bobby too much to deny him his chance. They had promised to do whatever it took, and it was her time to live up to that vow.

Chapter Two
Second Thoughts

✍

As soon as Mya had slammed the door behind her, Roarke wilted in his seat. He laid his head on the desk and took deep breaths to regain his composure. Had he really just done that? How had he done that? Apparently, his long-ago acting lessons had stayed with him more so than he ever would have imagined.

He pushed away from the desk to walk over to the glass wall of his office that looked down on the sound stage below, where a crew was in the middle of shooting *Wilder Hearts*. He leaned against it and stared at the bustle below him.

How he missed it. It was the first movie to carry his name that he wasn't directing, but his brother had wanted a shot. Roarke grimaced as the actors turned away from the camera to do half of their scene before anyone realized it was the wrong angle. Maybe he should pull Lenny out of the project.

He leaned his forehead against the cool glass and sighed. Mom would rake him over the coals if he didn't give his little brother a proper chance or if he stepped in now. She wouldn't understand that they were already a month behind in schedule and a few million over the projected cost. A smile teased his firm lips as he imagined what she would say if he told her that. *"What's more important? Money and schedules, or your brother's confidence?"*

His conscience pricked him and forced his thoughts from his family to what he had just done. He felt guilty, especially as he remembered the tears in her eyes. Why had she been so put off by the idea? He wasn't a gargoyle, by any means. Women occasionally fell at his feet. There was a lump in his throat brought on by disappointment. What had he expected? Her unqualified joy? Had he imagined she would eagerly drape herself spread-eagle across his desk? Dream on. She was an engaged woman.

The best thing to do would be to release her. Maybe tell her it was all a joke. His eyes fell on the script on his desk. *Playing His Game* had been the inspiration for today's meeting. Hell, it had been the only way he could finally engineer a meeting with her at all. Her beauty had mesmerized him on the two occasions she had been on the set before today. He had asked around about her, but no one knew anything. Each day, he held his breath as he waited for her to reappear. When she came on the set today, he had been determined to act on the opportunity.

He was distracted once again as her face popped into his mind. Mya was even more beautiful than he had thought when he saw her for the first time from the view his second-floor office provided.

She had been somewhat different in person though. For starters, she was about five-four, which was shorter than he had guessed. Her breasts were a nice surprise—firm and lush, and larger than he would have expected judging from the rest of her stature. They were just a bit more than a handful. Perfect.

Roarke stroked his goatee as he recalled her finely drawn features, straight nose, and sweeping cheekbones. Brown freckles adorned the bridge of her nose and swept across her cheeks to whisper secrets in her shell-like ears. How he longed to be those freckles.

Yes, guilt weighed heavily on him, but the anticipation over their first meeting already dimmed the annoying prick of his conscience. She was his to play with, although he didn't want to hurt her. She honestly believed he could keep Bobby from working again, so she would do whatever he asked. Roarke fought down a flush of embarrassment at the lie he had told. He had power, but not that much.

He fell into fantasizing about their first encounter before abruptly realizing the condo was still on the market and completely bare of furniture. He hadn't really believed it would work, and so he hadn't prepared a plan. The script called for the playboy to arrange weekly meetings in a hotel room he owned for the convenience of his myriad trysts. Having no suite in reserve, Roarke had impulsively settled for the next best thing. The keys to the condo he'd had on the market for over a month had been conveniently nearby, to his relief.

Unfortunately, because of a lack of preparation, he only had three days to get everything in place. He temporarily put a hold on the delicious erotic images parading through his mind to focus on practical matters. After all, they couldn't play the game without props.

Chapter Three
Sacrifices

 හ

By the time Mya and Bobby returned to their new apartment, she knew she couldn't go through with the bargain she had made with Roarke Thomas. They would find some way to repay the money. Maybe even enlist the help of an attorney. She wished she carried a recorder with her everywhere so she would have proof of his coercion. Too bad she wasn't the star of a movie or the heroine of a book. She might have been prepared for the bizarre situation had she been.

"Whadya think?" Bobby asked as he tossed the keys on the hall table before he unbuttoned his shirt. "Didn't I just blow your mind?"

Mya nodded, unable to summon a smile. She tried to recapture her previous enjoyment of Bobby's performance, but she was too preoccupied. How would she tell him? He would be so distraught.

His lower lip sank into a downward curve. "I can tell you loved it." He tossed the expensive red silk shirt onto the thick gray-green carpeting.

She noticed his sarcasm and forced a smile when she touched his bare arm. "You were wonderful, as always."

"Why didn't you say so before I had to ask you?"

"I've been thinking about something."

His eyes widened. "What could be more important than me?"

"Mr. Thomas called me into his office." She twisted a long strand of hair around her finger nervously. "He wanted…" She broke off as she searched for the right words. "Well, he started out by talking about you."

Bobby gripped her upper arms. "Really? What did he say? Did he love me?"

"He said he could make sure you have a long career." Mya didn't have a chance to add more.

"Yeah! He loves me."

"But, Bobby—"

"What?"

Mya bit her lip before continuing. "He wants something in return."

"I'll do anything."

"He wants me," she burst out.

Bobby blinked. "What?"

"He wants me to sleep with him to further your career." Mya's eyes widened when Bobby laughed. "What's so damn funny?"

"Seriously, what did he want?"

She glared at him. "He wants me to become his virtual sex slave for the remainder of shoot time."

He finally seemed to realize it wasn't a joke. "But that doesn't make any sense."

She frowned at him with confusion. "Huh?"

"He's surrounded by beautiful women all day. Why would he pick you?"

Tears flooded Mya's eyes.

He awkwardly patted her shoulder. "I didn't mean it that way, babe. It's just, he could have his pick of any starlet. I don't understand why he wants my fiancée."

She sniffled, trying to fight back the tears. Of course, he hadn't meant to hurt her feelings. And he had a point. Why plain old Mya when he could have any woman? "I don't know."

"What did you tell him?"

Instead of answering, Mya said, "He threatened to fire you and demand your advance back. He said you'd never work again if I said no."

"My God! He can't do that."

She nodded. "I thought maybe a lawyer…"

Bobby waved his hand. "Too much hassle, and we have no proof." His blue eyes darkened. "I want you to know that I'm not happy about this, but I won't hold it against you."

Mya stared up at him with a frown. "Are you saying you think I should…?" She shook her head, certain she had misunderstood. "You really want me to…?"

With a solemn expression, Bobby pulled her against him. "I don't think we have a choice."

"We can fight this," she said against his bare chest.

"Mya, we don't have the money for all that. If he fires me and I have to repay the advance, how will we manage? Especially if he ruins my career. I'll have to go back to Serpent Springs with my tail between my legs." He patted her back. "I don't want to share you at all, and definitely not with that pervert, but we're both making sacrifices."

She lifted her head and didn't fight the tears. "Not this, please. I'll work two jobs until we have enough to repay him. I'll even borrow money from my folks." The prospect filled her with revulsion, but she would do anything to avoid Thomas's bargain.

His fingers were tender as he touched her face. "I hate this as much as you do."

Her lips trembled as she recognized the acceptance in his eyes. "I can't do it, Bobby. I've never been with anyone else."

"We both promised to do whatever it took to help my career."

She closed her eyes and recoiled from his reminder, but was unable to deny she had made the vow. She was defeated when she dropped her head against his chest again and sobbed.

"It won't be so bad." Bobby's tone was soothing. "Once it's over, we'll pretend it never happened. It won't change things for us."

How could it not? The words were on the tip of her tongue, but Mya knew it was pointless to utter them. Bobby saw the long-term benefits of a short-term sacrifice. He was right—she knew that. Every fiber of her being protested it was wrong, but she knew it was the only option. She would grit her teeth, endure whatever that Thomas guy had in mind, and think of Bobby every step of the way.

Chapter Four
First Encounter

Mya took a taxi to the apartment on Flower de Boliva and used the key Roarke had given her to open the glass doors and access the elevator. She took it to the fourteenth floor, where she got out in the luxurious hallway. Her sandals sank into the deep carpet, which completely cushioned the sound of each step.

At precisely two-thirty, she let herself into the apartment. She tried to quell her nervous stomach as it protested her presence there. Her eyes widened at the bare living room and kitchen. There were no furnishings—not even pictures on the wall or a phone. The only items in the kitchen were a fridge, stove, and dishwasher. The white tile sparkled, and the scent of lemon cleaner still hung in the air.

Her legs shook as she walked down the hallway. Was he here yet? "Hello?"

"In here, Mya. The last room on your left."

The sound of his voice made her grimace as she made her way down the bare hallway. Two of the four doors stood cracked open, and each room was bare. A closed door separated her from him in the other room. She knocked on the black wood and felt ridiculously like she waited for someone important to admit her.

"Come in."

She took a deep breath, then twisted the doorknob and entered the bedroom. This room was furnished with a recliner positioned near the foot of the massive bed. He sat with his feet up on the footrest. A glass of amber liquid rested in the cup holder built into the elegant black recliner. A box lay on the bed.

"Welcome."

She frowned at him, refusing to answer. She didn't care how petulant her behavior seemed. It didn't hurt to remind him she didn't want to be here.

He waved her closer, and her reluctant feet obeyed. When she stood within touching distance, he handed her a sheet of paper. "What's this?" She stared at the crisp, white paper and tried to make sense of the black letters.

"My health report."

She dropped the envelope she held onto his lap before she looked at his page. Mya had no idea how to interpret it, but assumed he wouldn't have shared it with her if it revealed anything negative.

He opened the envelope and scanned the pages. "Excellent. You're on the Pill, I see."

"Yes."

Roarke took a drink from his glass. He fidgeted with the envelope, then sat up so abruptly the footrest folded in with a snap. "Would you like iced tea? It's all I have on hand." He winked at her. "I know tea isn't the stiff drink you probably think you need to get through this."

She shook her head and crossed her arms over her chest. She ignored his banter as she studied him. Was it her imagination, or did he seem lost? Mya dared to hope he had changed his mind. "What now?"

Roarke had fantasized this moment repeatedly for the last three days, but somehow it didn't seem to be going so well in real life. "Take off your clothes."

Her eyes widened. "Already?"

He shrugged.

She compressed her lips into a straight line. "Fine. Where's the bathroom?"

"Out here."

Mya shook her head.

He grinned up at her. "I only want to see what you're wearing under those shorts and that prim little shirt you have buttoned all the way to your neck."

With a glower, Mya unbuckled the belt on her khaki shorts and pulled it off. She maintained her glare when she dropped it on the floor. She tried to blank all thoughts from her mind as she fumbled with the zipper and button and pushed down the shorts. She shuddered when his eyes caressed the length of her leg from the hip to her toes in the rope sandals.

"Very nice." Roarke's cock hardened almost painfully, and he wondered if he could stick with today's schedule of events. "The shirt too."

Mya bit her lip as her trembling hands fumbled with the first few buttons. She saw his lips part as the shirt gaped open at her breasts. She struggled to prevent the flush as it blossomed on her cheeks. She finished unbuttoning the shirt and let it fall to the floor. *I have nothing to be embarrassed about. He's the one who should be ashamed.* Her pep talk didn't ward off an attack of self-consciousness as he eyed her critically.

Roarke shook his head and clicked his tongue. "Chain-store bra and panties, Mya? It's a crime to cover your luscious curves with plain white cotton."

She tossed her head back and resisted the urge to cover her breasts when his eyes lingered. "Why does it matter what I wear under my clothes? No one sees it."

"Bobby does."

She lifted a shoulder. "He doesn't care."

"Well, I do." He pointed to the box. "That is for you."

"No, thank you."

He smiled. "It's not a choice, Mya."

She frowned at him as she marched to the bed and ripped the box open. She faltered at the sight of the white teddy. Although she worked the makeup counter, Mya had picked up enough during her tenure with Macy's to know the material was real silk and probably very expensive. She was careful to ensure it didn't snag on the box as she lifted it out and laid it across the bed. "You want me to wear this?"

He nodded.

"But…" Mya couldn't think of a reason not to, and even the skimpy covering it would provide was preferable to complete nudity. "Where's the bathroom?"

Roarke quirked a brow, but decided to indulge her. "Through that door." He pointed to the door by the closet.

Mya scooped up the teddy and swept through the black door that contrasted so dramatically with the silver walls. The bathroom was as unfurnished as the rest of the condo, without so much as even a bath mat. The only personal touches she could see were two fluffy towels folded on the counter.

In an attempt to delay the inevitable, Mya opened the medicine cabinet to snoop, but didn't find even one bottle or tube. She closed the mirror and sat on the toilet. She shivered. It wasn't actually cold, but she was nervous. Forced to stand in front of Roarke in her underwear, she had been unnerved, but the teddy was so much more intimate, which made it even worse.

She firmed her lips before she unhooked the bra and slipped it off. The panties followed, and she laid both on the counter. Knowing the sooner she got dressed, the sooner the afternoon would end, Mya stepped into the teddy and pulled it up. She frowned at herself in the mirror.

The legs were French cut, with a narrow crotch made from sheer lace. A lace panel revealed a diamond of her midriff, the shadow of her pubic region, and a hint of cleavage where her breasts pushed together at the bottom of the cups. The neckline plunged to meet the top of the diamond, and two spaghetti straps held it up on her shoulders. She turned around to look at the back and realized it was completely sheer except for a band of lace that fell below her shoulder blades.

She stared at herself in the mirror and wondered how she could walk out there dressed in that. His eyes would eat her up.

How could she maintain a façade of indifference with her defenses — and body — stripped bare?

Her head whipped around when he tapped on the door. "What?"

"Are you coming out?"

"In a minute." She tried to keep the edge of panic from her voice.

"Don't make me come get you. A tryst in the bathroom isn't on the agenda. Today, anyway." His laugh sounded more like the purr of a large, predatory cat than a sound of amusement.

She heard him walking away from the door and breathed a sigh of relief, but knew her reprieve was short-lived. Mya bent over and flipped her hair forward as she fluffed out the heavy strands. She stood up and arranged the locks to hide her breasts where the pink areoles were clearly visible through the thin silk.

With another deep breath, Mya opened the bathroom door and plunged into the room. Momentum carried her within three feet of the bed, before she froze like a deer in headlights. His hungry expression caused shivers to race down her spine.

Roarke struggled to control his breathing as he stared at her. A grin teased the corners of his lips when he saw how carefully she had positioned her hair to cover her breasts. "Stunning, but I think the sandals clash."

Color flooded her cheeks, and Mya kicked off the brown rope sandals. She stood near him while her arms dangled at her side. "Now what?"

"Let's talk."

"Talk?"

He nodded and waved at the bed. "You sit there."

She wasn't thrilled at the idea of being on the bed, but it was a better alternative than sharing the only chair with him. Mya perched on the edge of the bed, crossed her legs, and folded her arms across her chest, even though modesty was a lost cause.

Roarke racked his brain as he tried to remember the questions he had written down and memorized. "How many lovers have you had?" He cringed when he blurted out the question. He had planned to ease into questions like that.

She glared at him, but didn't refuse to answer. "Just Bobby."

He groaned under his breath and suddenly felt like the most depraved man in the world. "Why?"

"Because I love him."

"No. I mean, why just Bobby?"

Mya blinked. "We've been together since I was seventeen and he was eighteen."

"How old are you now?"

"Twenty-one."

So young. Had he ever been that young or innocent? The eleven years between them might as well be eleven thousand. "You've never wanted to be with anyone else?"

She shook her head.

"How do you know you love him if he's the only guy you've ever had?"

Mya frowned. "Can we not discuss this? I'll do whatever you want sexually," she closed her eyes to summon the strength to continue, "within reason, but I want to keep you—this— separate from the rest of my life. Otherwise, I'll go crazy."

He shrugged. There would be time for them to become acquainted later. "Fine. Do you like sex, Mya?"

She gasped at the question, but couldn't refuse to answer. It fell within the parameters she herself had set. She wondered how honest she should be.

"Do you love it, or do you tolerate it?"

"It's okay."

Roarke choked on the sip of tea in his mouth. She moved so gracefully, with an overt sensuality that inspired certain expectations. That was not the answer he had expected to hear. "Just okay?"

She shrugged. What was she supposed to say? None of her female friends enjoyed sex much either. They sometimes giggled over what a fuss their partners made about the act.

"Have you ever had an orgasm with Bobby?"

Mya blushed. "Yeah, of course." Twice, back in the days when they had first gotten together. Since then, things had fizzled.

Roarke saw the blush on her face and the longing in her eyes. "I see. How did he do it?"

She cleared her throat. "I don't want to talk about this."

"Just tell me, Mya." He winked at her. "While we're talking, I'm not touching."

Her face grew even fierier. "He…" She cleared her throat again. "His tongue," she settled for saying. She knew she couldn't bluntly say one of the harsher terms and had always found the technical term to be even more awkward.

"Do you touch yourself, Mya?"

The way he kept saying her name caused tingles to course through her body. She frowned at her own response, disgusted that the sexy, grating tone could affect her at all. What was wrong with her?

Roarke almost laughed as she dropped her gaze from his. From her body language, he knew she did, and that she had been taught it was wrong. "There's nothing wrong with it. It's your body. Why shouldn't you know every creamy inch, curve, indent, and sensitive spot?"

"Can we…? Ask me something else!"

He lifted a shoulder. "As soon as you answer the question. Do you?"

She kept her gaze averted as she jerked her head up and down once.

"Are you good at it?"

Mya's hazel eyes clashed with his. "What?"

"Can you make yourself come?"

Exasperated, she asked, "Do you think I'd keep doing it if I couldn't?"

Her answer caught him by surprise, and Roarke laughed aloud. Her disgruntled expression only added to his amusement. He forced the grin from his face, because he knew his next words would piss her off. "Show me."

Mya jumped to her feet. "What's wrong with you?"

"I want to see how you touch yourself so I'll know how to touch you when it's my turn."

"Why would you care?"

She was honestly puzzled, and Roarke felt the first stirrings of anger for her inconsiderate lover. "I want you to get as much from this as I plan to."

She couldn't hold back a snort. "Right."

He shook his head, but didn't press the topic. "One of us will be touching you today, Mya. It's your choice."

Hot color invaded her cheeks. How was she supposed to choose? It almost seemed easier to let him do it and get it over with than to do something so personal in front of him. However, the thought of his hands on her made her muscles clench. She balled her hands into fists and felt the short nails carve half-moons in her palms. "I'll do it."

Roarke watched and tried to remain impassive as she propped pillows against the headboard and lay down. His breath caught in his throat when she parted her legs, and he caught a glimpse of the fine red-gold curls at the juncture of her thighs.

The breath exploded from him in a sharp gasp as she pushed the material aside to slip a finger into her pussy. As he watched, entranced, she began to massage her clit, shyly peeking out from its hiding place. His eyes flicked to her face, and he saw she was too embarrassed to be aroused. With amusement, he watched her manipulate herself for half a minute before she assumed a twisted expression, shuddered a couple of times, and relaxed.

"Can I go now?"

He laughed. "That performance might fool Bobby, but it won't work on me. We aren't leaving until you come—for real this time, please."

She scowled at him.

"Are you even wet yet?" By the mutinous set of her lips, Roarke knew she planned not to answer. "Shall I find out for myself?" He knew if he touched her he wouldn't be able to stop, and that wasn't part of today's plan. He had no interest in forcing her. He wanted to seduce every one of the lovely Mya's senses until she was as desperate for him as he was for her.

With renewed determination, Mya pushed her head back into the pillows, resolved to ignore his presence. She closed her eyes and focused on the sensations that coursed through her body as she caressed her clit. Random erotic images flew through her mind as she got wet. She brought a second finger into play to spread the moisture around and explore deeper inside her pussy.

Mya arched her hips off the bed as she touched herself with an expertise born of practice. She grew wetter as her fingers increased their tempo and brought her closer to the brink.

Roarke wiped at the sweat beaded on his forehead as his amazed eyes soaked up every second of her solo show. His cock throbbed with each beat of his heart, simpatico with each thrust of her hips. He longed to offer his assistance, but knew any reminder of his presence would shatter her passionate haze, and the temporary illusion that they were both here of their own free will. He couldn't bite back a moan as she completely encased two of her fingers, and her body started to shake. A cry broke from her, and he knew this was no performance.

She blinked when he moaned, suddenly reminded of his presence. She had almost forgotten he was in the room with her.

Even the renewed awareness of his presence couldn't stem the tide of her orgasm as it washed over her. She shook with fulfillment, while tears leaked from her eyes. For a long moment after the last spasm had passed, she lay on the bed and struggled to regain her breath and composure.

Finally, she lifted her head to find his intent gaze fastened on her. She had expected him to leer, or maybe stroke himself from his front-row seat. Instead, he wore a tender expression. She was too tired to analyze it, or play any more games for the day. "I'm leaving now. If you don't like it, do your worst."

Roarke glanced at his watch, amazed that an hour had passed. "You're free to go—until Tuesday."

"Don't remind me," she muttered as she rolled from the bed. She kept her eyes off him as she grabbed her clothes from the floor and rushed into the bathroom. She stripped off the teddy and kicked it across the floor so she could dress in her own clothes. All the while, she attempted to ignore the uncomfortable dampness in her pussy. She would shower at home.

On her way out of the bathroom, Mya saw her reflection and froze. She looked embarrassed, but there was also a glow to her cheeks, and a sated look in her eyes. Her entire body felt relaxed, but she frowned when she realized she was still aroused. With a wordless cry, she denied what she saw in the mirror. She wrenched the door open and ran from the apartment without a word spoken to Roarke. She couldn't outrun the truth though.

As she flagged a taxi and dropped into the back seat, Mya shied away from admitting that part of her—a very small part—had reveled in having an audience. No! She had not enjoyed the role of sexual plaything thrust upon her. She had hated every minute of it. Only the dampness inside her pussy countered her vehement denials of pleasure.

Chapter Five
Details

෨

When Mya let herself into the apartment, she was surprised to find Bobby sprawled across the three thousand dollar leather sofa. She glanced at her watch. It was just past four, although the afternoon seemed to have taken forever. "You're home early."

He shrugged. "There was a problem with one of the cameras. Lenny sent us home for the day."

She frowned. "They let you go for that?"

Bobby shrugged again as he got to his feet. "What happened?"

Mya dropped her keys and purse on the table and deliberately avoided his eyes. "It's over."

"You mean he called it off?"

"No. It's finished for today. I don't want to talk about it."

As she turned down the hallway toward the bathroom, Bobby followed her.

"Tell me about it."

She sighed. "No."

"You owe it to me to tell—"

She spun around in mid-step, catching him off-guard. "I'm doing this for you, Bobby. Don't tell me I owe you the details."

He nodded. "I'm sorry. It's just…I have to know."

"Why?"

"Was he better than me?"

She bit her lip, wanting to reassure Bobby, but not willing to set the precedent of divulging the details of her meetings with

Roarke. To continue functioning normally, she had to keep those separate from her real life. "Nothing happened today."

He cocked an eyebrow. "Don't lie."

"I'm not! He didn't touch me."

Bobby put his hand on her arm. "I just wanna know—"

She jerked away. "I told you nothing happened." Mya stormed to the bathroom and slammed the door behind her. She stripped off her clothes and started the hot water. She was bent forward to gather her hair into a large shower cap when she felt Bobby's hands on her hips. She stood frozen as he slid his hand down her bottom to touch her pussy. "What are you...?" She started to stand, but his hand on her lower back stopped her. "Bobby?"

"Reminding us both," he said as he stepped closer.

Mya realized he was naked as his cock brushed her thigh. Despite the way her body still tingled with arousal, she wasn't in the mood. "Not now, Bobby."

He pulled her up and wrapped his arms around her until her back pressed against his chest. "I need you, Mya. I have to know you're still my girl."

With a sigh, she submitted to his caresses and moaned when he brought his hand up to rub her nipples. His other hand forayed inside her pussy to ease his passage. "You're so wet."

It sounded like an accusation. "I didn't..." She broke off when she decided it wasn't wise to tell him she hadn't showered earlier. He would naturally wonder why she had needed a shower if nothing had happened. She sighed when he turned her around and lifted her in his arms. Bobby moved so that she was braced against the wall, and then slid inside her.

Her pussy tingled as it accepted his cock, and she leaned forward as he filled her. Mya grasped his shoulders and began to thrust with Bobby. She tried not to think of anything that had happened earlier in the afternoon. She managed to ignore her thoughts as Bobby continued to push her bottom against the wall with each deep thrust. She was poised on the brink when she felt his fluid fill her before his cock softened.

Mya could have cried with frustration when he slid out and sat her on the marble tile. She continued to ache for fulfillment, but he already had that sleepy expression he got after making love.

His expression was brooding. "Your cunt was soaking wet before I ever touched you."

She rolled her eyes. "How many times do I have to tell you that he didn't lay a hand on me?"

"Whatever happened, you liked it."

Mya turned away from him, too angry to speak.

His tone was still disgruntled when he said, "I bet that wiped away all memories of him."

Her mouth fell open, and she spun around to face him. "Is that what this was about? You were…" She floundered as she searched for a way to describe what he had done. "Was this about comparison?"

Bobby shook his head and pushed loose strands of hair behind his shoulders. "It's not like that. I just wanted you to remember what it's like with someone you love."

"But he didn't touch me!" Mya winced at the shrill tone and bit her tongue to hold back a scream.

His expression became sad. "How are we going to get through this if you won't be honest with me?"

"How am I supposed to do this if you insist on fucking me after each meeting to remind me who I belong to?"

His lower lip protruded. "I don't like sharing you."

She tossed her hands up. "Fine with me. I'll call Thomas and tell him to shove it."

Bobby's blue eyes grew dark, and he shook his head. "You can't. We have to do this."

She sighed. "Just let me cope in my own way. Don't ask for details, and don't make love to me to mark your territory."

After a pause, he finally nodded. "If that's what you want."

Before Mya could respond, he had hopped into her hot shower. She bit back her annoyance and sat on the toilet, knowing Bobby hated to share a shower unless they had sex under the pulsating stream. She wanted to tell him that she didn't want any of this, but his spontaneous rendition of *Another One Bites The Dust* made it impossible for her to speak.

When he finally emerged, she was too tired to pursue the conversation. Mya got in the shower and yelped when cold water pelted her. She slid the glass door open a few inches and leaned her head out. "All the hot water is gone."

Bobby carefully wrapped his long locks in a powder-blue towel. "I noticed that too. Probably because you left the water running."

She slammed the sliding door closed, satisfied with its protesting clunk and the way it rattled. Mya's body shook as she tried to control her anger and repress the tears that pricked the back of her eyes. It wasn't the lack of hot water—or even his ability to always make everything her fault—that made her so angry. It was a combination of the afternoon's events and his reaction—most especially his refusal to believe Roarke hadn't touched her. "I thought nothing would change," she whispered as the hair dryer turned on. She let cold water sluice the hot tears from her cheeks.

Chapter Six
Family Dinner

Roarke bit back a groan when Sam and Lisa made their big announcement. It wasn't that he wasn't happy for his oldest brother and sister-in-law, but he knew what he and Lenny were both in for as his mother's teary eyes fastened on the two of them. They sat at the opposite end of the white oak table, and both found their attention suddenly focused on their plates.

"When are you two going to give me grandchildren?"

Lenny's face reddened with embarrassment. "I'm not even married."

"It's no wonder since you never date."

Roarke shared an amused look with Sam. In point of fact, Lenny dated frequently, but Mom refused to acknowledge his male friends. She had dismissed his being gay as "just a phase".

To Roarke's discomfort, her brown eyes, the same shade as his, turned to him. He held up a hand in an attempt to ward off the interrogation. "Don't start, Mom."

She shook her head. "You need a woman, son. I want grandkids."

He pointed to Lisa. "All you have to do is wait a few months."

Deirdre didn't pay any attention. "You're thirty-two years old. It's time you married and settled down."

"It's the new millennium. People don't marry so young these days." How did she always manage to reduce him to feeling like the same guilty five-year-old who ate the whole blueberry pie she had made for Dad's birthday?

She shook her head as she pointed to Sam and Lisa herself. "Nonsense. You marry when you find the right one. It's as simple as that."

He sighed. "I haven't met the right one." Unbidden, an image of Mya popped into his head, just as quickly followed by the ring on her finger.

"All I'm saying is you have to start looking."

"Okay, Mom." Roarke concentrated even harder on the plate and pretended to be completely engrossed in his pot roast and carrots. Deirdre took the hint and dropped the subject.

* * * * *

After dinner, Roarke left the Mediterranean-style house, taking a seat on the railing of the porch. He took the script from his inside jacket pocket. It was dog-eared from his many readings. As always, the scenes following the initial encounter between the playboy and the girl did nothing to inspire him. As with most scripts, the passage of time was swift. By the next sex scene, the girl was a willing convert. Roarke felt his mouth twisting, knowing Mya wouldn't be so easily won over.

Fantasies about all the things he wanted to do with her came easily, but they all seemed too forward this soon into the game. Roarke didn't want to frighten her with his desire, and he didn't want her to hate him anymore than she already did. He had to come up with something for tomorrow's meeting, but so far nothing he had thought up was the right thing.

The sound of the screen door opening had Roarke looking up, hoping it wasn't Mom coming to continue their discussion. To his relief, it was Sam. "Hey."

"What are you doing out here all alone?"

Roarke shrugged as he bent the script in half vertically so he could stuff it back in his jacket. "I just wanted to get away."

The grin teasing Sam's mouth grew, giving him a boyish look. "From Mom?"

"Maybe." Roarke's smile gave his real answer. "Congratulations."

"Thanks."

"You ready for fatherhood?"

Sam shrugged, and a hint of doubt showed on his face. "It's scary." He leaned against the railing on the other side of the support post. "Ever give it any thought?"

"Nah. I'm too young."

"Four years younger than me, bud. That's not too young." Sam shook his head, which caused his brown curls to flop. "Mom means well, you know?"

"Yeah, I know." Roarke started to put the script away, but Sam took it from him. "Hey!"

"Another movie that's going to make you millions?" Sam flipped it open before Roarke could grab it back. His eyes widened. "What are these notes?"

Ruddy color swept across Roarke's cheekbones. "Nothing. Just director's notes."

"'Mya would hate this'." He flipped the script open to the middle. "'Possibility once I know Mya better'." Sam looked up. "What is this? There's no Mya listed on the front page."

He snatched the script from his brother's fingers and shoved it back in his jacket. "Nothing."

Sam crossed his arms over his chest. "C'mon. Spill."

"Honestly, it's nothing."

"Who's Mya?" His tone was casual, but his questioning eyes were sharp.

"No one. There is no Mya." Roarke averted his eyes.

"You never could lie very well." Sam chuckled. "Fine, don't tell me."

"She's just a woman." *A girl I'm completely crazy about.* "Nothing important." *Why can't I stop thinking about her?*

Lifting a shoulder, Sam said, "If you say so."

"She's driving me nuts!"

Sam quirked a brow. "What?"

"I can't stop thinking about her...fantasizing about her. She's in my dreams, dammit." To Roarke's surprise, Sam laughed. "You think that's funny?"

"I never thought I'd see you fall in love."

"I'm not in love." He couldn't be. She belonged with someone else. He had only a tenuous hold on her, and there was no way she could ever love him.

With a snort, Sam clapped him on the back. "I hope Mya realizes how lucky she is."

"Yeah, she's in seventh heaven," Roarke muttered under his breath.

Sam frowned. "Problems?"

"She hates me."

His eyes widened. "What did you do to make her hate you?"

Roarke hesitated. His actions weighed heavily on him, but Sam was probably not the best choice of confidant. He had very rigid moral views and would never understand. On the other hand, he gave sage advice. "We're playing a game together." He handed him the script once more. "This game."

Sam's eyes grew round as he read the brief synopsis of the script. "I take it she doesn't want to participate?"

"She's engaged to someone else."

He was succinct. "It'll never work."

"Maybe—"

"If you really care for the girl, don't make her do this."

Roarke's shoulders dropped as his brother confirmed what his own conscience had told him for days. "I know you're right."

"Good." Sam shoved the script into his hands. "If you're lucky, maybe you haven't ruined her life yet."

"Yeah." Yet. Despite his brother's words, and the prickle of his own conscience, Roarke knew he couldn't let her go. The game hadn't played out to its conclusion. And for him, the game was all too real.

Chapter Seven
Dancing

ಐ

Mya let herself into Roarke's apartment, unsure of what to expect. Her stomach clenched when she saw him propped against the counter in the kitchen. A blush swept across her face as she remembered the way he watched her at their last meeting. She dropped her eyes and frowned when she noticed he wore a tuxedo. She opened her mouth, but he spoke before she could ask about it.

He smiled at her as his eyes raked over the blue and gold sundress that displayed just a hint of cleavage. She looked wonderful—fresh and composed—but the outfit wasn't suitable for today's activities. "There's a box for you on the bed."

"Is every session going to start with dress-up?" Her tone was sarcastic. She ignored the flutter of excitement. She had never gotten many gifts from Bobby, but that was no reason to look forward to something from Roarke. It was sure to be another teddy, which was for him, not her.

Roarke shrugged. "Maybe." His sanguine response hid his anxiety over their upcoming meetings. Planning their meetings was nerve-racking, especially with him wanting each to be better than the last. He had a feeling she wouldn't be at all thrilled with the plans for their next meeting. He didn't even know how she would respond to today's events, and they weren't nearly as intimate. "Go get dressed."

Mya walked down the hall to the bedroom, alarmed to notice he followed her. "What are you doing?"

Roarke gave her a lopsided grin. "Watching."

"I don't—"

"I'm staying, Mya."

She glared at him, then walked over to the large beige box on the bed and carefully pulled off the blue satin ribbon. She lifted the lid and gasped. It wasn't lingerie as she had expected. Mya lifted the dress out to examine it more closely. It was a midnight blue shade with a velvet bodice and full satin skirt. There were no straps, so only her endowments would hold it up.

With a glance over her shoulder to gauge his reaction, she pulled the sundress off and draped it across the bed. Mya shivered as she felt his eyes slide over her body. She didn't have to turn around to know he watched her every move.

She unzipped the blue dress with trembling hands and dropped it over her head as quickly as possible.

"Beautiful, except for the bra straps."

Mya turned around and scowled at him. "It doesn't matter if they show."

Roarke shook his head. "It matters to me."

"Fine." She pushed the dress down to her waist and removed the plain white bra. She heard Roarke's indrawn breath and froze. Mya lifted her bowed head and met his hungry gaze. She could feel her nipples harden as his eyes settled on them. It was almost as if he was touching her. He lifted his eyes, and they locked with hers for a long moment. She had no doubts of how much he wanted to cross the bedroom and touch her.

The thought alarmed her, and she tore her gaze from his. Mya pulled up the dress and fumbled with the zipper, which she got halfway up her back. The back of the dress itself fell just below her shoulder blades. A slippery material that molded itself to her and caressed her body with every movement lined the bodice and covered her nipples. The sensation, combined with the way he looked at her, caused her to shiver again.

"There's another box too," Roarke said.

She turned her attention to the smaller box on the floor. She lifted it up and removed a pair of high-heeled blue satin pumps. Mya kicked off her sandals before she slid her feet into the shoes. As she looked at herself in the mirror, she realized her hair didn't look right with the dress. She obeyed a spontaneous impulse and opened her purse to take out a brush and plain black barrette she kept to pin up her hair.

Mya started to brush her hair, but stiffened when Roarke walked toward her. Without speaking, he took the brush from her and began to brush out her long hair. Her stomach clenched, and her breathing grew shallow as his hands moved through her hair, gently wielding the brush and smoothing through the strands. He didn't touch any other part of her, but she found herself wishing he would. That thought propelled her to step away. "That's fine."

He nodded and proffered the brush before he stepped away.

She gathered her hair into a ponytail and rolled it up, then fastened the barrette to hold it in place. Once more, she looked at the mirror, and her mouth bowed into an O of surprise.

She hardly recognized herself. She had never worn anything so elegant, not even for the prom. It seemed silly to waste the dress on whatever Roarke had planned, but she wasn't about to ask to keep it. She wouldn't feel comfortable wearing it again, and Bobby would throw a fit if she brought home a "gift" from Roarke.

Thoughts of Bobby dispelled her mental fog, and she firmed her mouth as she turned to face Roarke. His eyes darkened as he looked at her. His expression made Mya shift restlessly. "What's with the dress?"

"You can't do ballroom dancing without a dress like that."

Mya frowned at him. "Ballroom dancing?"

He nodded as he walked toward her. When he stood a few inches from her, he said, "Turn around."

Her expression was suspicious. "Why?"

Roarke grinned at her. "So I can finish zipping you up."

"Oh." She had been expecting something else. Mya turned around and stumbled a bit on the unaccustomed height of the heels. His hands steadied her while they slid down to the zipper. A shiver danced up her spine as his warm fingers pulled the zipper up to the top and locked it in place. For a brief second, his hands lingered on her shoulders, and then dropped away. Mya turned around, surprised to find her face within inches of his chest.

She stepped back and turned to the door, followed closely by Roarke. She left the bedroom and walked into the living room. Mya stood in the center of the room, wondering what would happen next.

Roarke walked into the kitchen and bent down to a cupboard. When he stood up, he held a portable stereo, which he set on the counter. He pressed a button and slow music wafted from the speakers.

He walked into the living room and stopped a few inches away from her. "You really are beautiful," he whispered. With a deep breath, Roarke put his arms around her and took one of her hands in his. He rested the other one on her back. "Lay your head on my chest."

Reluctantly, Mya did as he instructed and put her free hand on his waist. There was something so intimate about being this close to him. She felt exposed. Even more so than she had on Friday, when he had watched her in that teddy as she touched herself. That day, he hadn't laid a hand on her, but now his body pressed against hers. She could feel his rapid heartbeat against her cheek, and it echoed through her ear. He smelled of peppermint and spicy cologne. A curiously pleasant combination that was uniquely him.

He resisted the urge to pull her so tightly against him that they couldn't dance. If his feet didn't move continuously, Roarke knew his hands would start to explore, and she wasn't ready for that. He ached for her, but held off. He buried his face in her hair and breathed in her scent. He tried to tell himself to be content with her in his arms, despite the layers of clothes between them. He lowered his head to the bend where her neck and shoulder met and inhaled.

Mya's eyes widened when he moved to her neck. She froze as she waited for him to nip her, but all he did was breathe against her skin. Her stomach clenched, and her nipples hardened further, much to her embarrassment. As his facial hair tickled her neck, and his breath whispered across her skin, Mya's head tilted of its own volition to allow him better access.

Unable to resist, Roarke pressed a gentle kiss to the sensitive spot. His mouth curved upwards as she moved her head. A small sign of acceptance, but enough to nurture his hope.

She shivered when his lips touched her. Mya's eyes closed, and she snuggled a bit closer. A dull ache started in the pit of her stomach and soon spread downwards to her pussy. She sighed when he kissed her again.

His hands tangled in her hair, and he pulled the barrette out to let the mass fall free around her shoulders. He took a handful of the red-gold hair and rubbed it against his cheek. Roarke was relieved when the music suddenly stopped. He was shaky and knew he was almost out of control. He stepped away from her so fast she swayed at the abrupt withdrawal of his support.

Mya bit back a protest as his arms fell away from her. She lifted her heavy lids to look up at him with confusion. "What...?"

He smiled down at her and touched her cheek. "The CD ended."

She glanced at her watch. How had thirty minutes passed without her knowledge? She cleared her throat. "Yes. I was counting down the minutes." They both knew it was a lie, and Mya raised her chin. Her eyes dared him to challenge the statement.

He bit back a laugh. "You can leave now."

"Already?" She turned bright red when the question slipped out of her mouth. What was she thinking? She should be relieved that their meeting had ended so soon and without any unpleasant firsts. She shouldn't feel even a hint of disappointment. Mya was seized by the urgent need to escape before he could respond to her question. She hurried around him, but froze when his hand fell on her shoulder. She turned back to him with a frown of censure. "You said I could go."

Roarke smiled at her, pleased to note the flush of desire on her cheeks — or was it embarrassment? Either way, it indicated a reaction to him. Rather than answer, his hand moved to the zipper and lowered it for her. When he let go, she rushed past him to the bedroom. Her flight spoke of a desire to escape. If he judged from her response to his touch, she sought escape from her own reaction more so than him. A satisfied smile curved his mouth. He didn't want to endure another night of frustration, but it was a small price to pay to leave her in the same condition.

An image of a naked Waller, eager to hold Mya in his arms, chased away his smile. Unlike Roarke, she had someone who waited for her at home. Someone who would ease her frustrations. He almost abandoned his plan and stormed into the bedroom. Only the realization that he would lose all chance with her caused his feet to turn in the direction of the door.

Mya had just hung the dress in the closet when she heard the front door slam. She walked over to the bedroom door and peered out. From this angle, there was no sign of Roarke. She went back to the bed, scooped up her purse, and left the room. There was no sign of Roarke as she walked through the condo. The only proof of their presence was the stereo on the counter and her barrette on the floor. She bent down to retrieve it on her way out.

As she locked the door behind her, Mya wondered why Roarke had left in such a hurry. He hadn't said a word before he rushed out. Had she done something that upset or offended him? Her mouth twisted. She hoped she had so he would let her out of this ridiculous game. She ignored the little voice in the back of her head that said otherwise, ruthlessly squashing it as she hailed a taxi to take her home. Back to Bobby, where she belonged.

Chapter Eight
Roarke's Summons

ഹ

Mya didn't sleep well Tuesday night. Bobby had sulked the entire evening and didn't speak to her once. She was relieved to find him gone when she woke up later than usual on Wednesday. That made her feel guilty, but she was too consumed with a headache to worry about how she felt. She rolled from the bed and padded into the bathroom. After swallowing two Advil, she went into the kitchen to pour a cup of coffee.

She hissed with annoyance when she saw Bobby had shut off the warmer, despite the half of pot that remained in the carafe. She dumped out the contents and started a fresh pot. While she waited for it to brew, she went to the answering machine when she noticed the light flashed.

When Mya pressed play, she groaned. Her boss's voice was as brisk as usual, although her message was a surprise. "We won't need you today, Mya. I double-scheduled, and you have seniority, so you get the free day. With pay, of course."

She frowned and deleted the message. It wasn't like Chelsea to give anyone a day off. The next message offered an explanation.

"Mya, it's Roarke. I wanted to see you today. I can't wait until Friday. I handled your boss, so don't offer that excuse."

Damn, his voice was as sexy on the tape as it was in real life. She glared down at the machine and wished she could retort.

He continued. "You should have a delivery around ten-thirty. Be at my office by noon, wearing only what's in the box."

She stuck her tongue out when the machine beeped, indicating the end of the message. He couldn't see her response, but it made her feel better.

The doorbell distracted Mya, and her gaze automatically flew to the clock. 10:34. Her visitor could only be the delivery Roarke had spoken of.

She didn't bother to change from the silk pajamas when she answered the door. A petite UPS driver stood on her step, holding a small box. "Yes?"

"Are you Mya Lang...uh—"

"That's me." Mya signed the electronic box before she took the package. Once she had closed the door, she took the box into the bedroom and unwrapped it. She frowned when she lifted out the contents. It looked like a raincoat, with a zipper down the front, but was made from some lightweight tiger-printed material. The model on the tag was shown wearing it as a dress, with a scarf around her head, and blocky heels.

"He wants me to wear this?" She shook her head and held it against her. It was indecent. The material was so sheer it must be transparent.

She wanted to lift the phone and tell him to fuck off, but she restrained herself. Mya groaned, knowing she had agreed to play his stupid game, which made her at his beck and call. She left the scrap of cloth on the bed and went to shower.

When she returned to the bedroom, she slipped on a bra and panties before lifting the dress and unzipping it. She pulled it on and was surprised at how soft the fabric was. She zipped it up the front and looked in the mirror. It wasn't transparent, as she had thought. The interior fabric wove together to keep some secrets of the wearer.

She felt uncomfortable in the dress as she walked out of the apartment and went downstairs. Mya flagged a taxi, carefully watching the driver's expression for any indication that he could see through the dress. He seemed uninterested in anything at all, except her destination.

Once she had settled in the backseat, Mya found herself wondering what Roarke had planned for today. The unscheduled meeting irked her, but she thought Roarke was probably testing her obedience.

By the time the driver dropped her at the studio, Mya was fuming. She checked in with security with barely a word, afraid to let her tongue fly. The same man who had escorted her to the first meeting with Roarke led her up the stairs. He knocked and held the door open for her. He nodded as she walked inside, and then closed the door behind her.

Mya's eyes fell on Roarke, with his feet propped up on the desk. She glared at him. "How dare you rearrange my work schedule? I don't appreciate being summoned like a peasant to the king."

Roarke swung his legs off the desk and laughed. "I know, but I had to make sure you would come if I sent for you."

She walked forward and threw herself in the chair. She crossed her arms. "Do I have a choice?"

Roarke lifted a brow. "Yes."

Mya shifted. The choice she had was no choice at all. She sighed. "So, what do you want?"

"You're going to dance for me."

She rolled her eyes. "More dancing?"

A peculiar grin curved across his face. "Solo, this time." He slid his seat sideways and turned on a CD player. A heavy, pulsing beat issued from the speakers.

She shook her head. "I don't dance."

Roarke patted his lap. "Don't make me ask again."

Mya glared at him when she stood up. "You never ask."

He shrugged and leaned back. "Ever done a lap dance?"

Her eyes widened. "Of course not."

He laughed. "That's about to change."

Mya walked behind the desk and hesitated. "I don't know where to begin."

"With the music. Feel the rhythm and pick it up. Move your hips." His voice got progressively huskier. "Sit on my lap."

She bit her lip and tried to focus on the music. The beat was actually rather simple, and she swayed her hips to the music in no time. She deliberately kept her eyes off Roarke's face and concentrated on the ceiling. Mya sashayed toward him before she swung her leg over his chair. She paused and waited for the courage to touch him.

She looked down from the ceiling and saw his hands clenched around the arms of his chair. Sweat beaded his forehead, and he had a hard-on already. She hadn't even touched him yet.

Mya slowly lowered herself onto his lap. His cock pressed against her thigh. She flushed when she felt her pussy moisten.

"Don't forget to move with the music," Roarke bit out through clenched teeth.

She wiggled tentatively and felt him jerk in response. Mya grasped the back of the chair with her hands on either side of his head and rotated her hips in a circle. He groaned, and she pressed herself against him to grind her pussy against his cock. Wetness flooded her, but she was too into her performance to be ashamed.

"Take off the dress."

Mya obeyed his command without question. Her hands shook as she unzipped the dress, but she got the zipper down. She tossed the garment over her shoulder and returned her hands to the back of his chair.

Her breasts were inches from his face, and she sat on his lap and wriggled around. Mya frowned when she realized Roarke didn't wear an expression of bliss or even frustration. He looked irritated. "What?"

Roarke shook his head. "You didn't listen."

She lifted a brow. "I'm sorry?"

Roarke touched the strap of her bra, careful not to come into contact with her flesh. "I told you to wear just the dress."

Mya's eyes widened. "You meant without underwear?" Her mouth opened and closed. "That's indecent."

He grinned. "I prefer *naughty*." Roarke sighed. "And you were naughty for not listening." He reached for a pair of scissors from his pen organizer.

Mya's eyes widened when she saw the sharp shears. "Wh-what are you going to do?"

He ignored the question and slid the blade under one of her straps. He cut through it with one clean slice, and then did the same to the other one. He felt her stiffen when he slid the blade between her breasts. "I won't hurt you," he said with a rasp of irritation.

Roarke made short cuts through the white material. The bra was thin and cheap, and it easily surrendered to the sharp edges of the scissors. When he cut through the band of the bra, he peeled it from her, still not touching her breasts.

Mya instinctively covered her breasts. "You're crazy."

He laughed. "Maybe, but only for you. Now, move your arms and climb on the desk."

She bit back a refusal and dropped her arms. Mya tried to pretend he wasn't watching her every move when she lifted herself from his lap onto the desk. "Ouch." She fumbled under her bottom and removed a pen.

Roarke took it and put it in the pen organizer. "Turn more on your left side."

Mya shifted so she lay almost on her left side. She braced her hands behind her on the desk and put her feet on the arms of the chair.

Roarke swallowed when he was confronted with an unobstructed view of the crotch of her panties. They were thin cotton and almost transparent because of the moisture leaking from her pussy. He reached out to caress her puffy lips, but held himself back. "I think you like dancing for me." He forced an easy grin, which became more natural when he saw her embarrassed expression.

He took pity on her and turned his attention to the waistband of the panties on her hip. He slid the scissors inside and cut through the material. His hand lingered on her hip for just a second, before he forced himself to peel the material from her body. "Other side."

She looked pissed as she rolled onto her other side and silently endured his removal of the other side of her panties.

"Lean back and spread your legs."

Her eyes gleamed with anger. "No."

Roarke met her eyes, keeping his expression firm. "You chose not to obey me, Mya. This is your punishment."

"You bastard." Tears swam in her eyes as she leaned on the desk and propped her feet on each corner.

His fingers brushed against her wet pussy lips, and he felt his cock harden until it hurt. Roarke had to clear his throat before he could speak again. "Lift your hips."

When she complied, he stripped off the ruined panties and dropped them in the trash. She started to get up, but he put his hand on her stomach. "Don't move until I tell you to."

She grunted, but lay down again.

Roarke opened his desk drawer and removed the package he had purchased at a small shop off Hollywood Blvd. They specialized in catering to women's fantasies, but they had treated him with respect and not as a pervert when he wandered inside last Sunday.

He opened the plastic and removed the thin vibrator. It was made from some purple jelly material and might have been inspired from the phallus of some magical creature. It was anatomically perfect, except for the on/off switch at the base of the penis. He turned it on and saw her head lift. "Don't move," he said again, more forcefully, and she returned to her head to the desk.

Roarke parted her pussy and teased her clit with the head of the jelly vibrator. He felt her stiffen and jerk, and watched as her hips began to arch up in tiny increments. He slid the vibrator lower and teased her opening before he returned it to her clit. Once again, she arched against it, but didn't seem to be trying as hard to mask her response.

"Do you like this, Mya?"

She moaned, but didn't answer.

He grinned. "Do you like how it vibrates against your clit?" He allowed himself to touch her thigh. "Don't bother answering. I can feel your response."

He rotated the vibrator around her swollen clit, and then moved it down her slit again. "Would you like to feel this inside you?"

She whimpered.

He could see the way her feet arched and her hands clenched into fists as he pushed an inch of the vibrator into her slick pussy. He pulled it out and pushed it in deeper, enjoying the way she gasped with pleasure. "More?"

She didn't say anything, but she tried to buck her hips.

Roarke moved his hand from her thigh to her pelvis, where he pushed down with enough force to keep her pinned to the desk. "You have to ask for it, Mya. Tell me you want it."

She hesitated, seeming to be at war with herself. The tiny tremors convulsing her body gave her away. She finally relaxed and whispered, "Please."

"What do you want, Mya?" He bit down hard on his tongue as his cock transmitted what it wanted. He longed to throw away the vibrator and take possession of Mya himself.

"I want it." The answer was strained, but clear. "Please put it in me."

"What is it?" It was more than a little fun teasing her, but also painful. She wasn't the only one longing for release. "Can you say the word?"

She lifted her head and glared at him.

"You're moving, Mya." He withdrew the vibrator and turned it off. "I guess you can go now."

"Damn you, fuck me with that vibrator."

He didn't know which of them her outburst shocked more. Her face was bright scarlet, but he imagined his was too. He took a deep breath and forced himself to sound amused when he said, "Since you ask so nicely, how can I say no?"

She voluntarily laid her head on the desk and spread her legs even wider.

Roarke pushed the jelly vibrator deep inside her pussy, until she stiffened and gasped. He removed his hand and allowed her to thrust against the vibrator. She seemed not to want him to do anything, so he held it for her. He licked his lips as she thrust upward and rolled her hips. A tiny trail of her juices trickled onto his desk, and he groaned at the sight of the fluid.

He knew the exact moment she climaxed by the way she stiffened and arched her back. He immediately turned down the vibrator and pulled it out partway as her legs shook and her thighs tightened around his hand. He let out the breath he had been holding and tried to maintain his tenuous self-control. Roarke was too old to come in his pants without the assistance of a partner — or so he told himself.

She slowly sat up and covered herself with her arms and hands. She still seemed embarrassed by the way she had told him to satisfy her. Her eyes avoided his.

Roarke felt his cock diminish enough for him to move without pain, and he completely removed the vibrator. He patted her thigh. "First time?"

She nodded and kept her eyes averted. "I wanted one once, but Bobby..." She broke off.

"Felt threatened?" Roarke finished for her.

Mya nodded again and still did not look at him.

He put it back in the wrapping, and put the package in a plain brown bag. "Do you want to take it with you?"

She shook her head. "I don't ever want to see it again."

Roarke frowned and grasped her chin to pull her face around to his. "Why not? There's no shame in pleasure."

Tears streamed down her cheeks. "I begged for it. It's just a thing, but I begged for it."

He chuckled. "Actually, you ordered me to use it on you." Roarke could see her wince, and he dropped the vibrator into his drawer. "If you change your mind, let me know."

She nodded, but her expression revealed she would never ask for it. "Can I go now?"

He shifted as his cock throbbed, but nodded. "I'll see you Friday."

Mya didn't answer as she climbed off the desk and searched for the dress. She slid it on over her nakedness and fled his office. She didn't look back as she rushed into the ladies' room and washed her face. Then she locked herself in a stall and sobbed out her shame. She couldn't reconcile what she thought about herself with the wanton who had demanded Roarke fuck her with a fake cock. How could she have done that?

She sighed and unlocked the stall. She returned to the sink and washed her face again. She fixed her hair and met her eyes in the mirror. She had a flush on her cheeks, but also a sated look in her eyes. Maybe he was right, and it wasn't a big deal. He had teased her to a fever pitch. She couldn't blame herself if his manipulations overwhelmed her common sense.

She ignored the voice in the back of her head that accepted a full share of responsibility for the interlude. Mya left the restroom feeling considerably calmer. Roarke was to blame for her downfall, and she had no choice but to go along. She shouldn't be so hard on herself for getting a bit of pleasure from his twisted game.

Chapter Nine
Shopping

ȿɔ

As Bobby had done frequently during the past three months, he shopped on Thursday evening. Despite his cool attitude, Mya decided to accompany him since she needed a few things herself. They went to Macy's where she could use her employee discount.

Once he had selected two new outfits and a six hundred-dollar leather jacket she had raised her eyebrows at because of the heat, they made their way to the ladies' department.

Bobby shifted the purchases he held. "You won't be long, will you? This stuff is heavy."

She scowled at him. "I just followed you around for an hour. You could do the same for me." She motioned to the baskets near the register. "You could get one of those."

He sighed and positioned his body stiffly to show his displeasure when he returned with the blue basket.

Despite her protest, Mya found herself rushing through her selections, not wanting to keep him waiting. He was already angry with her, and she didn't want to upset him anymore. Her parents and sister were coming for a visit on Saturday, and Bobby should be his most charming. Not that it would matter to her family, since they didn't like him. Not that the feeling wasn't mutual.

"Aren't you done yet?" Bobby's tone was strident.

She blinked and realized she still held the same shirt as when she had drifted off. She bit her lip and looked at the price. Although money wasn't a big problem anymore, she wouldn't pay one hundred dollars for that skimpy thing. She shoved it back on the rack.

"Can we go now?"

"I need underwear." Mya surprised herself with the statement. She had just bought several sets of white cotton briefs and bras about two months ago. Even subtracting the pair Roarke cut off her yesterday, she still had plenty of sets.

Bobby sighed more deeply, but followed her across the aisle to the lingerie department.

Her mouth twisted with a mix of amusement and irritation when he checked out the underwear models featured in the large posters on the back wall. She turned her attention to the matched sets, an area she generally skipped over in favor of plain bras and packaged panty sets. She picked up an emerald set and held it against her. "Do you like this?"

Bobby's head jerked in her direction as he tore his attention away from the salesgirl he had been eyeing. "Yeah, it's fine."

His tepid response had her replacing the set and reaching for a more daring black pair. "What about these?"

"Nice." His tone lacked expression.

She heaved a sigh and reached for a scarlet set decorated with silver beads. "Do you like this one?"

He didn't even look at her. "It's great."

"Dammit, Bobby."

He turned back to her with a frown. "What?"

"I'm trying to get your input here."

He shrugged and shifted the basket in his left hand to the right. He threw the jacket over his left shoulder with a carefully measured move. "What do I care? No one sees your underwear."

"You do."

"So? Get whatever you want."

"Fine!" Mya grabbed the black set, and the emerald one. She was debating about the scarlet set when her eyes fell on a midnight blue pair. She lifted it from the rack, eyeing the plunging velvet bra and thong bikini pants. Could she wear something like that? It was very pretty. She smoothed a hand over the velvet cups. Roarke would like it.

Her head snapped up at the thought, and she shoved the set back on the rack. What was wrong with her? The ballroom dress came to mind, and she breathed a sigh of relief. Her brain had made an obvious connection between the blue velvet of the underwear and the blue velvet of that dress. Nothing more. She certainly wouldn't buy anything with Roarke's preferences in mind.

"Come on, Mya. I want to get out of here."

She put the scarlet set in the basket. The blue bra and panties beckoned to her, and she added them too before she followed Bobby up to the register. She ignored him when he grumbled over the prices as the girl rang them up. Mya turned a blind eye to his flirtation with Shelley the salesgirl and focused her attention once more on the blue set. She suddenly couldn't wait to slip into it. She would feel sexy and decadent, even if no one else saw it. *Roarke will see it.* She quickly blocked that thought as she followed Bobby from the store.

* * * * *

Later that night, after dinner, Mya slipped on a black teddy Bobby really liked, then slid into the bed beside him. He had his nose buried in a script, and he jumped when her hand fastened around his naked cock.

"What are you doing, Mya?"

She frowned at his angry tone. "Touching you."

He pushed her hand away. "I don't like it when you do that stuff."

Mya sighed and collapsed against the pillows. "I was just-"

"I should be the one who instigates all that."

She wrinkled her nose at him. "Why?"

"Because I'm the man."

She couldn't hold back a laugh.

He dropped the script and crossed his arms over his chest. "What?"

"That's silly. We have an equal relationship. That should include the bedroom."

He curled his lips. "I don't like it when you get all aggressive."

She forced herself to become boneless. "Is this better?"

Bobby grimaced before he turned his attention back to the script he picked up from his lap.

"Bobby, I want you…" She trailed her fingers across his biceps.

He shrugged her off. "Not right now. I'm busy."

"Fine!" She turned away from him and pulled the blanket over herself with a jerky movement. She viciously turned the knob on her bedside lamp. They didn't speak. He was too busy, and she was too angry. His rejection stung, and she forced back tears. She refused to let him know he had hurt her. It was long after Bobby had turned off his light and almost immediately started to snore before Mya was finally able to get to sleep.

Chapter Ten
Bubbles

ॐ

When Mya let herself into Roarke's apartment, she heard nothing but silence. She looked for him in the kitchen and living room, and then edged her way down the hall. "Roarke?"

"In the bathroom."

The closed door muffled his voice. She entered the bedroom and stood awkwardly in front of the bed.

"Come in."

"Oh." Mya walked over to the black door and pushed it open. Her mouth dropped when she saw he had transformed the bathroom into a lovers' dream. Dozens of tiny tea light candles lined the lip of the Jacuzzi tub. Soft music issued from the stereo on the counter, and a bottle of champagne and two glasses were at Roarke's elbow where the wall and Jacuzzi met to form a nook.

Most of all, there was Roarke, already in the bubbles. Everything below the tops of his nipples was hidden under the water, and she wasn't naïve enough to think he wore a Speedo. Dark hair lightly dusted his arms before it became more profuse across his chest. Mya stared at his nipples without thought, until she realized where her eyes rested. A blush swept across her cheeks, and she lifted her eyes immediately, while she tried to ignore the flush on her cheeks and the glint of amusement in his eyes.

"Come on in. The water's warm and slippery." Roarke's lips twitched, as she got even more flustered at his suggestive words.

Mya crossed her arms over her chest. "You want me to undress in here?"

He sighed. "I've seen all of you now, Mya. Does it really matter?"

"Yes!"

"Okay." With exaggerated movements, he took a washcloth from the wall shelf to cover his eyes. "I can't see you."

"Don't peek," she hissed at him as her fingers fumbled with the buttons on the side of her wraparound skirt. Then she pulled off the halter-top and paused for a long moment. She refused to acknowledge her disappointment when he didn't even try to steal a look. She had worn the blue set for nothing. She had constantly pulled the thong out of her bottom for no reason. Well, it was her fault. He would have looked if not for her instinctive protest about undressing in front of him. Mya sighed as she folded her shirt and laid it beside the skirt on the counter.

Roarke lifted his head in her direction without removing the washcloth. "What's wrong?"

"Nothing. Why?"

"You sighed."

A wicked idea occurred to Mya. "I got sticky from an ice cream cone on my way over."

He shrugged, and the washcloth remained in place. "The bath will take care of that."

"I think I might need a washcloth." She blushed as she asked for it. It had been the only one on the shelf.

Roarke froze and wondered if he had misinterpreted something. He handed her the cloth and kept his eyes squeezed shut. Against his brain's instructions, his left eyelid peeled up. He watched as she washed her chest with the cloth. She seemed to be oblivious to his presence. His other eye opened, and he gazed at her body.

After his initial double take, he realized she didn't wear the usual white bra and panties. His cock hardened at the sight of her flesh displayed in the blue thong and plunging bra. The material invited him to touch, and his mouth got dry as he imagined how it would feel to run his hands over the cups, then slide down her stomach to touch the velvet panties. He would start at the string waistband and touch the smooth skin at her hip before he moved his hands to her buttocks. Once he squeezed her cheeks, he would ease his fingers forward, until he touched her velvet...

She started to turn, and Roarke snapped his eyes shut. He heard the rustle of fabric against skin and barely managed to fight back a groan as he pictured the scanty panties as they dropped away to reveal her completely. It was a relief when she slid into the water, and he was able to open his eyes again.

When Mya turned around after she removed the underwear and pinned her hair up, she saw the flush on his cheeks. Obviously, he had seen her. She resisted the urge to preen for a compliment, and ignored the discomfort she felt because she had enticed him to look.

As she settled lower into the water and sat on the floor of the tub rather than a step, she realized it was indeed slippery. The water was perfectly warm and slid across her skin like satin. "What's in the water?"

"Bath oil."

She lifted a handful of bubbles. "Just oil?"

He nodded.

Mya sighed when she leaned her head back against the cushioned rim. The tub's lip made the perfect pillow. "It's wonderful."

"I buy it at a little shop on Fourth. They blend it for me." Although the clerk had been mildly surprised when Roarke asked him to add pheromones to the mixture, because he hadn't changed the ingredients since he first tried a sample. So far, he didn't notice a difference. He always wanted Mya, and he didn't need pheromones to stimulate his desire. It was impossible to tell if they had affected her in any way yet. "I'll give you the name and address before you leave, if you want."

She shook her head. "I'm sure I couldn't afford it."

He lifted a brow. "Sure you can, now that Bobby's career is taking off." His mouth twisted, and he was barely able to spit out her fiancé's name.

Mya couldn't hold back a sharp laugh. "I don't think he would buy it for me."

Roarke felt himself frowning. Instead of pursuing the obvious question—why not—he said, "You could always buy it for yourself."

She shook her head again. "Most of my check still goes to bills. A lot of Bobby's money was eaten up by...stuff."

Before Roarke could stop himself, he said, "He's used five hundred thousand already?"

Her mouth dropped open. "It wasn't five hundred thousand. It was about one hundred thousand."

He could add liar to his list of reasons to hate Bobby. Roarke could reveal Bobby's duplicity that second. He had records to back it up. He could show her that her fiancé had hidden four hundred thousand from her, and she still slaved away in a menial job for no good reason. He could deal their relationship a crippling blow. He looked at her confused expression, prepared to list the facts.

He could destroy her with the truth. Miserable, Roarke said, "Oh. I must be thinking of someone else." He averted his eyes to the champagne, because he knew he was a terrible liar. But she didn't know him, so she wouldn't be able to tell.

"Ah." Mya studied him as he opened the champagne with a pop. He barely lost any foam before he poured them each a glass. His shoulders were stiff, and he seemed to deliberately avoid her eyes. Had he lied to her? She pushed that thought away quickly, because she knew it would lead her to thoughts about Bobby she didn't want to explore. "Thank you." She took the glass he held out and sipped. Bubbles tickled her nose and caused it to wrinkle.

He stared at her and wondered if she knew how adorable she was. With her nose wrinkled, the freckles blurred together, and her eyes got crinkly, which gave her a giddy look. "Do you like champagne?"

She shrugged, but took another drink. "I've never really had it before. One glass years ago at my brother's wedding is all."

"Oh." Roarke watched as she drained the glass in four swallows. He almost felt wicked when he refilled it for her before he took a first sip from his glass.

Mya sat up, rolling her shoulders. "Does this have those jet things?"

"Yes." Roarke lifted a small panel on the wall to turn on the jets. Within seconds, the water bubbled around them, and the foam on the bath stirred agitatedly. He saw her roll her neck. "Are you okay?"

"Yeah." Mya took another sip of the champagne, allowing its bubbling warmth to spread through her, bringing a haze of relaxation with it. "It was a long day."

"Your neck hurts?"

"And my shoulders." Mya's eyes widened as he put his glass in the corner and slid toward her. "What are you doing?" Her voice emerged as a squeak, and she covered her breasts with her arms, even though he couldn't see them through the thick layer of bubbles.

"I'm going to give you a massage."

She shook her head as he took her arm and pulled her up and away from the edge of the tub. As he brought her back with him to his corner, she said, "You don't have to."

Roarke settled on the step and pushed her down so that she sat on the bottom of the tub with her back to him. "I want to."

"Really, there's no need—ahh." She moaned when his hands settled on her shoulders and slid across her skin with ease because of the oily water. As he worked the muscles, she slowly relaxed.

Roarke couldn't concentrate when she made breathless little sounds in the back of her throat. They grew more frequent as he dug his fingers deep into her skin to loosen the tension. As she grew relaxed, she leaned against him until her back pressed against his stomach. Her lower back was a mere inch from his groin, and he gave into temptation. He thrust his hips forward just a bit. He felt her stiffen when his cock touched her, and he redoubled his efforts with the massage.

Her eyes widened when he pressed into her back and Mya started to pull away, but the massage felt too good to stop. Her eyes grew heavy as the champagne and his touch made her too languid to move. Instead, she cuddled closer and left no room for Roarke to continue the massage. Her neck rested against his right forearm, and she rubbed her cheek against the wet hair. "That feels good."

"I'm not doing anything." His voice was husky, and he cleared his throat.

"Your hands…" She trailed off, unable to summon the energy to explain that the way he continued to apply pressure on a particularly painful spot caused it to relax.

Roarke lifted her and slid off the step so that he sat on the tub's floor. He settled her into his lap and held her against him. He wrapped his arms around her waist, and she didn't protest. To his surprise, she shifted so that she was closer to him and leaned her head back against his shoulder. She didn't mention his cock and where it pressed against her bottom, and he tried to ignore the pleasure/pain of his cock's proximity to her pussy, because he knew he couldn't make love to her yet.

When he slid his hand up her stomach to just under her breast, he held his breath. He waited for her protest for several endless seconds. When she still didn't say anything, he flicked his thumb across the turgid peak. She moaned a little, then shifted restlessly, and brought his cock more fully between her legs. *You're not doing anything today,* he reminded himself even as he thrust his hips up to nestle his cock nearer her pussy.

Mya felt him move again and knew she should pull away, but she was too sleepy. Her lids felt weighted, and she yawned. Besides, it felt too good to move. Why bother? They hadn't really done anything.

Roarke sighed when he heard her yawn. The explanation for her compliance became clear—too much champagne coupled with the hot bath and massage. "Are you sleepy?"

"Um hmm."

Despite his frustration, Roarke was able to smile at her hazy response. He moved away from Mya before he propped her against the side of the tub while he got out. His cock was painful, but he wouldn't do anything to relieve it while she was in this condition.

He wiped away the foam and some of the oil with one of the towels before he lifted her from the tub. They both needed to shower, but he didn't want to have to hold her up in the large shower stall while he washed both of them. She could remove the oily residue later, once she woke up.

She leaned against him, sweet and cuddly, while he dried her off. He lifted her again, and she sighed. Mya curled against him as though she had been made to fit in the cradle of his arms when he carried her into the bedroom. He balanced her with one arm while he pulled back the new cover, and then laid her on the silver silk sheets. He put the blanket over her before he returned to the bathroom to blow out the candles, shower, and get dressed.

Roarke dropped his pants when he realized he was at least a little sleepy. He looked at himself in the mirror, traded wicked grins with his reflection, and lifted his pants to put them back on the shelf.

He reentered the bedroom and stopped to look at her for a moment. She slept peacefully, and tiny sighs issued from her every few minutes. He walked over to the bed and slid in on the free side. She rolled right into his arms and pressed her bottom against his cock as he wrapped his arms around her. As they spooned, Roarke realized he really was tired, and his eyes closed too, until they were both asleep.

Chapter Eleven
After The Nap

80

Mya stretched, and her legs entangled with another pair. They felt different from Bobby's. She opened her eyes slowly and felt disoriented. Roarke lay beside her with his eyes wide open as he watched her. He had a strand of her hair wrapped around his finger. A gentle smile teased his lips. "What happened?" She sounded hoarse, and her head ached.

"You took a nap. I joined you."

"Oh." She frowned, while she tried to remember what had precipitated the nap. She remembered the bath and massage; the two glasses of champagne; deliberately enticing him to look at her... She groaned.

"What's wrong?" Roarke touched her cheek.

"I feel a little sick."

"It'll pass. A shower will perk you up."

She bit her lip and mustered her courage. She didn't feel like they had, but she needed to ask. "Did we...?"

Roarke's eyes widened. "Of course not!" He winced at his sharp tone, but couldn't pretend she hadn't offended him. "You were in no shape, and I'm not into passivity."

Behind his anger, Mya could see genuine hurt in his eyes, and it gave her a pang in the pit of her stomach. "I'm sorry." Why had she apologized? It was a logical assumption that he would have taken her when she was passed out. It would have fit in with his ruthless personality.

However, he wasn't truly ruthless. She could see that from the way he treated her. For two weeks, the opportunity to force her into his bed had been open to him. Mya was in no position to refuse him, but he hadn't pressed her. He hadn't done anything but try to please her. She was always the focus of their encounters. Roarke seemed concerned only with her gratification.

He shrugged. "Do you want that shower?" His tone was still cool, although he hadn't meant it to emerge that way. She had every right to assume he would take advantage of her. Hadn't he already?

She nodded and slid from the bed. When she stood up, Mya realized she was completely naked. She froze and scanned the room for her clothes.

Roarke's breath became trapped in his throat as he got his first real look at her nude perfection, instead of in stolen flashes and small increments. When he had lifted her from the bath, his attention remained focused on how to get her to the bed, rather than what she looked like. The lamp he had clicked on when he woke up served to illuminate the creaminess of her skin and cast shadows across her body, while it exposed other delectable parts. The oil from the bath left on her skin gave it a shiny, almost translucent quality. She was well proportioned, with pert breasts, and shapely legs. She had defined abs, and the muscles in her arms rippled under the skin as she reached for the sheet. She was lithe and toned. He could stare at her all day. He would love to touch her all night.

She broke his trance when she fastened the flat sheet around her, sarong-style. Most of her hair had come undone from the barrette, and it cascaded over her shoulders. He could easily imagine her as the queen of an island. He would gladly do her bidding; worship her always and get down on his knees to pray. He dismissed his fancies with a soft sigh. "There's a fresh towel for you on the counter by the sink."

Mya hurried into the bathroom to escape the hunger in his eyes—the hunger she suspected mirrored in hers. Her body still tingled, as if his eyes had been hands and had stroked her most private places.

She turned on the faucets and entered the spray. The water was almost hot enough to hurt, but it felt good too. As she washed away the traces of oil from the bath, Mya tried to wash away the uncomfortable truth that she wanted Roarke.

She touched the ring on her left hand. It was tangible proof she was Bobby's woman. Mya had no business thinking about Roarke the way she was. It was bad enough having to play his game, but she certainly shouldn't be enjoying it, or looking forward to the next round. She shouldn't imagine it was his hands washing her. She definitely shouldn't wish that she hadn't left that spacious bed. If she were still lying with him, he would be touching her. His hands on her body, not hers, as she slipped her fingers into her pussy.

Her breathing grew ragged as she imagined Roarke's hands on her. She leaned her head against the warm tile and entertained thoughts of asking him to wash her back. She fantasized that he would throw open the glass doors, storm into the shower, pin her to the wall, and make her his. There would be no time for protests. She would be caught in the onslaught of his passion—willingly, eagerly even.

Time! Mya's eyes popped open, and her hand fell away from between her thighs. What time was it? A security shutter covered the window in the bathroom, so she couldn't see out. She felt rested, and the shower had revived her. She felt like she had slept for hours.

Mya rinsed the remainder of the soap away and shut off the water before she stepped onto the bare floor. She took a folded towel from the counter and wrapped its fluffy folds around her. She lifted the other towel, which smelled faintly of soap and Roarke, and briskly dried her hair. She dropped it back on the counter and removed the towel around her. After a quick rubdown, she threw on her underwear, the wrap-around skirt, and the halter. She found her shoes under the sink.

Mya skipped all other grooming rituals and rushed back into the bedroom. Roarke sat in the recliner, wrapped in the comforter from the bed. She frowned at his nakedness. "Why aren't you dressed?"

"My clothes were in the bathroom."

"Oh." Mya frowned at her asinine question. "What time is it? I don't have my watch."

Roarke glanced down at his Rolex. "Three-twelve."

"In the afternoon?"

He almost laughed at her blatantly hopeful tone. "A.M."

"Shit!"

"Don't worry. I'll help you think of something to tell Bobby so he won't know."

She shook her head. "He already knows. It's my parents and sister I'm worried about. They'll be here in three-and-a-half hours. With the nightmare at the airports these days, we'll need to be there by five."

"He knows?"

Mya's head lifted at Roarke's cold tone. "What?"

"Bobby knows about our...arrangement?"

She lifted an eyebrow. "Yeah. Are you listening to me? I've been out half the night, and my family will be here soon." She went to the nightstand before she remembered he had no phone. "God! How can you live without a phone? I need a taxi."

Roarke struggled to suppress his anger as he rose from the recliner, leaving the comforter behind. "I'll drive you home. Your apartment is on my way."

She frowned. "Your way?"

"I don't live here, Mya." Despite his preoccupation with thoughts of strangling Bobby, he was able to muster a small laugh. "This place isn't even Spartan. No one could live here." But if she was in his bed, day after day, he would be willing to try.

He saw her anxious pacing and sighed. Without waiting for a response, Roarke went into the steamy bathroom to put on his clothes. When reentering the bedroom a few minutes later, he found Mya standing by the door. "I guess you're ready?"

She nodded. What was Bobby going to say when she showed up at this hour? How could she have been so careless as to fall asleep? The champagne and massage had been too much relaxation, and she had been so tired. Would he understand that? Would he believe that nothing had happened besides a bath and a nap? She closed her eyes and bit back a sigh. She knew the answer already. The best course of action was to not tell him anything. She would just apologize profusely and hope he dropped the issue.

Roarke followed her from the condo and struggled to keep up with the pace she set as they hurried to the elevator. She didn't slow down until they were in the parking garage attached to the lower floor. She was forced to wait for him as he led the way to a black Lotus, which he unlocked with the remote on his key chain.

Once in the passenger seat, she fidgeted with her purse strap, chewed on her thumbnail, and stole peeks at the radio's clock. The yellow-orange numbers seemed to glow brighter with each passing minute. "He's going to be so mad."

"He'll understand." Bobby must be very understanding if he would let Mya enter this ridiculous game. Roarke's mouth twisted. Or he was a selfish pig. How could he stand by and let Roarke coerce Mya into bed? If she were his fiancée, no man would ever touch her again. He would give up anything and everything for her. His career wouldn't have meant anything next to Mya. "Why are you with that bastard?" Roarke silently cursed himself when he blurted out the question.

Mya's attention had centered on rehearsing what she would say to Bobby when she got home, so it took her a moment for his words to sink in. "What?"

He shook his head, deciding discretion was the better part of valor. "Never mind."

She frowned at him and wondered why he had abandoned the question. She chose to answer anyway. "I love him."

Her voice lacked conviction. He had no trouble detecting the note of uncertainty in her tone. "Why?"

Mya's reaction surprised her. Whenever her sister asked questions like that, she fervidly defended Bobby. Her hackles rose whenever her family criticized him. Now she found herself at a loss and searched for an answer that wasn't trite. She opened her mouth, but couldn't find the right words. She breathed a sigh of relief when the Lotus turned onto her street. "It's the pink stucco building."

Roarke stopped in front of the building. "Do you want me to walk you up?"

Her eyes widened. "No!" She quieted her strident tone to a normal decibel. "This neighborhood is safe."

He wanted to protest, but Roarke knew she would have a hard enough time when she faced Bobby without him appearing on the doorstep. He could only imagine Bobby's reaction. "You don't have to go up."

His urgent words surprised her. Mya's brow furrowed. "Why wouldn't I?"

"He won't get violent, will he?"

She bit her lip. Bobby might get violent, but not with her. When they argued, which was infrequently, he had sometimes thrown things, or yelled and cursed, but he wouldn't hurt her. "I'll be fine."

It wasn't the answer he wanted, but Roarke settled for it. He took his wallet from his pants and flipped it open. He rifled through the contents for a moment before he handed her a card. "That's my private phone number and home address. If things don't go well, you can call me."

The moment struck Mya as surreal. The man who had forced her into a sexual relationship now offered to protect her from her fiancé. Shouldn't it be the other way around? She slid the card in her purse before she lifted the door handle. There didn't seem to be anything else to say, so she opened the door.

He put his hand on her arm. "When are your parents leaving?"

"Friday."

"Did you take vacation?"

"Yes." Would he ask for an extra day? Would she object? The ambiguousness of her feelings gave her an answer, but it wasn't one she wanted to examine.

"Let's skip this week." He gritted his teeth as he made the offer. "You obviously miss them, and you can't see them enough with them living in Washington. You'll want to spend this week with them, focused on them—not thinking about…other things."

She refused to acknowledge the dart of disappointment. "Okay. I'll see you next Tuesday."

He almost blurted out that he would be counting the days, but Roarke restrained himself. She didn't want to hear that. "Good night."

Mya surprised them both when she leaned over to kiss him. She pressed her lips to his for a brief moment, and then scurried from the car. She rushed up the walkway, idly noting her knees trembled, although it wasn't strictly nerves about the confrontation with Bobby that made her legs weak. She could still feel Roarke's lips against hers.

As she unlocked the entrance, Mya turned around in time to see Roarke pull away. She touched her lips and stared after him until his Lotus turned a corner. With a sigh, she entered the apartment building and trudged up the stairs.

Chapter Twelve
Confrontation

ဢ

Bobby had sprawled out on the leather sofa, and he snored as he slept. Mya let herself in and quietly lowered her keys and purse to the table. She was almost tempted to just let him sleep until four-thirty, when they would leave for the airport. There would be no opportunity for him to yell at her for the time being. With a sigh, Mya walked over to the couch to wake him, because she knew it was better to get the discussion out of the way. Bobby wouldn't forget it. He would just get angrier as time passed, until he eventually exploded. The last thing she wanted was a serious fight in front of her family.

His eyes snapped open when she touched his shoulder. Mya held her breath as she waited for his reaction.

He yawned and stretched. "What time is it?"

She glanced at the clock on the VCR. "Three fifty-seven."

Bobby swung his legs off the sofa as he sat up. "What's going on?"

"Huh?"

"What were you doing all night?"

"I fell asleep."

He looked skeptical. "For twelve hours?"

She shrugged and dropped into the loveseat. "It's been a long week."

"I'll bet your afternoon with Thomas was exhausting."

Mya closed her eyes and let his bitter words wash over her. She knew if she retorted it would only prolong the argument. "I'm sorry I was gone so long."

"Sorry? You were gone all day and most of the night, and that's all you can say?" He crossed his arms over his chest. "You owe me an explanation."

"I fell asleep," she said again, this time with a hint of anger in her voice.

"That's not all. We both know it wasn't anything so innocent as sleeping."

Mya's hazel eyes took on a green cast as she got angrier. "Whatever I was doing, it was for you. I can't leave until he tells me to." She felt a flush of guilt creep up her neck as she said the words. It wasn't just for Bobby anymore, and Roarke hadn't kept her prisoner. She had fallen asleep in his bed and slept in complete peace in his arms. She had even imagined him in the shower with her. Mya felt her face get hot as the blush crept upwards, and she tried to redirect her thoughts back to Bobby.

"You had better be home when I get here from now on."

"Or what?"

He glowered at her. "You won't like it."

Mya's lips thinned. "Here's the solution to me being gone. Grow some balls and stand up to Roarke."

His eyes turned glacier, and he lunged from the sofa. Mya cringed away from his quick movements, but he hurried past her. He was completely dressed and stopped only to grab a jacket from the closet as he strode to the door.

"What are you doing?"

"I'm going out. Maybe I'll stay gone twelve hours, and you can see how you like it."

Mya rolled her eyes at his petulance until she realized he had scooped up the car keys from the table. "You can't take the SRX."

Bobby turned to frown at her. "Why not?"

"My family will be here soon. We need to pick them up."

"You can do it. Or maybe Roarke will help you." With a twist of his lips, Bobby tossed the keys at her before he opened the door and walked out. He made sure to slam it behind him.

Mya ducked as the keys flew through the air, aimed at her. They careened into the black lamp on the table and sent it crashing to the floor. A bubble of hysterical laughter welled up in her, which begged for release. The confrontation hadn't been as bad as she had expected.

Mya forced down the laughter and the tears that tried to follow. She got up from the loveseat to clean up the debris left from the lamp. She fished the keys from the ceramic shards before she fetched the dustpan and whiskbroom from the kitchen. After she cleaned the mess, Mya went into the bedroom to change into jeans and a warmer shirt.

As she brushed out her hair, she met her eyes in the mirror. They sparkled with unshed tears and repressed anger. Her skin was pale, and her mouth trembled. Her parents would surely notice how upset she was. As usual, they would attribute it to Bobby, and she would have to let them. She couldn't explain the situation with Roarke. They would never understand why she let herself be used for Bobby's benefit. Her parents wouldn't understand that his success was their success.

As she laid the brush down on the counter, an uncomfortable thought popped into her head. She averted her eyes from the glint of knowledge in the mirror image's eyes, but the thought wouldn't go away.

Was she really doing it for Bobby, or had she become a willing participant in Roarke's game?

She tried to push the thought aside as she left the apartment and headed for the airport. She made good time through the moderate traffic and arrived a little after four-twenty. She stood in line for a while before she finally got back to the gate where their flight would arrive.

Mya sat in a chair and thumbed through a magazine without reading it. Instead, she found her thoughts once again on Roarke. Not Bobby, as they should be. She wanted to think of the perfect apology to smooth things over with her fiancé, but all her mind conjured were images of Roarke. His gentle hands as they moved over her body, or the way his muscles moved when he had walked naked from the bedroom to the bathroom. His taut buttocks…

Mya suppressed a groan, forcing her attention back to the magazine. The headline of the open page screamed *10 Easy Ways to Seduce Your Lover*. She scanned the article almost automatically. *Sexy lingerie: Check. Flirting: Uh… Touching him without a reason: Good idea.* When Mya realized she was mentally listing what she had done as opposed to what she hadn't, she closed the magazine with a snap and tossed it back on the small table beside her chair at the end of the row.

She got up for a juice from the machine and paced around the lounge for a while. When the plane finally landed, she walked over to the window to watch the ground crew direct it in. When the first passengers poured in, she dropped the empty juice bottle in a trashcan and turned her attention to the line.

Solidly in the middle of the crush were a tall man, plump woman, and beautiful girl. Mya raised her arm and waved to them wildly. Carly caught sight of her first and waved just as enthusiastically. Mya worked her way through the crowd as her family did the same.

Then she was standing before them, and they were all talking at once. Three sets of arms enfolded her, and she did her fair share of hugging. "I missed you," she said over and over. The tears in her mother's eyes brought tears streaming down her cheeks too. It wasn't long before Carly was joining in. Only Frank's eyes didn't tear, but his lips were trembling.

After the initial rush of greetings, everyone caught their breath, and they turned toward the exit and joined the crowd that struggled to get through LAX as quickly as possible. "Where's Bobby?" Patty's tone was polite, but lacked any warmth.

Mya shrugged. "He couldn't make it."

Frank grunted, but didn't say anything. Patty nodded, and Carly looked relieved. Contrary to her usual reaction, Mya found herself too apathetic to answer their unspoken criticisms. "Let's go back to the apartment and drop off the bags. After, we'll go have breakfast." Her stomach rumbled and Mya realized she hadn't eaten since lunch yesterday. With the upheaval of the last few hours, she shouldn't be able to even think about food.

"I'm starving." Carly rubbed her stomach. "That airline food's a killer."

Mya chuckled. "I remember a time when you scarfed it down."

Her sister shuddered. "Don't remind me."

They stopped at the baggage carousel before they made their way to short-term parking. Mya opened the hatch of the Cadillac SRX so Frank could load their luggage.

"Nice." Carly caressed the deep purple paint. "Spendy?"

Mya nodded, more than a little sick at the amount of money Bobby had put down on the vehicle. There had been no choice with his bad credit, and he had been determined to have it. When she had protested at the extra two thousand for a custom paint job, he had assured her there was more money where that came from. As always, he had been confident of his prospects. That was before Roarke and his ultimatum. Mya's lip curled. His future was secure, for only the bargain price of her body.

"I hope you put some back."

"We did, Dad." She avoided his eyes when she thought of the small amount left in the checkbook.

"That boy will drain you dry—"

"Dad, don't start."

Frank slammed the back. "I'm just saying you have to be sensible about money when you're with a man like Bobby."

"Frank." Patty touched his arm while she shot him a look. "Remember what we talked about on the plane?"

"She needs to realize what she's getting into. And when they have kids—"

"Frank!"

He snorted as he walked around to the back passenger side.

Mya sighed as she walked to the driver's side and unlocked the door. She disengaged the other locks and slid inside. As she left the lot, she wondered at her lack of anger with her father's words. Maybe she had missed them too much to pay attention to the same old criticisms. Maybe she was finally mature enough to overlook their poor opinion of Bobby. *Maybe Dad's right.* Mya forced a smile for her sister when Carly handed her the parking slip, while trying to brush aside that thought. So what if Bobby was a little careless with money? It was part of his personality, and she loved him—warts and all.

Her stomach cramped. She frowned at her reflection in the mirror on the visor. She was just hungry. That was all. It had been hours since she had eaten.

Chapter Thirteen
The Gym

෨

Bobby spent the first two days of her family's visit in near silence, when he was home at all. This seemed to suit Frank, who was more cheerful than usual around her fiancé. By Monday, Mya was relieved when he went back to work. To her surprise, Patty and Frank decided to spend the day sightseeing alone and left the two sisters on their own.

Around six in the evening, Carly threw herself down on the couch. "I'm bored."

"We could go to a movie."

"Eh." Carly shrugged. "What do you normally do?"

Mya scrunched her brows together as she tried to remember the last time she had done anything on a Monday. "Well, I normally work until nine-thirty. When I get home Bobby and I go to they gym."

Carly's blue eyes sparkled, and she leaned forward so quickly her short, auburn, pixie-cut flipped up. "Cool. Let's go."

"You don't have a membership."

She lifted a shoulder. "I'll pay for a guest pass. I've been dying to work out."

"There's a small gym downstairs."

"No pool, and the machines suck."

"That's why we pay for a membership." She got up from her perch on the loveseat. "All right. I am stiff." She stretched reflexively. "I remember when I couldn't drag you away from your computer or video games."

A rueful smile curved Carly's lips. "That was me. No argument there."

"Did you bring you workout clothes?"

She shook her head. "Can I borrow something?"

"I don't know if I have anything that will fit you since you've gotten so skinny." Mya bit back a grin at her sister's blissful smile. She liked to praise Carly's accomplishment whenever the opportunity arose.

They rummaged through the closet, and then took a taxi to the gym since Bobby had the SRX. Once inside, Mya watched with amusement as her sister flirted shamelessly. She left Carly to her activities to do her workout. When Carly finally joined her, she made Mya exhausted as she watched. It was a relief when they were finally on their way out.

Until they ran into Roarke. Carly had her head turned to watch a guy as he pumped iron, and she ran right into a solid male body. She turned with a giggle. "I'm so sorry."

"No problem. Mya?" Roarke's eyes scanned her body in the form-fitting Lycra pants and bra-top. Why was she even sexier in the workout clothes than the teddy he had bought her?

She tried to suppress the excited quiver in her stomach as she smiled at Roarke. "Hi."

Carly's man-eater grin was in full force, as she batted her eyelashes up at Roarke—not too far, Mya noted with a grimace. Unlike her, Carly was tall. Her head came to his shoulder. The perfect level for them to kiss. Her mouth twisted at the thought, and she tried to ignore the twinge of jealousy while she watched her sister focus her charms on Roarke.

"You know each other?" Carly had positioned herself just a few inches from Roarke after they collided.

"Roarke owns the studio shooting Bobby's movie."

Roarke held out his hand. "You must be Mya's sister."

Carly grasped his hand. "I'm Carly, the baby of the family."

He cleared his throat as she stroked her fingers across his palm. Roarke's eyes skimmed over her lithe figure in the shorty-shorts and t-shirt, knotted under her full breasts. "Could have fooled me." He disentangled his hand while he looked at Mya from the corner of his eyes just in time to catch her pouty frown.

Mya winced at her sister's girlish giggle. She sounded so fake and idiotic. Surely, men didn't really fall for that routine. Her eyes narrowed when she saw Roarke's smile widen.

"You're so sweet." Carly angled a bit closer to him. "Your wife must just adore you."

A blush crept into Roarke's cheeks, and his eyes locked with Mya's. "I'm not married."

"Your girlfriend..." Carly trailed off and blinked rapidly at him as she twined a short auburn strand around her long finger.

Mya glowered at the two of them as they made spectacles of themselves. Roarke was much too old for her sister, and Carly shouldn't flirt with every man she met.

"I-I'm not seeing anyone." Roarke cleared his throat and bit back the urge to chuckle when he saw Mya's frown turn down farther.

"Really?" Carly hooked her arm through Roarke's. "Why don't you come with us to the Juice Hut, and we'll all commiserate our single status together?"

"Mya's not single."

Carly shrugged and leaned closer. In a pseudo-whisper, she said, "She should be."

He didn't even bother to refute her statement. "I really can't, but thanks." If Mya got any angrier, her eyes might pop out of their sockets. As fun as it was to tease a response from her, Roarke didn't want to hurt her or make her angry with her sister. Carly's lower lip, glossed in bright coral, protruded. "Why not?"

"I haven't worked out yet."

She trailed a finger down his well-defined arm. "With muscles like these, you can afford to skip one session."

Gently, Roarke pulled his arm from hers. "Not if I want to stay looking like this."

She heaved a sigh before she turned to Mya. "Well, I hope my sister has your number, because I need someone to show me around."

Roarke's expression was serious. "I'm not the right guy for that."

Carly studied him for a moment, and then nodded. She lost her flirty expression, and her spine straightened. "Your loss."

He laughed at her confident tone. "I don't doubt it." *But my heart belongs to someone else.* He left the words unuttered, but couldn't resist one last look at Mya before he headed to the locker room. The only logical explanation for her anger was jealousy. He frowned as he ran up the stairs. Unless she was afraid he would try to play his game with Carly, and she wanted to protect her. He sighed as he pushed open the locker room door. He knew he still didn't have her figured out.

Chapter Fourteen
Confessions over Carrot Delights

ဆော

"Try the Carrot Delight. You'll love it."

Mya read the ingredients listed on the board and grimaced. Carrots, zucchini, kiwi, and pineapple? "Yuck."

Carly bounced up to the counter and gave the clerk a bright smile. "Hiya."

"Hey." He was young, and he blushed as his eyes were drawn to her breasts. "What can I get you?"

"Two Carrot Delights."

"No, Carly—"

The boy looked up from the register and tapped his finger against the register to indicate he waited for the order to be completed.

"Two Carrot Delights," Carly said again.

"And one of those." Mya pointed at a chocolate chip biscotti.

Carly shook her head, which made the short hair fly around her face. "No, not the chocolate, Billy." She smiled at the clerk again and leaned across the counter a bit so he could look down her shirt. "Two of the honey, oat, and berry."

Mya faked a gag. "If I have to drink the carrot thing, I'm darn well getting some chocolate to choke it down."

Her sister heaved a sigh, but nodded to Billy. "Two Carrot Delights, a honey, oat, and berry biscotti, and one chocolate chip biscotti."

The boy bagged the biscotti in a white sack and slid it across the counter to Carly. As he turned to the blenders, Carly walked over to a table to put the bag down. She slid into a chair. "I'll get 'em when they're ready."

With a shrug, Mya sat down at the small table, noticing two of the male patrons at a nearby table were staring at her sister. She couldn't blame them. Carly was definitely the beauty of the family. She took the biscotti her sister passed, sinking her teeth into it with a crunch.

"So, who's that Roarke guy?"

She nearly choked on the biscotti. "I told you. He owns the studio where Bobby's working."

Carly lifted a brow. "Give me a break, sis. He's a lot more than your fiancé's employer."

Heat suffused her face. Mya used a napkin to blot at her cheeks and hoped it hid the color. "I don't know what you mean."

"It's obvious you're fucking." Before Mya could respond to that, Carly had bounded to the counter to get their drinks. When she returned with the slimy orange concoctions, she picked up where she'd left off. "There was a vibe between you two."

Mya rolled her eyes as she stared at the Carrot Delight with trepidation. "You're imagining things."

"I wasn't imagining that you were seething with jealousy when I flirted with him."

"What are you talking about?" Mya had meant her voice to be cool and level, but it sounded defensive.

"You were so pissed at both of us, and he was enjoying egging you on."

"Carly—"

"I'm young, not dumb."

"We aren't sleeping together."

Carly lifted a brow. "But you want to."

"It isn't like that."

"Well, how is it?"

To her shock, Mya blurted out the whole story. She didn't gloss over anything that had happened, not even their first encounter, or the way she had ordered Roarke to use the vibrator. When she finished, she waited for her sister's appalled reaction.

"What a jerk!"

She shook her head. "Roarke's really not that bad. When things first started, I thought I would hate him, but now—"

"I'm not talking about Roarke. Bobby, your bum fiancé, is the jerk. I can't believe he told you to go through with it." Carly's blue eyes had darkened with anger. She picked up her biscotti and broke it in two with a cracking sound. "Why are you still with that creep, Mya? You could do so much better."

Mya sighed. "Can we focus on the main issue?"

With a snort, Carly bit into half of her biscotti. "Fine. What's the problem?"

"What do you mean, what's the problem? Any day now, Roarke's going to want to have sex."

Carly leaned closer and lowered her voice. "Go for it."

"Huh?"

"It's your last chance for a fling." Her mouth twisted. "Your precious fiancé even sanctioned it."

"It isn't right—"

"Mya, I can see you're hot for this guy."

Mya broke eye contact by picking up the Carrot Delight and taking a tentative sip. "Ugh! It tastes like cold vegetable soup."

"You'll get used to it." Carly waved her hand. "Don't change the subject."

"Okay, I'm attracted to him." Mya's face turned crimson, and she lowered her voice. "I have this fantasy of him just pinning me to the wall and taking me. I don't have a chance to protest or talk him out of it." She closed her eyes and waited for her sister to castigate her. Her eyes popped open when Carly laughed. "Why are you laughing? I'm dreaming of being raped, and you think it's funny?"

Carly shook her head. "First off, it isn't rape. You just want him to take control. It's not like you wouldn't participate if he did pin you to the wall."

Mya nodded reluctantly. It was no more than the truth.

"And it's so obvious why you want him to be in control."

"It is?"

She nodded. "Yep. If Roarke pushes the issue, you get what you want, but you don't have to feel guilty for betraying Bobby."

Mya slammed back against her chair and her head spun. She felt as if her sister had physically hit her with the truth. "My God. You're absolutely right." She ached for Roarke, but her persistent loyalty to Bobby wouldn't allow her to act on those thoughts. She had to believe he forced her or swayed her judgment before she could let it happen. Otherwise... "I'm a slut."

Carly touched her hand. "You're a normal girl who has never had a decent lover."

"Bobby—"

"Sucks! You told me yourself that he doesn't do it for you."

Mya curled her arms around her torso. "I didn't say it like that."

Rolling her eyes, Carly said, "I can read between the lines. So, admit you want Roarke, and you can have him. He'll dispense with the seduction and just fuck you until you can't stand up."

"Carly! Where did you get such a foul mouth?"

"Girls' locker room after softball practice." She was nonchalant.

"I can't do that to Bobby."

666

666

666

6666

6666

"He's giving you permission. You started out playing this game for him, but don't you think you should get something out of it?"

Mya nibbled on her lip. "Well—"

"Of course you should."

She squirmed at the thought of blatantly asking Roarke to make love to her. "I can't tell him I want him to…"

A wicked grin encompassed Carly's face. "Play him for a while."

"Huh?"

"Turn the tables on Roarke. Start seducing him. Wriggle your bottom, touch him for no reason, flutter your lashes at him, and dress seductively. It works every time."

Mya snickered. "Like you would know, Miss Cocktease. You're the eternal virgin."

"Hey! I'm only eighteen." A strange smile flashed across her face. "And I'm not a virgin anymore."

"What? When?"

"There's a TA at the college—"

"You don't go to college."

Carly sighed deeply. "I'm trying to tell you what happened, okay? Don't interrupt."

"Sorry."

"I was registering for my fall classes when we met. He's six years older than me, so he said he was too old to take me out."

"But you persisted?"

Carly nodded. "I seduced him." She lifted a shoulder. "Things are progressing."

"Do you love him?"

Carly's world-weary expression was replaced by a look of excitement. Her blue eyes shone, and her lips quivered. "Yeah. I think I do."

Mya laughed. "Why do we Langelles women always fall for older men? Dad's nine years older than Mom."

Carly shrugged. "Bobby's only a year older than you. It's not really the same thing."

"O-of course not," she stuttered out as her face got hot again. "I don't know what I was thinking."

Carly snorted, but let it pass. "You going to finish that Carrot Delight?"

"Hell no!" After shoving it across to her sister, Mya went to the counter to order a banana orange smoothie. For the first time since she had started playing Roarke's game, she felt buoyant. She was already planning ways to implement her own rules into the game. He wouldn't know what hit him.

Chapter Fifteen
Gifts and a Revelation

૬૭

Friday, there was a knock at the door a little after eight in the morning. Mya heard no one stir, and Bobby continued to snore beside her. With a yawn, she rolled out of bed, fumbled on a robe, and padded on bare feet to the living room. Carly had curled in a ball on the foldout leather sofa, and a thin line of drool ran down her cheek.

Mya bit back a grin and peeked through the peephole. An impatient looking UPS man stood on the other side. She removed the security lock and eased open the door. "Hi."

"Good morning." He glanced down at his board. "I have a delivery for Mya Lang, uh, less?"

She winced at the mispronunciation. "I'm Mya Langelles."

"Sign here."

Mya took the board from him and signed her name in the electronic box. After she returned his reader, he lifted a large box from the hallway.

"Who's it from?" Mya tried to get a glimpse of the corner, but he held it too high for her to see.

"I don't know. Do you want me to set it down for you?"

She smiled. "Please." Once she had stepped aside, Mya led him to the kitchen table where he put it down. After he left the apartment, she took the shears from the wooden block and set to work on the box.

Her sister came into the kitchen, still in her pajamas. "Whacha doing?" Carly's yawn caused the words to be a bit garbled. She dropped into a chair. "Who's that from?"

Mya shrugged. "I don't know. There's no return address."

"Hmm." Carly lifted a corner of the tape with her acrylic nail and pulled it off the box in one smooth motion.

Between them, they had the large box opened in a few seconds. Mya frowned when she saw another, smaller box. She lifted it out and grunted at the unexpected weight.

"Pretty." Carly caressed the light pink and cream marbled box. "There's a card." She lifted the envelope from the box and slipped a nail inside to open it.

Mya snatched it from her sister's lean fingers. "Do you mind? It is for me."

Carly shrugged. "Fine." She turned her attention to untying the ribbon on the pastel swirled box.

The glue on the pink envelope resisted Mya, so she ripped the side. A thick cream card fell onto the table, and she lifted it.

Pamper yourself.
R

"What does it say?" Carly abandoned the ribbon to snatch the card from Mya's fingers. "Oooh. I wonder what he sent you?"

Mya's hands shook with excitement as she snipped the ribbon Carly hadn't gotten to, and then lifted off the top of the box. "Wow."

Carly peered into the box. "What is all that?"

Her movements were careful when she lifted out a wire basket filled with glass jars of varying sizes. "It's bath oil, shampoo, and lotion." Mya unscrewed the bath oil to sniff it and instantly recognized the scent. "He has this specially made."

"What else is in the box?"

Mya laid the basket aside and lifted out a portable spa unit. "Oh, my God. I've been dying for one of these."

"I have to try that before we leave tomorrow." Carly reached for the box to take it from her.

Mya slapped at her hand lightly. "Wait your turn."

"There's more."

"Yeah." Next in the box was a satin black robe with midnight blue piping. The matching slippers invited her feet inside, and Mya slid them on. "Oh, these are amazing."

"Is that everything?"

"Yes… No." Mya pulled out a smaller box. "You want to open this?"

Carly nodded and reached for it eagerly.

Mya delved into the box once more and found only a card inside. When she held it up to the light, she saw it was actually a day-pass for Rendezvous Spa. The subtitle said 'Where Lovers Come Together'. The pass was valid for Tuesday only, and she could arrive anytime after ten. "Look at this."

"Look at this," Carly said at the same time.

They both giggled as they looked up. Mya handed her the card after she took the hairbrush from her sister. The white bristles were softer than any she had ever touched, and Mya didn't doubt the back and handle of the brush were real silver. Abstract swirls were etched into the brush, and her initials were engraved on the handle. Mya ran a finger across the M.I.L. "How did he know the initial for Isabelle?"

Carly giggled. "I have no idea."

Something in her tone caused Mya to raise her head. "Did you —?"

"I might have answered a few questions for him when he called here Wednesday night."

Mya shook her head. "He just happened to get through to you?"

"No. Roarke said he had to hang up three times before because Mom answered."

"Oh." She and Dad had gone to pick up dinner on Wednesday night. They had left Mom and Carly—who claimed to be too tired from shopping to move—at the apartment. Bobby, as usual, had worked late. What would Roarke have done if she had answered the phone? Or if Bobby had?

"So, it looks like you've got a date with him for Tuesday." Carly tapped a peach nail against the thick spa pass.

Mya sank into a chair and wriggled her toes in the satin slippers. She felt decadent. "I'm not sure I can go through with what we talked about."

"Sure you can."

She bit her lip. "I can't get past what I'll be doing to Bobby."

Carly sighed. "He'll never know the details. It's not like you're going to tell him if you enjoy fucking Roarke."

"But I'll know! How can I pretend like I don't or ignore what I've done?"

Carly's eyes wrinkled, and she fidgeted. "You know I don't like Bobby, right?"

Mya's eyebrow raised by itself. "Well, duh. None of you have ever bothered to keep the animosity under wraps."

"But you don't know why I hate him."

"Hate?"

Shrugging, Carly began putting the items back in the box. "When I was a freshman, a lot of people were mean to me since I was so fat."

"You weren't fat. You just hadn't outgrown it all yet."

With a snort Carly said, "I was fat, but that's not important to the story."

"Okay."

"Some of the boys used to tease me by asking me out. I was no fool. I knew it was a big joke, so I ignored them." Carly's eyes dropped to the table. "A few took their games a step farther. They would touch me."

Mya frowned. "Touch you?"

"My boobs, mostly. They were a lot bigger then."

"I'm so sorry, Carly. Why didn't you say something?"

"It was your senior year. You were busy with your own stuff."

"I would have done something."

Carly's eyes shimmered with unshed tears. "What could you do?" She swallowed. "Besides, it was the impetus I needed to make changes."

"What does this have to do with Bobby?" Mya's stomach clenched with dread.

"He was one of those guys."

"Bobby used to touch your breasts?"

Carly looked ill. "That wasn't enough for him. When I stopped crying and trying to get them to leave me alone, most of the guys lost interest in their cruelty. Not Bobby." Her mouth twisted. "One night at a football game…" She blinked. "I even remember which one. The Serpents were beating the Eagles fourteen to two. You were cheering and everyone loved you."

Mya shifted in her seat. "That's not true."

Her sister nodded. "It is. People were always drawn to you. I used to hate you for that."

Mya's head dropped forward. "Oh." She looked up when Carly touched her hand. "I never meant to hurt you."

"I know. It wasn't your fault I wanted to be like you. I outgrew all that petty crap a long time ago." Carly heaved a sigh. "Anyway, that isn't part of what I'm trying to tell you."

"What happened?"

"He and two of his buddies—Ryan Peters and Chris Cahill—cornered me by the bleachers. He kissed me."

Mya felt a wash of relief that it wasn't anything worse, but Carly continued before she could say anything.

"He pushed up my shirt, and one of the guys put their hand down my pants…" Carly wiped at a tear on her cheek. "They didn't rape me or anything, but the three of them left some bruises on my breasts. I was sore for a while and had an aversion to boys touching me at all for months."

Mya shook her head unconsciously. She wanted to deny what her sister had said. "Why would he do that?"

Carly shrugged. "He's an asshole?"

"That was years ago—"

Her mouth twisted. "Yeah. I'm sure he's outgrown it." Her tone held an edge. "Anyway, shortly after that, you two got serious and I started working out. He never bothered me again."

Mya's mouth dropped open. "We were dating at the time?"

Carly nodded. "So, it's not like he's innocent, Mya. Enjoy your fling with Roarke. Then, if you must, marry Bobby."

"I don't know what to say."

Carly shrugged. "It was years ago, and I'm over it now. I just thought it was time to tell you."

"So I can do an eye for an eye?"

"No. So you can realize that Bobby isn't as great as you think, and that you owe it to yourself to explore other options before settling down with him. You've never had anyone else, Mya." Carly's eyes shone with unshed tears. "I don't want you to make a mistake."

Angry words rose to her tongue, but she swallowed them. It pained her, but she no longer felt the urge to defend Bobby as she had in the past. Her sister's revelation was just one more incident in a pattern that had started to emerge. Her eyes dropped to the ring on her finger, and she was briefly tempted to pull it off.

That thought scared her and Mya tore her eyes from the small diamond. Things hadn't been great lately, but she still wanted to marry Bobby. Didn't she?

Her eyes drifted to the day-pass for the spa, and her heart rate increased with anticipation. Carly was right. She deserved to get something out of the mess her life had become. Bobby had even encouraged her to participate in Roarke's game.

The thought of another lover caused Mya's stomach to clench with excitement and nervousness. What if she liked it so much that she didn't want Bobby anymore? But if she didn't do it, she would never know. That could be worse than anything else that might happen. How would things be with her and Bobby if she always looked back with regret and wondered what if?

Carly cleared her throat. "Can I try out your spa?"

Mya pulled the box closer. "Not until I do."

"Hurry up, sis. I'm leaving today."

With a laugh, she rose from the table and carried the box with her down the hall. Once more, Carly had persuaded her to see both sides. Mya only hoped her confidence wouldn't fade with her sister's departure.

Chapter Sixteen
Rendezvous

℘

Mya arrived at Rendezvous a little after eleven on Tuesday morning. She had been delayed by the need to run a few errands for Bobby and pay some bills. As of yet, she hadn't found the time or opportunity to ask him about what Carly had told her and anxiety shadowed her hazel eyes.

The spa was located in a small white brick building amid upscale shops, a wholesale makeup supplier, and a wig manufacturer's outlet. Mya pushed on the golden bars of the clear glass door to open it and caught her breath when she stepped into the interior.

Pale pink walls and bright fuchsia carpets pleased the eye. A richly polished reception desk was in the corner, almost hidden by a mass of greenery that sprouted from wicker pots. A gorgeous woman sat behind the desk. She had shiny dark hair, glossy red lips, and a perfectly proportioned body.

The corner of Mya's mouth quirked as she wondered if she was supposed to believe a visit to Rendezvous would transform her into that. She shook her head and walked to the desk.

"Good morning." The receptionist's voice was as perfect as the rest of her.

"Hi." Mya clutched the pass in her hand.

"How may we help you?"

Mya resisted the urge to look around for the others that made up "we". Instead, she handed the woman her pass. "I have a reservation."

With one brisk nod, the receptionist took the card and consulted a book beside her. "Welcome, Ms. Langelles."

Mya's eyebrows shot up when the woman actually pronounced her name correctly. "Thanks."

"Mr. Thomas is waiting for you in the lounge."

Mya swallowed hard. "He's here already?" Hadn't she expected him to be though? Why else had she hurried through the morning's schedule and gotten more impatient with each delay?

The woman nodded. "If you'll follow me, I'll show you the changing rooms."

"Changing rooms?"

"Our clients generally prefer a more relaxed state of dress while undergoing a session."

Mya nodded and tried to look knowledgeable as she followed the receptionist, whose impossibly high heels sank into the thick carpet without a sound. They went down a hallway that featured the same wall coverings and carpet before they stopped before a light pink door labeled Women's. "Now what?"

"There are robes or terry sarongs to choose from." The woman pushed open the door. "There's also a selection of slippers and flip-flops."

"After I change, where do I go?"

"Inside is a door marked Lounge. If you go through it, you'll find Mr. Thomas."

"Thanks." Mya's smile felt wobbly as she walked through the door the receptionist still held for her. She surveyed the room and looked for the robes. Her eyes slid past the pink marbled floor and wall tile, pink lockers, and shower stalls to a large closet against one wall.

She walked over to examine the choices. The robe selections were varied—from a crimson silk robe that might have fallen two inches below her hip, to a full-length light blue terry robe. The sarongs were fashioned like a wraparound towel, but secured in place with Velcro.

She flipped through the selections and chose an emerald silk robe with a hood. It would be thin enough to allow Roarke a view of her body, but wasn't completely see-through. She slid it from the hanger and picked up a pair of cork thongs, which she took to a locker. She dropped the robe and shoes on the bench and removed her slacks and vest top quickly. She had worn her hair up in a clip, and she left it that way as she slid on the robe. She dropped the shoes on the floor before she pushed her feet into them.

The silk slid across her bare skin with every step she took, and the sensation made Mya shiver. She stopped in front of the wall-length mirror to admire herself. The emerald went well with her hair and brought out green glints in her eyes. Her nipples poked through the thin fabric because they had hardened from the sensuous sensation of the robe as it slid across her flesh. The hem ended mid-thigh and exposed the length of her legs to their best advantage.

With a smile to herself, Mya walked out of the dressing room, through the door marked Lounge. She froze three steps into the room when she saw another couple waited. They looked up at her, and then returned their attention to magazines.

Roarke sat in a leather recliner with his feet propped up, as he sipped from an espresso cup. He wore a thin black robe that ended just above the knee. When he saw her, he lifted a hand to wave her over to him.

Mya walked across the burnt umber carpet and tried to ignore the presence of the other man and woman. They seemed oblivious, which alleviated some of her self-consciousness. She resisted the urge to tug on the robe's hem, because it would only cause the bodice to drop lower. It was a relief to stop beside Roarke, who got up from the recliner. "Hi." Mya's voice trembled, and she didn't know if it was from nerves or the sight of his body revealed through the silk robe that molded itself to him.

"Good morning, Mya." Roarke touched the three-quarter sleeve of her robe. "Beautiful color on you."

She smiled up at him and ducked her head slightly. "Thanks." She wanted to compliment him, but her tongue felt too thick.

"Would you like to start with a massage, manicure and pedicure, or a mud bath?"

Her forehead furrowed. "Mud bath? What is that?"

"I've never tried it, but Lisa said it's very relaxing. Apparently, they immerse you in this tub full of mud with a gel mask over your eyes. They use aromatherapy to scent the air and play soothing music."

Mya couldn't keep a grimace from her face. "I'm not anxious to climb into a vat of mud."

He laughed. "Then what shall we start with?"

"Manicures?"

It was his turn to grimace. "That will be a new experience for me, but Lisa said this was a...nice place." Roarke winced, realizing he had almost revealed exactly what Lisa had said—a romantic place.

Mya's stomach clenched at his repetition of the name Lisa. Who was she? An ex-girlfriend, maybe? Or maybe someone who had played Roarke's game in the past? Maybe she still played it? He did have five other days in the week when he didn't see her. Who knew what he did with all that time? Mya tried to sound casual when she asked, "Who's Lisa?"

Roarke bit back a grin as he saw her eyes darken and hands clench. Her tone had bordered on glacial. Jealous? He certainly hoped so. He was tempted to let Lisa play a different role, but it wouldn't be fair—especially if she ever met Mya. "She's my brother's wife."

"Oh." Mya refused to acknowledge her relief.

A side door opened, and Roarke waved to the woman entering. She wore a long red dress with gold flowers. A tiger lily was tucked behind her ear, and her eyes looked exotic. They were a vivid green, lined with dark kohl, and edged by thick lashes.

Another product of the Rendezvous regimen, Mya thought with uncharacteristic cynicism. Was that the kind of woman Roarke wanted her to be? Her stomach churned at the thought. She could never be exotic or alluring.

She smiled as she came over to them. "Yes, Mr. Thomas?"

"We're ready now."

"Where did you want to begin?"

"With manicures and pedicures."

She nodded. "Follow me, please."

"That's Claudia," Roarke said softly to Mya as they left the lounge and entered another hallway. This one had beige walls and blonde hardwood floors. "She's our personal attendant for the day."

"Oh." Was he attracted to her? Mya's eyes narrowed as she watched Roarke's face and searched for any sign of attraction to the blonde. His expression remained bland, and some of her anxiety dissipated.

They passed into a small room where Roarke and Mya sat in chairs with their feet elevated. Two other attendants joined Claudia, and they set to work on the manicures while she did Mya's pedicure, followed by Roarke's.

Mya watched him from the corner of her eye. She grinned as he eventually relaxed his stiff posture. She couldn't imagine Bobby being so extravagant as to take her to a spa and sit through a manicure/pedicure. He would scoff and call it girly or worse. But Roarke seemed to enjoy the experience.

After the attendants had finished, Claudia led them back into the hallway, to another room. Two massage tables stood side by side, and a petite Asian girl in a white cotton dress sat in a chair. She flipped through a magazine with an air of boredom.

"Miko, will you please see to Ms. Langelles?"

With a nod, she rose from her seat. Miko laid the magazine on the chair and patted the table on the left. "Lay down on your stomach, please."

Mya's fingers trembled as she undid the bow on the sash. From the corner of her eye, she saw Roarke's eyes drop to her hands, then shoot up as she pulled the robe off. She ignored her nudity as she lay on the table.

Miko draped a towel across her buttocks before she lifted a bottle from the rack nearby. Before she put her face into the opening of the massage table, Mya watched Roarke shed his robe and lay on the table beside hers. There was a flush along his cheeks, and she wondered if it came from her nakedness or from his own nudity. When Claudia draped a towel over Roarke's rear, Mya sighed. She turned her face into the hole in the table and tried to imagine she was boneless. As Miko's fingers began to work their magic, she couldn't bite back the occasional groan of pleasure. She had never had a professional massage before and suddenly understood why they were so popular.

Roarke gritted his teeth with each sound of pleasure she made. His hands clenched into fists and freshly manicured nails dug into the flesh of his palms. He tried to enjoy Claudia's ministrations, but he wanted her hands to be Mya's. He was still tense when the massage ended thirty minutes later.

"Would you like lunch before the mud bath?" Claudia asked them as they rose and slipped back into the robes.

Mya's stomach rumbled to remind her she had skipped breakfast. "Please."

"We have a sushi bar, or we can have items delivered if you would prefer?"

Roarke shrugged to indicate the decision was Mya's.

"The sushi is fine."

Claudia led them into a small room with one table and two chairs. She brought menus, and they ordered. Within minutes, plates of marinated sushi chunks and handrolls were before them. Hot oolong in delicate bone china cups accompanied their meal.

"How do you feel?" Roarke tried to wield the chopsticks to pick up a roll, but dropped it every time.

"Wonderful. I'm so relaxed."

With a growl, Roarke laid aside the chopsticks and picked up the sushi handroll to pop in his mouth. "Me too." His shoulders were still tense though. He had been unable to truly enjoy his massage because his attention had focused on his attempts to incorporate Mya's groans and moans into a different sort of scenario that still played out in his head.

Mya bit back a giggle as she watched him eat the sushi. She laid aside her chopsticks and picked up the rolls with her hands to make him feel better. The sushi disappeared quickly, and her stomach felt pleasantly full fifteen minutes later.

Almost as soon as they had finished, Claudia returned. "Are you ready for a soak?"

Suppressing a shudder, Mya got to her feet. "I guess."

"Yeah." Roarke tried to sound enthusiastic, but the thought of a mud bath didn't appeal.

She ignored their reluctance as she escorted them from the private dining area. Through the last door on the left, they entered a large room with a tub sunk into the floor. What looked like brown slime churned lazily. It was thinner than traditional mud, and there was no foul odor in the air.

Mya breathed in deeply and recognized jasmine and lavender from the myriad aromas. They blended to form a fragrant cloud spread by humidifiers in each corner of the room and sent out as a barely visible mist. Low-pitched Spanish guitars serenaded them through discreetly placed speakers.

"If you would like to wear something into the tub, there's a selection of swimwear." Claudia pointed to a rack with men and women's accessories.

Before Roarke could answer, Mya smiled. "I want to try it *au naturale.*"

Roarke's eyes widened when Mya winked at him. He blinked and tried to determine if she really had winked. Had she tried to flirt with him? Did she want to tease him? He frowned and dropped the robe with an air of challenge while he waited for her to do the same.

Mya struggled to appear nonchalant as she untied the sash to remove the robe. Claudia took it from her and bent down to pick up Roarke's. Mya kept her expression bland as she turned to him. "Are you ready for this?"

"Uh—" He cleared his throat. "Yeah."

"You can go in." Claudia handed them each a gel mask. "This will relax you, but if you prefer not to wear them…"

Mya took hers and slipped it over her head. She was careful not to snag the elastic strap in her hair clip as she positioned it on her forehead. With the knowledge that Roarke's eyes rested on her, she sashayed to the steps of the tub. With a grimace, she took the first step into the mud.

She stopped as it began to ooze around her toes. It was warm and smooth, rather than slimy, as she had expected. She took a deep breath for courage and walked down the other three steps until the mud was at mid-thigh. She felt her way around the side and dropped onto a bench. The mud surged to her neck. The mud squelched when she pulled an arm free to push the mask down over her eyes. The mask was cool and tingly, while the parts of her immersed in the mud were warm. "Coming in, Roarke?"

He swallowed. "I guess." Roarke took a mask from Claudia before he strode to the steps. His first couple of steps were confident, before the mud engulfed his legs. He shivered at the not-unpleasant sensation and forced himself to walk deeper into the pool. The mud resisted him slightly, and he forced his way through so he could take a seat beside Mya. Once settled, he pushed the mask over his eyes and leaned his head against the pillowed ledge. He gradually let the rest of his body sink into the thin mud.

"I'll be back in awhile," Claudia said cheerfully. A second later, the door closed behind her.

"This is amazing." Mya sighed and scrunched down until the mud touched her chin. "It looked so—"

"—disgusting," Roarke put in.

"But it feels so—"

"—relaxing."

"Yes." Mya slid closer to him as she leaned her head against the ledge of the tub. "How do you think they make this?" She felt him shrug.

"You probably don't want to know."

She tried to imitate Carly's girly giggle. "Yeah. Once you remove the mystique, what's left?"

"How it feels?" His voice was husky.

Mya slid her hand from her thigh to his skin. Her flesh glided smoothly over his as she brought her hand up higher. "It feels great to me," she said in a throaty whisper.

Roarke froze as her hand brushed his stomach and hesitated. What did she plan to do? Was she...? His breath hissed through his teeth as her hand wrapped around his cock. "Mya—"

"Hmm?" She struggled to sound innocent as she stroked him from head to base. The mud squished through her fingers and eased her way, but also interfered with her ability to feel him. In case he had the same problem, she squeezed her hand and tightened her grip.

Roarke gasped as she increased the pressure of her cupped hand. She continued to stroke him and circle the head of his cock with her thumb with each upward stroke. His cock grew rigid in her grasp, and his hips bucked as the muscles in his groin tightened. He had never felt anything like it. The mud slithered between them to fill in the gaps between her fingers and clenched hand. She seemed to completely engulf him, and he knew he would come if she didn't stop. "You shouldn't."

Mya's grin was wicked, and she was glad he wore a mask. "Relax. Enjoy the mud."

"But…" Roarke trailed off as she flicked her finger across the very tip of his cock. This wasn't part of his plan. She wasn't supposed to touch him at all yet. He wasn't supposed to touch her either — not today, anyway. That would come later.

His mind went blank as she increased the tempo of her strokes. Roarke tried to focus on his seduction scenario, but soon his body's response overwhelmed his ability to think. He relaxed completely and gave into the urge to thrust.

Mya slowed down her hand as he began to participate. She continued to caress him and apply pressure as she stroked up and down his cock, but he did most of the work. Her pussy grew wet as she imagined the expression on his face. With her free hand, she slid the mask aside so she could see him at the moment he reached satisfaction.

His forehead furrowed and his lips drew back to expose gritted teeth as his cock spasmed in her hand. Warm liquid splashed onto her fingers, and she knew he had come — as if his blissful expression couldn't have told her that.

With a satisfied smile, Mya lowered her mask so he wouldn't know she had peeked. She relinquished her hold on him as he leaned against her. He buried his face in her hair, and the corner of his mask touched her ear. His lips pressed against her cheek.

"Why?"

Mya searched for an answer, but nothing sounded right in her head. Rather than answer, she rubbed her cheek against his mouth and received a small kiss.

"Come home with me." Roarke abandoned his carefully thought out plan. He needed to have her today. He couldn't wait any longer. Not days and certainly not weeks.

She hesitated over her response. She had expected him to ask, but hadn't given much thought to her answer. It was what she wanted too, but it was irreversible. Once she gave in to her desire, she couldn't undo her deeds. She would have to live with the consequences for the rest of her life.

"Mya?"

The need in his tone cut through her confusion. "Yes. I'll come home with you."

Chapter Seventeen
Making Love

ဆာ

Mya stared out the window of Roarke's black Lotus, lost in her thoughts. It was some time before she noticed they weren't headed in the direction of his condo. "Where are we going?"

"My house."

She bit her lip and wondered if she should protest. The condo was their meeting place. His home seemed almost too intimate. Too personal. She closed her eyes as her body twinged with desire. It didn't matter where they made love, as long as it was soon. "Okay."

He turned down a quiet street lined with large homes, but nothing that was too ostentatious. The Lotus turned into the third drive on the left and stopped before a two-story Mediterranean with terracotta tiles. Roarke opened his door, but didn't get out. "Are you coming in?"

She knew this was the last chance he would give her to back out. Mya moistened her dry lips, and then grasped the handle of the door. She let it speak for her as she opened it and slid out. "This is your house?"

Roarke got out of the car, and they walked up a set of wide, shallow steps made of textured cement and painted white. "For about six months."

"Why did you move from the condo?"

He took time to unlock the door and let her precede him into the deliciously cool interior before he answered. "I got tired of living in a building where there was no privacy." He grimaced as he recalled the neighbor who always dropped by — sometimes to borrow something or invite him for dinner. In reality, she had consumed him with her eyes on each impromptu visit. Never mind the huge rock she had worn on her hand.

The irony didn't escape Roarke as he caught sight of the diamond on Mya's finger. He dropped his keys on the standing table near the door with a twist of his lips. How his ethics had plummeted.

Mya eyed the spacious interior—white floors, white walls, and black furniture—with round eyes. She had never been inside a house like it. A step separated the entryway from the rest of the house, and she stepped up and walked into the living room. A massive entertainment center dominated one wall of the room. She recognized a flat-screen television and small speakers in the corners of the room that provided surround sound. Bobby would love this place.

But he wouldn't love what she planned to do here. A sudden chill seized her, and Mya rubbed her bare arms.

"Would you like me to turn down the air conditioner?"

She shook her head and licked her lips again. "I'm thirsty. Could we get something to drink before…?" Mya trailed off, unable to say the words even though she had been the one to bring them to this point.

He nodded. "Follow me." Roarke led her into the bright kitchen and walked to the fridge. "What are you in the mood for?"

Mya shrugged. "Water?"

He pushed aside a bottle of juice to take two bottles of water from a flat on the second shelf. After he had handed it to her, they stood in the middle of the kitchen to drink. Once they quenched their thirst, an awkward silence developed between them. Roarke racked his brain for something to say, but drew a blank. All he could think about was her naked form sprawled across the crimson silk sheets on his bed upstairs. How did he get her from here to there though?

Mya sat the bottle on the counter and cleared her throat. "Can I see the rest?"

His eyes widened for a moment before he realized what she meant. "Sure." He took her hand to lead Mya through the rooms on the lower level. They climbed the curved staircase together and emerged onto the second floor. He showed her the guest rooms and his office before he stopped in front of his bedroom door. "This is where I sleep."

Mya swallowed audibly as he pushed open the white door. She still held his hand, and she could feel the moisture between their palms. Was it his sweat or hers? Maybe both.

She followed him inside and caught her breath. A huge four-post black lacquered bed took up most of the middle of the room. Black furniture that matched the decor was stationed strategically around the walls to maximize space. Highly polished hardwood absorbed the clunk of her sandals' heels as she walked farther into the room and stopped before the fireplace. A luxuriant black rug stretched across the floor in front of the hearth, and she almost knelt to touch it. Only the knowledge of how gauche her actions would be restrained her.

When she turned around, she found Roarke's solemn eyes on her. "It's beautiful." Mya kicked off her sandals as she walked over to the bed. It rested on a pedestal, so she didn't have to bend down to touch the satiny red comforter draped across the bed. She turned back to look at him again and saw the hunger in his eyes that she knew was reflected in hers. She forced a smile as she sat on the bed. "This is so comfy."

He nodded as he walked over to her. "You should try lying down on it."

Mya stretched out until she lay completely on the bed. Her stomach quivered with nerves as he sat down beside her. "Heavenly."

Roarke ran a finger down her bare arm. "Absolutely." He moved his hand to the top button of her vest shirt where it met at the valley of her breasts. The lacy cups of her red bra were just visible from this angle.

Mya put her hand on his. She wasn't sure if it was to stop him or urge him to continue. He must have taken his cue from the desire that burned in her eyes, because he flicked open the top button, then the next and the next, until all five had been undone. Mya closed her eyes as his hand settled on her stomach to rub back and forth in slow circles.

Roarke's breath caught in his throat as he eased open the vest shirt to stroke her stomach. His hand traveled up to her left breast, and he rubbed the nipple through the lace of the padded cup. He groaned as she squirmed against his hand. Her lips were moist and invited him to kiss her. He shifted positions so he could lean down to press his lips against hers.

Her eyes flew open as he brought his lips against hers. They had only shared one kiss, and it had been almost platonic. As his tongue traced her lips, Mya moaned low in her throat. When he pulled his hand away from her breast, she protested wordlessly.

Roarke chuckled as he buried his hands in her hair and pulled her closer. Their tongues met, and she stroked hers across his, which made him shudder. He rolled Mya onto her back and settled on top of her. Her mouth was instantly more accessible, and he pushed his tongue in deeper and elicited a moan from her.

Mya's eyes widened as he explored the interior of her mouth. His cock pressed into her thigh and strained against the confines of his clothing. She was so hot. Had she developed a fever? She didn't think she had ever felt like this before—not even in the throes of an orgasm.

Roarke pushed her away slightly to smile up at her. "You're so soft."

"And you're so hard." Mya couldn't hold back a giggle. She wriggled under him and pressed her thigh against his cock.

"I'm amazed after the incident at the spa." He winked at her. "You inspire me to new heights, love."

As Roarke kissed her again, Mya wrapped her arms around his shoulders and held him tightly. His tongue traced a path from her mouth to her ear, where he nibbled on the lobe. Their eyes were inches apart, and she got lost in his blue depths. It was as if she had drowned in an ocean of… What? There was vulnerability in his eyes that she saw beneath the heat of passion. Approval, joy, and tenderness mingled with his obvious desire. Did he see the same things in her eyes? Was her love for him blatantly obvious?

She gasped at the thought, which drew a concerned look from Roarke. He immediately stilled his mouth on her lobe. How could it be? When had it happened? Did she really love Roarke?

He looked up at her with an uncertain expression. "Are you all right?"

Mya nodded, unable to speak. The gentle expression on his face was like nothing she had ever seen from Bobby. It was obvious he cared for her and was compassionate. Both qualities Bobby lacked in his makeup. This man was everything her fiancé should be, but wasn't. She should be feeling guilty, but all she felt was the joy that swept through her when she realized she was finally in love.

"Mya?" His eyes had darkened. "Are you okay? Do you want to stop?"

She shook her head. If she opened her mouth, the words would fly out. That could ruin everything. What if Roarke didn't feel the same? It was a game to him, and any declaration of love might send him away. She couldn't lose him—not yet, anyway. While she couldn't keep her emotions hidden forever, she could for an afternoon.

Roarke pushed the shirt off her shoulders and unfastened the front clasp of the bra. As her breasts spilled free, he pressed his face to them and basked in the moment. He'd had a few lovers, but didn't think he had felt this way before. However, he had never been in love before now. He didn't shy away from the revelation as he had done in the past. This time, he embraced it, determined that she would feel the same way about him. Someday, Mya would be his, not Bobby's, if he had patience. In the meantime, he had her body, if not her heart.

A groan ripped from his throat as Mya pushed her hands under his shirt and flicked her nails across his nipples. He moved his face to take possession of one of her plump pink nipples. He grinned around the bud in his mouth when she groaned and ground her pussy against him. Maybe now wasn't the time for patience.

"Roarke."

"Hmm?" He laved the nipple as he squeezed her right breast.

"Roarke!" Her tone was more insistent, and Mya slid her hands down his stomach to the fly of his pants. She stroked the length of him through the cotton material, pleased to feel him jump under her hand.

He moved his lips from her nipple. "What do you want?"

"You."

He grinned. "Soon." Roarke slid off her and stood up to remove his clothes. As Mya started to undo her slacks, he said, "Let me."

She paused and stared up at him. He joined her on the bed, clad only in a pair of black silk bikinis. Mya ran her hand across his buttocks. "Nice underwear."

Roarke fumbled with the button and zipper on her pants and finally got it open. He touched the lace of her red panties and flirted with the lips of her pussy. "Yours too."

She shrugged. "I had some advice about underwear."

His chuckle turned to a gasp when her hand traveled around to grasp his cock. He pulled her away. "Not yet."

"But—"

"In awhile. This time, I want to be inside of you."

She lay back as Roarke pulled off her pants. Mya's eyes felt heavy, but the rest of her body tingled with desire. She held out her arms as he knelt on the bed, but he ignored the invitation.

Instead, Roarke settled down more toward the foot of the bed, between her thighs. He pushed them apart to make a nest, and then stroked her warm pussy through the lacy red panties. She arched against his finger and moaned. He propped his chin on his elbow so he could see her eyes. "Do you like that?"

She rolled her eyes at him and hissed as he plunged his finger inside her shallowly. She could feel the warmth of his digit surrounded by the lace, and the sensation made her tighten her thighs.

Roarke gently slapped her left thigh. "Relax."

Mya's mouth dropped open when he did that, but she wasn't offended. It was obvious he wanted to play with her, and she found she liked it. "You like to spank?" Her voice was a throaty whisper.

Roarke shrugged. "Only naughty girls." He blushed at the lie. He had never spanked a woman in his life.

A grin teased at the corners of her mouth. "I'll have to see how naughty I can be."

Roarke's eyes widened at her words, and he wondered if she really wanted him to spank her. With an air of experimentation, he pulled on her hip so one of her cheeks was exposed. He lightly tapped his hand against the flesh revealed by the thong. To his surprise, she giggled and purred at the same time. "You like that, don't you?"

Mya held up her thumb and forefinger to indicate a little. She was too breathless to speak as he pulled down her underwear. His hand came down on her butt again, with just a bit more force. As he did that, his other hand went to explore her pussy. The combination left Mya a confused mass of sensations. When she arched against his fingers, his hand hit her buttocks with more force, which caused a sting to linger. It was impossible not to rub her pussy against his fingers though.

Surely, her cheeks were pink now, but she didn't care. It felt too good to ask him to stop.

He bit back a laugh as she turned into a babbling, giggling hedonist before his eyes. He watched carefully until her eyes closed, and she clenched her hands together. He moved quickly and rolled her onto her back to bury his face between her thighs.

Mya screamed as his tongue invaded her pussy. She felt him jerk, before he stopped. "Keep going," she forced out through clenched teeth.

"Are you okay?" His voice was muffled.

She nodded before she realized he probably couldn't see her. "It surprised me." She wriggled against him and waited for his heavenly tongue to begin its conquest. When he flicked it over her clit, she cried out again.

As Roarke continued his velvety kisses, he felt her body shudder and twitch with each flick of his tongue. She sobbed with pleasure, and moisture flooded his mouth. Right before she was about to come, he withdrew.

Mya's eyes popped open. "What are you doing?"

He grinned at her angry tone. "I want us to go together."

She shook her head. "I can't...not during... Please?" She wanted to scream as he slid up her body, farther and farther away from her pussy. "Don't do this, Roarke. I need to—"

"Explode," he finished for her as he positioned his cock at her entrance. "You will. I promise."

She sighed. It would do no good to protest. She resigned herself to another disappointment as he slowly filled her. She moaned at the length of him, and her body adjusted with an ease that surprised her.

Having his cock buried inside her wet pussy felt like heaven. Roarke let her moisture flood him as he stayed in her and didn't move. As her hips started to buck, he let her body persuade him to move. He withdrew almost completely, and then filled her pussy again. Mya's harsh breaths expressed her pleasure more than any words could, and Roarke did it again.

Mya trembled on the edge of climax, but she knew that he wouldn't last long enough to push her over the edge. She closed her eyes and gritted her teeth as he plunged into her pussy again. She felt his finger stroke her clit and her eyes popped open. She stared into his blue depths as he continued to thrust into her while he manipulated the nub. She threw her head back as shockwaves washed over her from the epicenter between her thighs. Mya buried her hands in his hair as she climaxed and thrust against him with a sob as her pussy convulsed.

He couldn't wait any longer. With her first shudder, as her muscles tightened around his cock, Roarke let his climax sweep over him. He pulled her closer, and she strained against them. For a moment, it was as if they were one person as their satisfaction pulsed through them. Their heartbeats were simpatico, and a mingled cry came from both of their throats before Roarke collapsed on top of her and held her against him. He rubbed his face in her soft hair as her hands moved to his back. He never wanted to let her go, and he pulled her even closer.

Mya held onto him as if he was her lifeline. Maybe he was. She wanted to stay with him forever, but she knew she would have to leave. First, she had to settle things with Bobby before she could think about a discussion of the future with Roarke.

* * * * *

"Are you sure you want to take a cab? I can drive you."

Mya shook her head as she did up the last button on her vest top. "A taxi is fine. You look too comfortable to move."

A rueful grin curved across his face. It was true he didn't want to move. The only thing that would make the moment more perfect was if Mya stayed with him. He almost asked her to, but knew she would refuse. Bobby expected her at home, and the afternoon's events hadn't changed that. She was still Bobby's girl—for now.

She hesitated at the doorway and looked back at him. She half-hoped he would ask her to stay. When he didn't, Mya sighed and twisted the knob. "I'll see you Friday?"

Roarke put his hands behind his head and snuggled against the pillow. "Unless you want to see me sooner?" He kept his tone deliberately light in an attempt to mask the serious undertones.

She wanted to, but Mya was afraid of his reaction to her sudden enthusiasm. She couldn't handle a rejection right now until she sorted things out with Bobby. Either way, she knew she couldn't stay with her fiancé—not after she had realized she loved Roarke. Even if it was all just a game to him, it had become serious to her. It wouldn't be fair to Bobby to pretend that she still loved him just to have a safety net in case things ended badly with Roarke. "I can't. Work and all…"

Roarke sighed. "Friday it is. Do you want me to walk you down?"

She shook her head. "I'll be fine." Mya wanted to say so much more, but in the end she turned and left the bedroom. She was halfway down the stairs when she heard him call out to her. Her heart stuttered and she hoped he was about to ask her to stay. She gripped the banister and turned around. "Yes?"

He stood at the top of the stairs in the nude. "You left your earrings on the night stand."

A horn honked in the driveway to indicate the taxi had arrived. "Bring them with you Friday." Mya hurried down the stairs and out the door before she blurted out a confession or begged him to let her stay. It was too soon, and she was too uncertain. Besides, she owed Bobby an explanation before she stayed overnight with Roarke—if he wanted her to.

Chapter Eighteen
Dinner with the Producer

ဆ

When Mya entered the apartment, her eyes fell on Bobby. He stood in the entryway in a suit and tie. His blond hair was in a slicked-back ponytail, and she could smell his cologne from the door. "What's going on?"

"Jesus Christ, Mya. It's almost seven. You have to get dressed."

"Why?" Mya pulled her hand away as he reached for her. "What's going on?"

"We're having dinner with Tony Scarpeti."

She raised her eyebrows. "Why didn't you tell me sooner, and who is Tony Scarpeti?"

"He's doing a movie, and I might get the lead." Bobby's blue eyes sparkled with excitement. "Tonight is about striking a deal—maybe."

She shook her head. "Why didn't you give me some warning?" Mya winced as her shoulders grew stiff. Already the relaxation of the afternoon spent with Roarke had dissipated.

He frowned at her. "Mr. Scarpeti invited us today. I couldn't say no."

Mya knew their discussion would have to be postponed until after the dinner. "What time are we meeting him?"

"Eight."

"Eight!" She looked down at the slacks and vest she wore. "I'll never make it."

"Hurry." He took her arm to push her toward the bathroom. "And make yourself beautiful."

She put her hands on her hips, frowning up at him. "Why?"

Bobby's eyes shifted away from hers. "I've heard he has an eye for the ladies. It can't hurt if you impress him."

With a disgusted sigh, Mya marched down the hall to the bathroom. Thankfully, she had taken a shower at Roarke's before she left. She applied makeup and twisted her hair into a loose bun. Afterward, she stripped off her clothes and dashed down the hall to their bedroom.

She locked the door behind her so Bobby couldn't walk in. It was crazy when she considered how many times they had seen each other naked, but she no longer wanted him to see her undressed. It would feel like she had cheated on Roarke.

After she put on underwear and stockings, Mya took a black dress from the closet and grimaced at the thought of wearing it. The heat that enveloped the city would transform the frock to a furnace, but it was her only formal dress, so she had no alternative. She slid the simple silk sheath over her head while she shoved her feet into black pumps. When she hurried from the bedroom, she found Bobby in the hall, where he leaned against the wall. "Zip me?"

He grunted and set aside his drink as Mya turned around. Bobby lifted the zipper, and then put his hands on her hips. "There's something different about you."

"Huh?" Mya fought back a blush as she turned back to face him.

His eyes narrowed as they examined her. "You're different."

She rolled her eyes. "We don't have time for this. There's traffic—"

Bobby shook his head. "You look different."

Was it an afternoon of great sex or the knowledge she was in love that made her look so different? Mya shrugged unconsciously and tried to divert Bobby's attention from her. "Mr. Scarpeti won't like it if we're late."

He nodded. "Yeah, we should go." He eyed her critically. "Take your hair down."

"What?"

"You should wear your hair down."

"That style doesn't suit this dress."

His lip curled. "Mya, the fashion guru."

Her spine stiffened. "I prefer economy over fashion. It's something you could learn about."

Bobby glared at her. "I want you to wear your hair down. I said you had long hair, and I want you to show it off."

"Too bad. It's hotter than hell out there." Mya turned from him and scooped up her purse and car keys on the way to the door. "Coming?"

"Yeah." Bobby snatched the keys from her hand and strode from the apartment. He didn't seem to care if she kept up.

Rather than run after him, Mya walked at a sedate pace. When she got to the parking garage, she found him behind the wheel. He glowered at her when she opened the door. With a cool smile, she climbed into the SRX and slammed the door as he accelerated from the space. Mya shook her head at the way he drove and fastened her seatbelt without comment.

The ride to Cirque was laden with a tense silence that she felt no inclination to break. Once she opened her mouth, Mya knew the truth would fly out, and she didn't want to ruin Bobby's deal with Tony Scarpeti. Their breakup was imminent, but she didn't want it to be acrimonious. Not that she wanted to be friends with Bobby either.

Bobby left the SRX with a valet and took her arm. He wore a charming smile, and Mya tried to keep the frown off her face. Always the consummate actor, her Bobby. A small smile found its way through her lips. Not really her Bobby for much longer. Was she a terrible person to feel so relieved? No longer would she have to pander to his ego or give in to his wishes. She sighed quietly and received a warning look from him.

The maitre 'd greeted them with a sneer, but quickly humbled himself when Bobby gave the name Scarpeti. "Ah, yes. Mr. Scarpeti waits for you in the lounge."

They followed him into the small lounge where a handful of people waited. Mya saw a dark-haired man and woman at a table and assumed they were the Scarpetis. Instead, the maitre 'd led them to a lone man. He was in his forties, with thick black hair, intent dark eyes, and olive skin. He was on the chubby side, but still handsome.

"Bobby," she hissed at him.

"What?" he asked out of the corner of his mouth.

"Why did you bring me? This is obviously a business dinner, or he would have a date too."

Bobby shrugged and disengaged his hold on her to extend his hand to Mr. Scarpeti. "Hello, sir."

"Bobby." He spoke with the tiniest trace of an accent. Mr. Scarpeti shook his hand and flashed three shiny gold rings. Then he turned to smile at her. "You must be the fiancée."

Mya held out her hand. "Mya, Mr. Scarpeti."

He took her hand, pressing a kiss to the palm instead of shaking it. "Call me Tony. Did you want a drink, or shall we go to our table?"

Mya left Bobby to answer as she discreetly wiped her palm on the dress and followed them across the restaurant to a round table in a quiet alcove. She remained quiet as they discussed the movie and concentrated first on the menu, then on her food. She tried to hide her boredom, but a yawn escaped her.

"Look at us." Tony shook his head. "We're discussing business when we could be discussing pleasure." He winked at Mya.

She frowned at him and automatically pressed her back against the linen of the chair. "This is a business meeting, so please don't feel like you have to entertain me."

He frowned at Bobby before he regarded her intently. "It is just business for you?"

She shrugged. "What else would it be, sir? This is about Bobby's career, after all."

He stroked his chin and suddenly laughed. "Ah, I see." His mirth disappeared when he turned to eye Bobby. "You have not represented this arrangement honestly, Mr. Waller."

"I'm telling you, she'll do it." Sweat beaded Bobby's forehead.

Once more, Tony's eyes studied Mya. "I think not. There is nothing about the woman to suggest she is accustomed to these sorts of games."

Bobby shook his head. "What about Thomas?"

Mya's mouth fell open. "What does Roarke have to do with anything?"

Tony shook his head and laid aside his napkin. "I have had enough of this, and I think you will be busy explaining long into the night, Waller." He opened his wallet to peel off a few bills and tossed them on the table. He rose and nodded to both of them. "Good night."

Before Bobby could say anything, Scarpeti had walked away from the table. "Bastard!" He slammed his hand on the table and turned to glare at Mya. "This is your fault."

She bit back a retort as she pushed away from the table. Most of the Mandarin Quail remained on her plate. "We need to leave. Now!" She didn't look back to see if he followed as she marched from the restaurant. She stood on the curb near the valet and waited for Bobby to emerge.

He stopped beside her, obviously angry. Bobby took the stub from his pocket and tossed it to the valet. "The SRX."

The red-jacketed valet nodded and hurried to the lot. When he pulled up with the SRX a minute later, Bobby tore around to the driver's side. As the valet got out, Bobby pointed to a tiny scratch on the bumper. "Look what you've done to my car."

The young man shook his head. "No, sir. I didn't—"

"You incompetent moron! I'll have you fired for this." Bobby grabbed the lapels of his red jacket and shook him vigorously. "You're going to pay for that."

Heat filled Mya's cheeks as she hurried forward. She wrenched on Bobby's arm. "Stop it. You know that scratch was there before. You made it on the way home from the dealership."

The kid pulled himself free and hurried back to his kiosk on legs that trembled.

Bobby glared down at her. "Don't contradict me."

"Don't act like an ass in public. You're taking your anger out on that kid." She scowled at him before she walked around to the passenger side. Bobby had already climbed inside, and Mya's mouth dropped open when he locked her side. She glared at him, but refused to plead for entrance. She turned on her heel to reenter the restaurant, where a bank of payphones lined the wall.

By the time she emerged into the heat again for the taxi that stopped at the curb, Bobby and the SRX were gone. Mya almost directed the cab to take her somewhere besides their apartment, but she had nowhere to go at the moment. Besides, she wanted to toss Bobby's ring back at him.

Chapter Nineteen
Moving Out

ॐ

Bobby didn't arrive at the apartment for several hours after Mya got home. By the time he sauntered in, as if nothing had happened, she had moved her things to the guest room. She was curled up on the couch under a throw and wore the robe and slippers Roarke had given her. She could almost pretend she was back on his silk sheets again.

He stopped in the entryway when he saw her on the couch. "You're still up?"

She shrugged. "We need to talk."

"I'm tired." There was a petulant cast to his lips.

"You shouldn't have stayed out until three in the morning." Mya resisted the urge to ask where he had been, because she really didn't care anymore.

"I'm a grownup. I can do what I want." He tossed the car keys on the table with a thunk.

Mya shrugged again. "What was the dinner with Scarpeti about?"

"Never mind."

"Tell me."

Bobby strolled into the living room and propped his hip against the couch. "I told him you would be very nice to him if he gave me a role in his movie."

Her mouth dropped open. "You were trying to pimp me out?"

He shook his head. "Just furthering my career."

"At my expense!"

Bobby scowled at her. "You don't seem to mind trading your body for my benefit."

If he had been closer, Mya knew she would have slapped him. Instead, she curled her hands around the blanket. "I wouldn't have done it."

"Yeah, right." Bobby sneered at her. "I'm sure Scarpeti's gifts are even nicer than Thomas's. Your mercenary little heart would have gone pitter-patter for him."

"I'm not avaricious." Mya gained her feet. "And I'm not the one hiding four hundred thousand either."

He blanched. "So, Roarke told you about that?"

She shrugged. A tiny part of her had hoped he would deny the heated accusation, but she had known Roarke hadn't lied to her. "Where is it? I'm entitled to some of that."

"You didn't do shit for it."

"I put up with you, and I bartered my body for your success."

Bobby strode toward her and grabbed a handful of her hair. "It wasn't anything you didn't enjoy, now was it?"

A cold smile curved across her face. "Absolutely right. I've enjoyed every minute with Roarke. He's fabulous in bed."

Bobby's hand curled into a fist, but he slammed it against the couch. "I'm going to bed."

"We haven't finished here."

"Finish yourself, babe." He strode down the hall and slammed the bedroom door behind him.

"I should be good at that after having fucked you for four years," she screamed after him. Mya had the urge to follow and tell him that they were through, but her heart still pounded with fear. She had seen the rage in his eyes, and she knew he had almost hit her. She would let his temper cool before she confronted him when he got home from work tomorrow night.

* * * * *

Mya let herself into the apartment after work the next day. It was almost four, and she knew Bobby would be home within a couple of hours. That gave her plenty of time to get everything packed that she hadn't gotten to last night so she could be ready to leave. Not that she knew where she would go yet. The money in her purse wouldn't see her through more than a few days at a hotel, and she had already emptied the joint account she shared with Bobby. It seemed unlikely that she would see any of his hidden four hundred thousand dollars. She racked her brain for a solution as she walked down the hallway to the guest room.

She frowned as she passed the partially opened door to the master bedroom. She could hear voices and heavy breathing. Her heart stuttered as she slowly pushed open the door, somehow unsurprised by what she saw.

Bobby was in between the legs of a brassy blonde woman several years older than he was. Her large, round breasts jiggled as she thrust against his face. Moans came from her, punctuated with, "Fuck me, love."

Tears stung Mya's eyes at the casual betrayal she saw before her. It didn't matter that their relationship had died. How could he bring some woman into the bed they had shared together? Her eyes narrowed as the blonde tossed back her hair. Mya gasped when she recognized Roni Sherwood, Bobby's agent.

They jumped apart at the sound, and Bobby turned to face Mya. "You're home early." He sounded defensive, but there was a note of satisfaction in his voice.

Their movements had been stiff and obviously rehearsed. When she looked in his eyes, Mya realized the scene was a setup. She was supposed to walk in and catch them while they fucked. She felt sick. "How long?"

"Three years," Roni said with a giggle. "I'm the reason Bobby moved you here. We met in Seattle—"

"—she saw potential in me—"

" — and here you are." Roni shook her head. "How could you not know, Mya?"

She shrugged. "I was an idiot?" Mya turned her head to look at Bobby. "Why keep me around if you want to be with her?"

Bobby, stark naked, stood up. "I brought you along so you could support us while I acted. When I got the role in *Wilder Hearts*, I thought I could finally get rid of you."

"He's going to marry me." Roni held out her left hand to show off a large diamond.

Mya's nausea increased. Part of Bobby's advance had gone to that ring. No wonder Roni never talked about her fiancé. "So, why didn't you?"

"Thomas wanted you, so you were useful for a while longer."

His words hurt, but not as much as she would have expected them to if she had ever imagined he could say something so cruel. She was angrier at her own naïveté than Bobby's manipulation. "Is the money all gone?"

He nodded. "Most of it, anyway. We bought a condo, and I got Roni the ring. With planning the wedding and settling a few debts, there isn't much left."

Mya's grin was cold. "I hope it lasts awhile longer since I just cleaned out the last couple thousand in the checking account."

His expression darkened. "You bitch! I want half of that."

"Most of it came from my hard work."

He started toward her, but Roni's voice stopped him. "Let her have it, darling. You have fantastic prospects. We don't need two Gs. And what else does she have to keep her warm now that she won't have you?"

"You're right, babe." Bobby sneered at Mya. "Get out of my apartment."

Mya giggled, either because she was hysterical or giddy. "I had already planned to. I packed most of my stuff last night."

He frowned. "You're leaving me?"

She nodded. "Yep."

"Why?"

"It turns out Roarke is better at a lot of things than you are. Foremost, he knows how to love me."

Bobby's eyes widened. "You're in love with him?"

"Oh, yeah. And he's in love with me." Mya resisted the urge to cross her fingers. Her pinkie brushed against the tiny diamond on her finger, reminding her of one more thing she wanted to do. She wrenched the ring off her finger and flung it at Bobby. Her lips twisted into a smile when it nailed him on the cheek. "Maybe you can return that to the crackerjack box where you found it." Then, head held high, she marched from the room to gather her things.

In the guest room, Mya locked the door and threw the rest of her stuff into a case. Before she left, she picked up the phone to call Carly. When her sister answered, she blurted out, "I'm leaving him."

"Finally." Carly seemed unsurprised. "Where are you going?"

"I don't know. A hotel, I guess." Mya bit her lip because she knew how expensive apartments—even a shithole like the one she had shared with Bobby for eighteen months—could be. "I don't know where I'll go after that. Wanna move to L.A.?" she asked, half-hopeful that her sister would agree.

"Sorry. I'm moving in with Troy."

"Wow! Dad must be blowing a gasket." Frank hadn't accepted it well when she moved in with Bobby, not even when they got engaged. Mya could only imagine his reaction to his baby's plans to move in with an older man.

"He likes Troy, but he's not thrilled." Carly sighed. "Anyway, where will you go? Are you coming home?"

"I can't yet."

"Why not?"

"I'm in love with Roarke."

"I know," Carly said easily. "It was all over your faces."

"His too?"

"Uh huh."

Mya bit her lip, not so certain. "I don't know."

"Trust me."

"Well…" She trailed off so she wouldn't voice her doubts. She hadn't thought beyond the end of things with Bobby and had no idea how she would confess her feelings for Roarke. She chuckled suddenly.

"What? What's so funny?"

"I just realized I have a place to stay." If she was careful, he would never know she was there. Roarke had said he never used the place—only for their meetings. "You have my cell number, right?"

"Somewhere. Why?"

"The place I'm going doesn't have a phone." All it had was a bed and bathroom. When she and Roarke got together, that was all they needed.

Chapter Twenty
The Balcony

ഉ

Mya had carefully hidden her things in the guest room because she figured Roarke wouldn't venture in there. She had risked the addition of a few items to the cupboards and fridge and hoped her luck would hold. When Friday arrived, she was satisfied she had removed all traces of her occupation. She had even washed the silk sheets that morning, and then returned them to the bed when she got back to the apartment after work. She was sprawled across them when she heard Roarke's key turn in the lock shortly before two-thirty. She held her breath as she heard his tread on the carpets. To her relief, he bypassed the kitchen and living room to enter the bedroom.

Roarke froze when he opened the door to find Mya draped across the bed. The silver of the sheets lent her skin a pearly sheen, and her hair, spread out across the pillows, contrasted sharply with the silver. "Uh…hi."

She smiled up at him. "Hi." Mya trailed a finger down her bare hip.

"You're early."

She shrugged. "I got off early."

He entered the room and stopped before the bed. She was gorgeous as she lay before him with one knee curled up to shyly obscure the triangle between her thighs. When she licked her lips, he groaned. "So—"

"Yeah?"

Roarke shook his head, unable to think when she was spread so temptingly before him. What had he planned for today? He couldn't remember now. His eyes widened when she stood up from the bed, trailed fingers through her hair, and made her breasts jut up.

Mya rolled her hips as she walked over to him and ran her hands down the smooth cotton of his short-sleeved white polo. She stopped to rub a nipple and press herself against him. "You're wearing too many clothes."

He cleared his throat, thrown off-kilter by this side of Mya. "You think?"

She nodded.

"Okay." To Roarke's surprise, her busy hands moved across his body to pull and push at his clothes until she had removed his shirt and unfastened his pants. "Mya." He tried to push her hands away as they moved to his waistband.

"Surely you don't have a problem with this?" She looked up at him through the veil of her lashes. "You aren't old-fashioned, are you, Roarke?"

He shook his head as he swallowed audibly. His hands dropped to his sides, and Mya pushed his trousers down. She paused to allow him to kick off his shoes and have him step out of the pants. Navy briefs quickly followed them.

She was on her knees before him and looked up at him with an uncertain expression. An impish grin teased Mya's lips as she tossed his slacks and underwear into the corner near his shirt. She touched the head of his cock with the tip of her tongue to catch a dewy drop of his arousal.

Roarke groaned when Mya's mouth slid down around him. She didn't take him in completely, but she tortured him with quick flicks of her tongue and intermittently applied suction. He arched forward and pushed himself deeper inside the moist recesses of her mouth as she swirled her tongue around his cock. He paused to see if he had gone too deep. He looked down and saw she was a bit surprised, but didn't seem to mind. "Are you okay?"

Mya couldn't speak or nod, so she used her thumb and forefinger to form an OK sign. She continued her ministrations.

She worked her tongue around the circumference of his cock as she sucked rhythmically. When she felt his body start to quiver, Mya pulled her mouth away.

He groaned, and the lines of his face contorted into a grimace. "Why did you stop?"

A wicked grin curved her mouth. "I want to be with you when you come."

Roarke bit back a sigh. It was no less than he deserved since he had done the same thing to her last time. He pulled Mya into his arms and nestled his face at the bend of her neck and shoulder where he nibbled softly. She pressed closer and pushed her nipples into the light dusting of hair on his chest. He heard her moan and moved his head to swallow the sound with his lips on hers.

He kissed her until she went limp in his arms, and then pushed her back onto the bed. Once again, Roarke knelt between her parted thighs to kiss the damp tangle of reddish-gold curls that hid her pussy. Mya shuddered and twitched, but pushed him away when he would have continued. "What's wrong?"

"I had something else in mind." She stood up and took his hand to lead him outside to the balcony.

Roarke resisted as they got to the sliding glass door. "What are you thinking?"

"It's such a nice day. I just want to go outside." She turned to bat her lashes at him as she had seen her sister do a hundred times. "Please, can't we *come* outside?" She licked her lips.

Who could see them so high up? Would anyone care if they did see a couple as they made love in the middle of the afternoon? Roarke's body tightened as he realized the thought of an audience didn't repulse him. He didn't drag his feet as he followed her out onto the patio. He winced as the soles of his feet touched the hot cement. There was a moment of vertigo as he realized he stood on a balcony fourteen floors up, stark naked. When it passed, his gaze fastened on Mya, surrounded by a halo of bright sunlight that kissed every inch of her. Not a bad idea, he decided, with a twitch of his lips.

His eyes widened as he saw the chaise lounge that hadn't been there before. "Did you — ?"

"I picked it up after work." *Yesterday*, Mya added silently. She lay down on the floral-print cushion and held out her arms.

Roarke gingerly lowered himself on top, careful not to crush her. He balanced his weight on his arms. He grunted when she pulled him down to rest on top of her. The tip of his cock pressed against her moist pussy, and she wriggled her hips. "Mya," he said in a warning tone.

She giggled, not at all repentant. Mya lifted a breast to offer him a taste. She moaned as he dipped his head to accept her invitation. As he suckled on the turgid peak, Mya shifted slightly until they were aligned. She thrust her hips upward to take his cock inside her.

Roarke's eyes popped open, and his mouth fell away from her nipple. "You can't be ready." However, her body confirmed she was, and he thrust his cock deeper into her pussy.

"I think I could always be ready for you," Mya whispered as she arched her neck to press her lips to his. She tried to maintain control of her emotions as Roarke thrust in and out of her, which caused the lounger to groan in protest. When sweat beaded her forehead — not from the sun, but from the willpower it took to hold off her orgasm — Mya pushed him away.

"What the hell?"

She laughed at his stunned expression. "So cranky." Mya grasped his cock in her hand.

"Why are you torturing me? Haven't you made up for Tuesday yet?"

She shook her head. "I want to try something."

He groaned and wondered if he was too old to keep up with Mya. His climax was perilously close, and she seemed barely affected. Roarke's eyes narrowed as he caught sight of the perspiration on her face and the way her chest heaved with each breath. Or maybe she was just a great actress? "What did you have in mind?"

She couldn't find the words to tell him what she had in mind, so Mya took his hand to lead him to the wrought iron railing. She turned to look down at the city. "Stand behind me."

His eyebrows rose when he realized what she wanted. "Are you sure?"

Mya nodded.

"Well…" They could always return to the bedroom if she didn't enjoy the position. With a shrug, Roarke stood behind her and lifted her hips as he thrust his forward. Once he had her positioned, he released her slowly until she had taken all of his cock. He looked over her shoulder and saw the way she gripped the railing with a white-knuckle grasp. To his surprise, she wrapped her legs loosely around his thighs. Her toes pressed into his buttocks. "Do you do yoga?" he joked.

"Aerobics that require a lot of stretching." Mya lifted her pussy up his cock, and then sank onto it again. "Move, Roarke."

He obeyed the command in her tone and thrust into her as deeply as he could.

"Faster."

"You sure are bossy," he teased, but complied.

Mya groaned as she felt his cock push against the walls of her pussy and rub near the clit with each thrust. She had never felt anything like it. Eagerly, she returned his thrusts and ground her pussy against him in small circles. It was difficult to maintain her hold on the railing and, at some point, his arms wrapped around her stomach to hold her against him, while she braced her forearms on the railing. As an orgasm tore through her, Mya gasped, too drained to cry out or speak. Her pussy continued to convulse around his cock, and Roarke thrust into her repeatedly.

He bit his lip and hoped the small dart of pain would help him prolong the moment. Roarke wanted to make her come repeatedly, until she was about to pass out, but when her pussy tightened around his cock for the second time, he gave in to his body's demand and released wave after wave of satisfaction into her.

It was only when the pleasure passed that he realized his legs and arms trembled, and she shook with mingled exhaustion and pleasure. With a gentle movement, he disengaged their bodies and lowered her to the cement. Once she was steady, he put his arm around her waist, and they stumbled into the bedroom to fall across the bed.

With a small reserve of energy, he was able to bury his hand in her hair. "Where did you get the idea for that?"

She shrugged. "I was staring down at the city, and it just came to me."

He frowned. "When?"

Mya struggled not to blush as her mind worked furiously. "Uh, the last time I was here. That's when I got the idea."

"That long ago?"

She nodded quickly. "Now that we can, I decided what the hell."

He chuckled. "If you keep throwing caution to the wind, you'll be the death of me. I think I'm too old for the sexual Olympics."

Mya snuggled closer. "You were in fine form, sir. I don't think you're ready for the senior events yet."

He put his arm around her and pulled her even closer. A fine trace of sweat dotted her skin and heat poured off her. Her back was already red. "You're going to have a sunburn."

"Small price to pay," she said around a yawn.

"You should take a bath to get some of the heat out."

Mya laid her head on his chest. "I don't think I'll lose any heat if we get into a bath together."

He stroked her hair as a pang hit his stomach. Time grew short, and moments like these would soon be only a memory he could use to torture himself. He wondered if Bobby had told her yet. "Have you and Bobby talked about the movie?"

She shook her head. "Not lately."

He struggled to concentrate as her hand moved across his stomach and slid lower to flirt with his semi-hard shaft. "Lenny told me yesterday that it's nearly in the can. Two or three more scenes at most."

Mya's hand froze, and she struggled to remember how to breathe. "Really?"

"Yeah. Apparently they've made a lot of progress in the last three weeks." Damn his brother. He was always a screw-up—even when he did something right for a change.

"I see." Her lips wobbled, and she was glad she had her face pressed against his chest. "When will it be done?"

"Probably by Friday. The cast has agreed to work through the weekend if necessary, so Monday at the latest."

Mya slowly lifted her head and tried to read his expression. "Our deal is near the end?"

He nodded and tried to keep his expression bland. "You'll soon be free of me." He silently pleaded for her to protest or declare she never wanted it to end.

His light-hearted tone cut through Mya's heart, and she blinked back tears. "Yes. This is probably our last meeting."

He cleared his throat. "Yeah."

She pulled away from him. "I think I'll take that bath now."

By the set of her shoulders, he could tell she wasn't in the mood for him to join her. "After I take a shower, I should be going. I have plans..." To sit home alone and wallow in despair.

Mya put a hand on his arm. "Stay with me tonight."

"Here?"

She nodded. "It's our last night together." He obviously didn't want to continue their liaison. She drew in a ragged breath to hold back a sob. While it humbled her pride to ask, she didn't want to miss her last chance to hold him.

He swallowed back the uncomfortable lump of moisture in his throat. "Okay. What about Bobby?"

Mya shrugged. "He can live without me tonight."

There was sadness in her eyes that he wanted to ask about, but Roarke knew he was the last person she would want to confide any relationship problems to. He had ruined his chance to ever be more than her lover when he had forced her into this game. Lucky for her, it almost over. She would be able to move on to her role as Bobby's wife and put the ordeal behind her. Unlike Roarke, she wouldn't be haunted with what-ifs for the rest of her life.

Chapter Twenty One
Mya's Fantasy

ဆာ

The sting of the sunburn woke Mya sometime late in the night. She lifted her head from Roarke's shoulder and rolled out of bed. She looked back to make sure she hadn't disturbed him as she padded into the bathroom.

She opened the shower stall and turned on the water as cold as she could stand it. Mya wasn't burdened with clothes, so she stepped directly under the spray after she adjusted the head to make it a softer stream. She gasped as the icy water pelted her, but it felt too good against her sunburn to move away from.

She leaned against the shower stall and let the water fall over her naked back. Mya felt tears prick the back of her eyes and tried to swallow them back. She didn't want to turn into a blubbering mess in Roarke's presence. The only thing worse than to lose him would be to have him to stay because he pitied her.

Mya lifted her head when she heard the door slide open. Roarke stepped in with her and shivered at the cold water. She hoped he would dismiss the tears on her cheeks as water droplets. "I didn't mean to wake you."

He didn't speak. Instead, he lifted and pushed her against the wall.

"Roarke, what are you—" Mya's eyes widened as he entered her with one quick thrust. Her pussy was ready for him and welcomed him eagerly. She melted against him and clutched his shoulders.

He grunted and thrust into her as he moved one hand to play with her clit. He wore a grim expression, as if determined to force an orgasm from her.

Mya couldn't believe the feelings that coursed through her. She felt out of control and primitive. She wanted to completely lose her conscious self in his flesh, and she concentrated on her orgasm, consumed solely with her needs. She dug her nails into his back and ground her hips against his, equally determined to come.

She leaned forward and pushed her pussy down hard on his cock. His hand was trapped between their bodies. Her entire body convulsed as an orgasm washed over her. She clenched around his cock and heard him moan, but he didn't come.

When Mya could breathe again, she relaxed against him and laid her head on his shoulder. "That was wonderful."

"Be quiet."

Her eyes widened at the command, and Mya frowned when he turned off the shower and stepped out. "What's—"

He frowned at her, but didn't answer.

She gasped when he pressed her against the bathroom wall and entered her again. She could only cling helplessly to him and match him thrust for thrust as he slammed into her until he elicited another orgasm. He continued to thrust. "Please, no more," she whimpered. "I'm too tired."

Roarke ignored her whispered words and lifted her higher.

She pushed against his chest. "I want to stop now."

He grasped her wrists and pinned them to the wall on either side of her head. The only thing keeping her in place was his lower body as he thrust in and out of her. There was a feral gleam in his eyes when he threw his head back and cried out. She felt him fill her, and she came again, although she had been certain she was too exhausted.

As their trembling subsided, he released her wrists and lowered her to the floor. He put his arms around her and held her close to his pounding heart. He sounded out of breath when he asked, "Did I hurt you?"

She hesitated. Her wrists stung from his tight hold, and her pussy felt sore and achy. Blotting out those tiny pains was the flush of satisfaction that swept across her body. "No." She pressed her face against his chest. "I liked it." She felt him chuckle.

"It looks like Carly was right."

Mya's head whipped up so quickly her neck popped. "What?"

He pushed hair off her face and smiled down at her. "Carly told me you had a particular fantasy. I waited for the right moment—"

"She told you about that? When?"

He nodded. "She called me yesterday. After complaining about how difficult it was to get through to my office, she told me about your fantasy. "

She froze. "What else did she tell you?"

"Nothing except this fantasy." He grinned. "Why? Is there more?"

"I can't believe she told you about that!" She felt anger welling up inside, but it was mixed with gratitude and relief—a peculiar combination. She owed Carly gratitude because Mya knew she wouldn't ever have had the courage to tell Roarke she wanted him to just take her without asking her first. She was relieved her sister hadn't said anything about where she was staying.

He faltered. "I'm sorry if you wanted it to stay just a fantasy. It started out as role-playing, but I lost control."

Mya touched his face. "So did I. I'm glad she told you."

He looked relieved. "You enjoyed it?"

Mya giggled. "Three times. Even when I was sure I couldn't take anymore."

"I know the feeling." He turned around to show her his back. "I thought you had dug into my spine a couple of times—not that I didn't enjoy it."

Mya gasped at the red marks on his back and blushed. She was pleased to have marked him. He would have a reminder of her for at least a few days. It would have to be enough.

Chapter Twenty Two
Bobby Pays a Visit

&

Saturday morning, Mya had a visitor. When the doorbell rang, she froze. No one knew she was here except Carly. Who could it be? She walked quietly to the door and looked out the peephole to see an elegantly attired blonde that stood on the other side of the door. She wasn't familiar. Maybe a neighbor?

"Miss?" she called.

Mya's heart stuttered, and, for one crazy moment, she wondered if the woman could see her through the door.

"Are you home? The security screener said she thought you were here."

Mya reluctantly opened the door. "Sorry. I was in the back room."

The blonde nodded and extended a perfectly manicured hand tipped with bright pink nails. "I'm Katie Winslow, Mr. Thomas's real estate agent."

"Oh?"

"I came by to see if I could arrange a visit. I have a couple dying to view the place." When Katie laughed, she flashed straight, white teeth. "I know Mr. Thomas temporarily took it off the market, but they really want something around this neighborhood. They've seen the pictures, and they love it."

Mya stood aside. "Come in, please."

"No time. Sorry." Her blonde hair never moved an inch when Katie shook her head. "Would Monday work for you—assuming Mr. Thomas is willing?"

"I'll be gone by then." Mya swallowed the lump in her throat. "I'm going home later today."

Katie's dazzling green eyes sparkled. "Excellent. So your lease is only temporary?"

"Yes."

"Thank you. I'll contact Mr. Thomas."

"Okay."

"Have a nice day." With a sunny smile that was nearly as bright as the yellow of her shorts suit, Katie hurried off down the hall.

Mya closed the door behind her and had made it halfway to the guest room before she realized she had to stop the realtor from calling Roarke today. She sprinted across the room and into the hallway to arrive at the elevator just in time for the doors to close in her face. She leaned her head against the cool metal and accepted she wouldn't be able to catch up with Katie Winslow in time.

She trudged back to the apartment with her shoulders slumped. She had to be out within the next couple of hours. Thankfully, most of her things were still in cases. She had only to finish up with her things and arrange for transport to the airport. She hoped she could move up her flight, or she would have a four or five-hour wait at LAX.

* * * * *

An hour later, Mya had nearly finished packing her bags when the doorbell rang again. Her stomach jumped with nerves as she anticipated an angry Roarke on the other side. Maybe just a puzzled one. The best she could hope for was the realtor had forgotten something.

She walked to the door and looked through the peephole. Her mouth dropped open, and she fumbled with the lock to open the door a couple of inches. "How did you know where to find me?"

Bobby shrugged. "I followed you the first time you met with Thomas. I took a wild guess that you'd be here."

She frowned at him. "Shouldn't you be on the set?"

"We finished early this morning." His mouth twisted. "Going to invite me in, or does your sugar daddy not allow visitors?"

"I don't want you in here." Mya started to close the door.

Bobby pushed against the wood and gained an inch at a time until he had forced his way inside. He took the door from her grasp and slammed it. "You bitch!"

Her eyes widened. "What?"

"What did you tell Scarpeti?"

She shook her head. "I don't know what you're babbling about. Now get out of here before I call the police."

His smile was cold. "You can't 'cause there's no phone here."

"I have my cell phone."

"I deactivated your service a couple of days after you left me."

"You told me to leave." Mya pushed the hair out of her eyes and wondered why she had bothered to counter his statement. It wasn't as if she hadn't wanted to leave him. "Whatever. Just go."

He grabbed her upper arms in a tight grip. "What did you tell that bastard?"

"Nothing." Mya tried to pull away, alarmed by the anger that emanated from him.

"Liar." He shook her. "You musta told him something. He said he didn't like how I treated you, and he'd heard shit about me."

"You didn't get the part?"

"No."

Mya wrenched her shoulders free. "I've only met him once. He figured out what your game is, Bobby. You can't blame your failure on me. I won't let you anymore."

Bobby slapped her. "I didn't fail," he screamed at her. "This is your fault. You're going to fix it."

"I can't. I had nothing to do with it." Mya cradled her stinging cheek. She backed away when Bobby lunged at her. "I'll scream this place down."

"These condos have thick walls." He smirked at her. "Roni and I viewed an empty one in this building a couple of weeks ago. The realtor was quick to point out the level of privacy. We really considered it, but in the end, I decided I couldn't live in the same building as you and your lover."

Mya whimpered as she tried to put more distance between them. When her back hit the wall, she cried out. Bobby lunged forward and pressed his face into hers. "Let me go."

"You have to fix things. I need that role."

"I didn't do anything."

"Stop lying." Bobby slapped her again. "I'm not leaving until you undo whatever petty thing you've done." He pinched her arm. "And you may not leave at all unless you get this sorted out. I've got hours."

"My parents are expecting me. Carly knows where I am."

"Nice bluff, but I know you wouldn't go back to that hellhole with loverboy here in L.A., waiting in the wings." Bobby pulled a cell phone from his pocket and punched in a series of numbers with so much force the phone warbled. "Talk to Scarpeti." He thrust the phone at her.

She took it reluctantly. Nothing she could say would change the director's mind. Her only hope was to dial Roarke's number instead. She whimpered when Bobby pressed his cheek against hers so he could hear the conversation, making it that much more difficult to reach Roarke.

* * * * *

Roarke had just gotten out of the pool when he heard the phone in the house ring. He dripped water behind him when he padded into the kitchen to lift the receiver of the nearest extension. "Hello?"

"Mr. Thomas, this is Katie Winslow."

"Hi, Katie."

"I wondered if I could show a couple around the condo on Monday?"

He forced back a twinge of regret. It was time to put it back on the market. He had no further use for the place, and the memories would be too bittersweet to revel in. "Yeah, that's fine."

"Excellent. Can you be there at one?"

"You need me present?"

"I think this couple will make an offer on the spot. It will facilitate the process if you're there. I like to have someone around anyway, but the current tenant said she would be gone by Monday."

Roarke frowned. "Current tenant?"

"Yes. She said she was going home today, and the rental term was ending."

"What did she look like?"

There was a pause before she answered, and she sounded uncertain. "She had long red hair. Quite pretty. Young—"

"Mya." Roarke's mouth moved, but no sound emerged. "She was going home? Did she say where?" To Bobby's or back to Washington?

"No, Mr. Thomas. Just that she would be gone later today."

"I have to go."

"What about Monday?"

"I'll call you back." Roarke dropped the phone back onto the cradle before he hurried upstairs to slide his feet into sandals and throw on a t-shirt. He didn't even bother to change out of his swim trunks before he rushed from the house and slid onto the leather seat of the Lotus. He didn't notice the unpleasant dampness from his shorts as he sped through the afternoon traffic. He focused on his arrival at the condo before Mya left for good. He had to know why she had stayed there, and why she wanted to go home. Most of all, he had to know if they had a chance.

When he screeched to a stop at the curb in front of the building, Roarke yanked the keys from the switch and slid from the car. He didn't remember to engage the alarm as he ran into the building.

"Mr. Thomas." The security attendant smiled at him.

He nodded at the young lady. "Do you know if the tenant in my apartment has left yet?"

She shook her head. "Not that I know of. Her visitor hasn't come down either."

"Visitor?"

Her smile turned feral. "Sexy guy with long blond hair and a ripped body."

"Bobby," Roarke snarled as he hurried to the elevator. Why was he here? Had he come to plead with Mya to take him back? Had Roarke wrongly assumed Mya had left the jerk?

The elevator seemed to creep up the floors, and Roarke barely resisted the impulse to continuously press the 14 button. When the doors finally opened, he sprinted down the hall to his apartment and fumbled with the key as he ran.

To his surprise, he found the door unlocked. His anger and confusion started to fade, as he grew concerned. Roarke pushed opened the door and entered the living room. He froze, and his eyes widened at what he saw.

Mya lay on the floor. She appeared to be unconscious. Blood covered her face, and her hair was sticky with crimson splashes. Bobby paced around her while he sobbed into his cell phone and babbled about Mya's scheme to ruin him, then begged the other person to stay with him anyway.

A red haze passed over Roarke's eyes, and he threw himself at Bobby. He knocked the phone from his hand as they both fell onto the carpet, inches from Mya. He grabbed a handful of Bobby's tank top to lift him. "What did you do to her?"

Bobby's eyes darted around. "Nothing. I found her like this."

Roarke's fist slammed into his face. "I should kill you."

Tears spilled from Bobby's blue eyes. He pressed a hand to his the cut on his mouth in an attempt to staunch the flow of blood. "Don't hurt me," he mumbled through his hand and swollen lip. "I have an audition Monday."

Roarke fumbled for the fallen phone and grasped the edge of it to pull it closer. He heard a frantic voice on the other end of the line and hung up on her. His hands shook as he dialed 9-1-1.

"What are you doing, man?" There was an edge of panic to Bobby's voice.

"Calling an ambulance and the cops."

He shook his head at Roarke. "No, please don't. They'll put me in jail."

Roarke hit him again. "You're lucky I'm letting them deal with it." As Bobby sagged against the carpet, the operator picked up. "I need an ambulance at 1427 Flower de Boliva. My girlfriend has been assaulted."

Once he had hung up Bobby's phone, Roarke knelt by Mya and felt her neck. A sob ripped past his throat when he found a strong pulse. "Mya, baby, open your eyes."

She blinked up at him. "Roarke?"

He pulled off his t-shirt to gently wipe the blood from her forehead and eyes. "What did he do to you?"

"Hit me." She felt weak and half-wondered if he was actually there. Her hand trembled as she lifted it to touch his sable hair. "You're here?"

"Yeah. Katie Winslow called me." A shaky smile split his face. "She inadvertently let it slip that I had a tenant."

Mya's eyes closed as dread swept through her. "I'll leave. I have a flight—"

He touched his finger to her lips as he heard sirens. "We'll talk later. Right now you need a doctor."

Within minutes, someone pounded at the door, and Roarke reluctantly left Mya to let the two firefighters in. "Where's the ambulance?"

One of the firefighters said, "They'll be here soon. We all answer calls."

"Oh, yeah."

Thirty seconds after their arrival, two EMTs entered through the opened door. Two cops, who insisted Roarke speak to them rather than stay with Mya, quickly followed them. He gave a brief statement, but broke away from them as he saw one of the EMTs head for the door. "What's going on?"

"We're going to take her to the hospital for x-rays. You can ride along if you'd like."

One of the cops came up behind Roarke. "Have you checked out the other guy?"

"Yeah. He's groggy, but there's no need for him to go to the hospital."

"It's okay to arrest him?"

"Knock yourself out." He hurried from the apartment before they could ask any more questions.

Roarke started to go to Mya, but the officer put up a hand. "We'll need a formal statement—"

"Tomorrow," Roarke said brusquely. "I'm going to the hospital with her right now."

The cop sighed. "First thing tomorrow, right?"

"Yes, sir." Roarke hurried to Mya and the other EMT. "How is she?"

"She'll be okay. Maybe a broken cheekbone though."

Roarke's rage bubbled up once more as he glared at Bobby. A surge or rage filled him, and he wished he had done worse than a couple of punches. "Will she need to stay in the hospital?"

"I doubt it."

The other EMT arrived with a stretcher, and they carefully loaded Mya onto it. She opened her eyes and reached for Roarke as they pushed her across the carpet. "Don't leave me."

He took her hand. "I won't." Not ever, he swore silently.

Chapter Twenty Three

The Game Ends

Roarke ignored Mya's protests and carried her into his house from the car. He lowered her onto the leather sofa and winced once again at the white bandages on her forehead and across her cheek. Both covered stitches, but Bobby hadn't broken any bones. "Do you want more pillows?"

She was propped against two of the throw pillows on the couch. "Less, please." After he removed one, she touched his hand. "I haven't had a chance to say thank you."

"You don't have to."

She yawned and tried to fight off the effects of the pain medication for a while longer. "I do. You rescued me." A small smile formed across her lips, which made her wince as the abraded spot at the corner of her mouth stung with the movement. "And you haven't yet demanded an explanation for why I was squatting in your apartment."

Roarke grinned at her. "Squatting? What a charming phrase."

Her eyes turned serious. "I should have asked you, but I was afraid you'd say no. I didn't have anywhere else to go."

"We can do this later."

"No. I need to tell you now." Her forehead wrinkled. "Did you call my family for me?"

"You only asked four times." He squeezed her hand. "Yes. I told them you would call tomorrow."

She bit her lip and winced as her teeth raked across the split area. "I hope I can get my flight changed."

"You're in no shape to leave yet." He let go of her hand and moved to the loveseat. "If you must go, at least wait a few days."

She swallowed back tears, because she knew if she started to cry she wouldn't be able to stop. "I have to go."

"Why?"

"My reason for being here is gone." She dropped her head. "It probably never existed."

He frowned. "You must have a life here outside of the one you shared with Bobby."

"Not really. He didn't like me to make friends." She grimaced. "Oh, he always found something wrong with anyone I introduced him to, but I knew he was just too insecure for me to have friends that weren't part of his life."

"Your job?"

She shrugged and felt a sharp pain shoot down her spine. "I can do that anywhere. I think I want to go back to school. I never got a chance to go to college because I was supporting Bobby's career."

"Go to UCLA."

A sharp laugh escaped her lips. "I can't afford that."

He raked a hand through his already mussed hair. "I'll pay for your tuition."

Mya studied him intently. "Why would you do that?"

He slid his eyes from her piercing gaze. "It's the least I can do after ruining your life."

"You didn't ruin anything. You freed me from my own stupidity."

Roarke's eyes widened, and he met her gaze once more. "What?"

"I would have stayed with Bobby, forcing myself to ignore his faults, because I thought I loved him." She bowed her head so that her hair covered her face. "It wasn't until I met you that I realized what love really is."

His throat grew tight, and Roarke's voice emerged as a squeak. "Huh?"

She trembled with vulnerability. Once she said it, she couldn't take back the words. "You never meant for me to, but I fell in love with you." A rueful grin tugged at her mouth, but she forced it away because she didn't want the flash of pain that accompanied it. "How could I not when you so enthusiastically set about seducing me?"

"Do you mean that?" His heart pounded in his chest, and Roarke struggled to breathe.

"Yes."

He shook his head. "You can't know for sure. We know so little about each other."

Mya lifted her head. "We know so much about each other," she corrected. "The rest will come in time. I know I love you."

"How can you be so certain?"

"I've never felt this way before. My heart races when I'm with you, and I think about you all the time when I'm not. I can't wait to see you—"

"—and hate leaving you when our time ends," he said.

Her eyes widened, and she held her breath. Did his words mean he felt the same? "How do you feel about me?"

Roarke stood up. He came closer and knelt on the floor beside the sofa so he could put his arms around her. He didn't squeeze her into a hug because of the bruised ribs, but he pressed a soft kiss to her mouth. "I love you."

She threw her arms around him, and then stiffened at the pain that shot through her. "How long have you loved me?"

"I'm not a romantic fool—"

Mya snorted.

He gave her a repressive look before continuing. "But I think I loved you the moment I laid eyes on you. I didn't admit that romantic notion to myself, at first. It took me a while to realize that it wasn't just lust, and by then I couldn't live without you." He frowned. "When did you realize you loved me?"

"The first time we made love. You were so gentle, and you cared so much about pleasing me. I think I recognized your love, and it forced me to acknowledge my own. I just didn't realize it at first." She touched his face and smoothed her finger across his mustache. "I was terrified."

"Why?" He shook his head. "Dumb question. You were engaged to Bobby—"

"Mostly it was because I didn't know how you would react. Obviously falling in love wasn't part of your game." Mya's frowned at him. "Exactly how long have you been playing this stupid game anyway?"

Roarke held up one finger. "Just with you."

Her mouth fell open, then closed with a snap. "But you seemed to know exactly what you were doing." She glared at him. "Like you'd done it many times before."

He laughed. "I got the inspiration from a screenplay on my desk. The playboy seduces a naïve innocent. He ends up falling for her. Hard."

Mya didn't know whether to laugh or hit him. "You started all this because of a script?"

He nodded.

She shook her head. "What if the author had never written it?"

His stomach clenched at the thought, but he tried to smile. "I still would have stolen you from Bobby."

She smoothed a hand through his hair. "You didn't steal anything, Roarke. You didn't sneak your way into my heart or bed through seduction or coercion. What I gave to you was given freely."

"What's that?"

"My heart."

He closed his eyes and leaned his forehead against hers, careful to avoid the bandage. "Will you stay here in L.A.?"

"Do you want me to move in with you?"

Roarke shook his head, and then nodded. "Yes, but I want you to marry me too."

"Really?" Her eyes sparkled. It was more than she had dared to hope. Mya had vaguely thought he might keep her around as his mistress, but she had never expected a proposal. "I'll probably say yes."

His eyes darkened. "Probably?"

She grinned at him. "As long as my family likes you. They hated Bobby, so they must be excellent judges of character." She giggled at his pained expression and brushed her lips against his. "My sister likes you. That's good enough for me."

"Is that a yes?"

"Yes."

Epilogue
Happily Ever After

ඦ

Several months later, Mya entered Roarke's home office to find him deeply engrossed in a dog-eared script. She plopped her robe-covered fanny onto the corner of his desk. "Whatcha doing?" She twisted the gold bands on her finger absently. It was still difficult at times to believe she was his wife. Some days, she still couldn't believe she had married him a little over a month ago. The new definitely hadn't worn off.

He lifted *Playing His Game* to show her the title. "Debating about whether to option this. I don't want my secret weapon to leak out."

"I think you should. It could be a very romantic movie."

He frowned. "The ending is unrealistic."

Mya nodded sympathetically as she scooted her bottom to move closer to him. "Who would believe something like that could have a happy ending?"

Roarke dropped the script onto the desk and slid her in front of him to wrap his arms around her waist. "You don't think anyone would believe that?"

"Nah. You should probably ask the writer to change the ending."

"It is for Hollywood. People are a sucker for love stories with a happy ending."

Mya giggled as he moved his hand from her waist to venture under the white silk robe she wore. She could tell the exact instant when he realized she wore nothing under it by the way his eyes widened and his breath became ragged. Her pussy drenched his fingers as they dipped inside her. "You should leave it as it is. I know I'm a sucker for a happy ending."

Also by Kit Tunstall

෨

A Christmas Phantasie

A Matter of Honor

Ablaze

Beloved Forever

Blood Lines 1: Blood Oath

Blood Lines 2: Blood Challenge

Blood Lines 3: Blood Bond

Blood Lines 4: Blood Price

By Invitation Only

Dark Dreams

Eye of Destiny

Heart of Midnight

Lions and Tigers and Bears *(Anthology)*

Pawn

Phantasie

About the Author

જી

Kit Tunstall lives in Idaho with her husband, son, and dog-children. She started reading at the age of three and hasn't stopped since. Love of the written word, and a smart marriage to a supportive man, led her to a full-time career in writing. Romances have always intrigued her, and erotic romance is a natural extension because it more completely explores the emotions between the hero and heroine. That, and it sure is fun to write.

Kit welcomes comments from readers. You can find her website and email address on her author bio page at www.ellorascave.com.

Why an electronic book?

We live in the Information Age—an exciting time in the history of human civilization, in which technology rules supreme and continues to progress in leaps and bounds every minute of every day. For a multitude of reasons, more and more avid literary fans are opting to purchase e-books instead of paper books. The question from those not yet initiated into the world of electronic reading is simply: *Why?*

1. ***Price.*** An electronic title at Ellora's Cave Publishing and Cerridwen Press runs anywhere from 40% to 75% less than the cover price of the exact same title in paperback format. Why? Basic mathematics and cost. It is less expensive to publish an e-book (no paper and printing, no warehousing and shipping) than it is to publish a paperback, so the savings are passed along to the consumer.

2. ***Space.*** Running out of room in your house for your books? That is one worry you will never have with electronic books. For a low one-time cost, you can purchase a handheld device specifically designed for e-reading. Many e-readers have large, convenient screens for viewing. Better yet, hundreds of titles can be stored within your new library—on a single microchip. There are a variety of e-readers from different manufacturers. You can also read e-books on your PC or laptop computer. (Please note that Ellora's

Cave does not endorse any specific brands. You can check our websites at www.ellorascave.com or www.cerridwenpress.com for information we make available to new consumers.)

3. *Mobility*. Because your new e-library consists of only a microchip within a small, easily transportable e-reader, your entire cache of books can be taken with you wherever you go.

4. ***Personal Viewing Preferences.*** Are the words you are currently reading too small? Too large? Too... ANNOYING? Paperback books cannot be modified according to personal preferences, but e-books can.

5. ***Instant Gratification.*** Is it the middle of the night and all the bookstores near you are closed? Are you tired of waiting days, sometimes weeks, for bookstores to ship the novels you bought? Ellora's Cave Publishing sells instantaneous downloads twenty-four hours a day, seven days a week, every day of the year. Our webstore is never closed. Our e-book delivery system is 100% automated, meaning your order is filled as soon as you pay for it.

Those are a few of the top reasons why electronic books are replacing paperbacks for many avid readers.

As always, Ellora's Cave and Cerridwen Press welcome your questions and comments. We invite you to email us at Comments@ellorascave.com or write to us directly at Ellora's Cave Publishing Inc., 1056 Home Avenue, Akron, OH 44310-3502.

THE
✟ ELLORA'S CAVE ✟
LIBRARY

Stay up to date with Ellora's Cave Titles in
Print with our Quarterly Catalog.

TO RECIEVE A CATALOG,
SEND AN EMAIL WITH YOUR NAME
AND MAILING ADDRESS TO:

CATALOG@ELLORASCAVE.COM

OR SEND A LETTER OR POSTCARD
WITH YOUR MAILING ADDRESS TO:

CATALOG REQUEST
c/o ELLORA'S CAVE PUBLISHING, INC.
1056 HOME AVENUE
AKRON, OHIO 44310-3502

erridwen, the Celtic Goddess of wisdom, was the muse who brought inspiration to storytellers and those in the creative arts. Cerridwen Press encompasses the best and most innovative stories in all genres of today's fiction. Visit our site and discover the newest titles by talented authors who still get inspired - much like the ancient storytellers did, once upon a time.

Cerridwen Press

www.cerridwenpress.com